Praise for the Baby Boomer Mysteries

"*Mistletoe Can Be Murder* is a delightful break from the depressing news, from any clutter you may have in your life, or from the drear of gloomy weather. Santangelo writes in a gentle style that pulls the readers in and engages them immediately. She hands us a tossed salad of characters who are believable, diverse, whimsical, and intriguing—and she manages to choreograph all of them skillfully throughout the plot. Find a cozy chair, head to your porch rocker, or stretch out on a beach...this is a fun read."
—George Eastman, Playwright, "Harry Townsend's Last Stand"

"This witty and fast-paced story kept me guessing until the surprise finale. *Mistletoe Can Be Murder* will delight your senses and make you chuckle your way through the book. A charming whodunit!"
—Nancy J. Cohen, Author of the *Bad Hair Day* Mysteries

"Christmas is coming and Carol Andrews is at it again! It's not like she goes looking for trouble, but while she and her husband are staying at an upscale hotel because their furnace is being repaired, they come upon a hotel receptionist lying injured outside in the cold. A murder occurs and Carol suspects everyone of the crime from her son-in-law's mother's boyfriend to her new neighbors. Funny and heartwarming, *Mistletoe Can Be Murder* is a wonderful addition to one of my favorite series."
—Allison Brook, Author of the *Haunted Library Mystery* Series

"Susan Santangelo's *Mistletoe Can Be Murder* is the perfect blend of family drama, humor, and murder. The author's gentle ribbing of husbands will make you laugh out loud while her well-placed clues and list of suspects will keep you guessing until the end."
—Ang Pompano, Agatha Nominated Author

"Relatable, kind, smart, opinionated and hilarious are all reasons I love cozy character Carol Andrews. Santangelo has the gift of creating characters who pull readers into the story and make them feel as if they're right there with Carol and company, solving mysteries and laughing all the way to the end of the book! Another winner in the series!"
—Jerri Cachero, Cozy Mystery Reviews

For Lucile —
Merry Christmas!

Mistletoe
Can Be Murder

Every Wife Has a Story

A Carol and Jim Andrews *Baby Boomer* Holiday Mystery

Tenth in the Series

Susan Santangelo

Susan Santangelo

SUSPENSE PUBLISHING

MISTLETOE CAN BE MURDER
by
Susan Santangelo

PAPERBACK EDITION
* * * * *
PUBLISHED BY:
Suspense Publishing

COPYRIGHT
2022 Susan Santangelo

PUBLISHING HISTORY:
Suspense Publishing, Paperback and Digital Copy, June 2022

ISBN: 978-0-578-38982-0

Cover and Book Design: Shannon Raab
Cover Artist: Elizabeth Moisan

Baby Boomer Mysteries

Acknowledgments

Thank you to my wonderful family—David, Mark, Sandy, Jacob and Becca. And especially to my husband Joe, who keeps me on my toes and inspires me every day.

A big thank you to my First Readers Club, especially Marti and Bob Baker, Judy O'Brien, Carole Goldberg, Sandy Pendergast, and Cathie Leblanc for their helpful comments and suggestions.

Thanks to Elizabeth Moisan for once again providing artwork for the front cover.

A big thank you to all my long-time friends from New England for their ongoing support, and to the friends I've made in Clearwater, Florida, especially the members of the Clearwater Welcome Newcomers Club, St. Brendan's CCW, my pals at The Attic, and Roxy Grinov from the Clearwater Beach Library.

To all my friends and cyber friends from Sisters in Crime, especially the New England, Northeast Florida, and Gulf coast chapters, thanks for sharing your expertise with me.

Boomer and Lilly send special doggy love to Lynn Pray and Courtney Lynn Ross, Pineridge English Cockers, Rehoboth MA.

To Shannon and John Raab, Abbey Peralta, Amy Lignor, and everyone at Suspense Publishing, who help me in so many ways, you're the best! I'm so proud to be a member of the Suspense family.

To all the bloggers who love mysteries as much as I do and support the genre in every way, especially Dru Ann Love, Lori Boness Caswell, Jerri Cachero and Diva Cat, a huge thank you!

And to everyone who's enjoyed this series—the readers I've met in person or via Zoom book events; those who have e-mailed me; those who've posted online reviews for the books; and followed me on Facebook, Twitter, and BookBub—thanks so much! Hope you enjoy this one, too. And keep those chapter headings coming!

To Barbara Pearson Rac and Linda Michaud:
With love and gratitude

Mistletoe
Can Be Murder

Every Wife Has a Story

A Carol and Jim Andrews *Baby Boomer*
Holiday Mystery

Tenth in the Series

Susan Santangelo

The week before Christmas, Midnight

It was a dark and stormy night. No, that's not true. It was a dark and freezing night. My husband, Jim, and I should have been warm and cozy, fast asleep in bed like normal people. But, sad to say, we're not normal people; we're dog people. Our lives are ruled by two English cocker spaniels, Lucy and Ethel. When they have doggy needs that must be attended to, no matter what the hour is...well, I'm sure you get the idea. Which was why, as I explained to the policemen, we happened to be outside in the middle of the night to discover the dead body.

Chapter 1

I really don't mind getting older, but my body is taking it badly.

"What exactly is your problem, Carol? I'm afraid I don't get what you're so upset about. You and the family will still be together. It's really no big deal."

I glared at my very best friend since our grammar school days, Nancy Green, incredulous that, after all the things we'd been through together, this woman, who can read my mind better than any other human on the face of the earth, who's supposed to support me in good times and in bad, in sickness and in health, no matter what, till death...oh, wait a minute. That's the marriage vows, isn't it? Forgive me, I digress. But Nancy was my maid of honor back on that fateful day almost forty years ago, so it's completely understandable that, in my current emotional state, I'd revert to my marriage vows. At least, for me, it's understandable.

My name is Carol Andrews. I live with my retired husband, Jim, in the bucolic community of Fairport, Connecticut, nestled on the shore of Long Island Sound. I was born here, went to school here, got married here, had two wonderful children here, and plan to stay here in my beautiful antique house on Old Fairport Turnpike until I die. Which I hope won't be anytime soon. To some of you, that may sound boring, but let me assure you, my life is so busy these days that sometimes I marvel at all the things I've accomplished at the end of every day. Especially since our daughter, Jenny, now married to her grade school sweetheart, Fairport Police Detective Mark Anderson, has made us grandparents for the very first time with the birth of the most wonderful baby ever born—CJ. Jenny and I are very close. In fact, sometimes I worry that we're too close, as she's been known to turn to me on occasion when she and Mark have had a little spat, hoping to get advice from dear old Mom that will make everything rosy again. I've made it a rule never to get involved in my children's personal lives, except under exceptional circumstances. Like, when either of them *really* need my advice. Or I see they're making a huge mistake and I need to speak up and stop them. Well, wouldn't you?

It's a lot easier to stay out of Mike's personal life than Jenny's. Our only son chose to move away from home the minute the ink was dry on his college diploma, and after knocking around Europe for a while, finally settled in South Beach, Florida, where he got a job as a server at a small restaurant. In no time at all, with a little financial help from us, he bought out the owner and turned the restaurant into a trendy eatery called Cosmo's. The rest, as the old saying goes, is history. He even paid back the money we originally loaned him—with interest. Now if he'd just find a nice girl and settle down...oh, wait. I shouldn't say that. In case I haven't made that clear on numerous occasions, I never interfere in the lives of my children.

Which brings me to my current problem. You'll be surprised to know that it's with Jenny, my darling daughter. And her insistence that she and Mark will host Christmas at their small condo this year, rather than have it here, where it's always been.

"You know how important celebrating Christmas has always been to us," I said to Nancy. "It's practically...sacred." I nodded my head, pleased with my brilliant choice of words. "It's one of our most sacred family traditions."

Nancy raised her left eyebrow and gave me a skeptical look. "I doubt Jim would agree with you," she said. "He'd remind you about all the times you complained about being in the kitchen during Christmas, knocking yourself out preparing one meal after another and never getting to really enjoy the holiday yourself. All you did was peel potatoes, stir the gravy so it wouldn't have any lumps, and say that nobody ever appreciated all the hard work it took to make Christmas so special or offer to help you. I could go on and on. But I won't." She gave my hand a squeeze. "Because I love you and I don't want to upset you."

"You mean, you don't want to upset me any more than you already have?" I turned so Nancy wouldn't catch me wiping my eyes. I knew she was right, darn it, but there was no way I'd ever admit it.

"And by the way, how do you happen to know how hard it is to put together a gourmet Christmas feast?" I asked. "You haven't cooked a real dinner in your kitchen since you moved into that house ten years ago. In fact," I added, warming to my subject even more, "I'm not even sure you know the house has a kitchen."

Bingo. I knew I'd scored a direct hit because of the shocked look on Nancy's face. The truth hurts. But I wasn't finished quite yet. I had one more zinger in my arsenal. "Wait a minute, I'm wrong; I apologize. You know you have a kitchen because you store all the white boxes from your takeout orders in the refrigerator."

Nancy's shoulders started to shake, and I instantly felt terrible. I had gone too far. I threw my arms around her, and I could feel her whole body tremble. "Please don't cry. I didn't really mean all those hurtful things I said."

Nancy pulled away from my grasp and swatted me. "You doofus. I'm not crying. I'm laughing. You really got me good. And you're right. I shouldn't criticize you." She put out her hand. "Truce?"

"Truce," I said. "Best friends forever. Never to be put asunder."

Nancy grinned at my horrible choice of words. "That's true, although sometimes I think we were more mature in fifth grade than we are now." She checked her smartwatch for the time. "Oops, I gotta go. I have a house showing in fifteen minutes on the other side of town to a hot prospect. I hope I'm the one who finally sells this property. Even in this competitive real estate market, it's been for sale for almost a year."

She gave our two English cocker spaniels, Lucy and Ethel, goodbye pats and me a regal wave. I'm embarrassed to admit that, for the first time in a long time, I was glad to see her leave. I don't take criticism very well. It hurts my feelings, especially on the remote chance that criticism was warranted. I knew I'd brood about Nancy's remarks for the next several hours, even though we'd technically made up. Yes, I know, stupid. I resisted the urge to slam the kitchen door after her, which I thought showed great maturity on my part.

Get over yourself, Carol. Nancy's just jealous because you have a warm, close family unit and she doesn't. Not that she'd ever admit that. Nor would I ever tell her that, because I am a generous, kind, solicitous person without a mean, critical bone in my body.

As if reading my mind—it's scary the way she does that—Lucy gave me a stare that could only be described as critical. Sheesh. Now even my dog was on my case.

My phone pinged with an incoming text. I squinted at the screen and realized I hadn't heard the usual sound of squealing tires that happens when Nancy makes a hasty exit.

Nancy: *Maybe u insist on running Christmas without caring what anyone else wants because of CJ. U never did share well.*

Chapter 2

A woman has the last word in any argument.
Anything a man says after that is the start of a
new argument.

I'd love to tell you the snappy response I texted back to my former best friend...but I can't. Don't get me wrong—it's not that I don't trust you. As a matter of fact, I didn't tell Lucy and Ethel, either. I can't tell you my response because I didn't send one. I couldn't think of a single thing I could write that would convey to Nancy how totally unfair I thought she was being. Correction: not unfair. Cruel. Just when you think you know someone after half a century of friendship (give or take a few years), they stab you right in the back.

Not to brag, but I've always been a wonderful, sharing, caring human being. And I've always been unappreciated. By every single person I was trying to be caring and sharing with. Or to. Whatever. Especially Nancy.

"For example," I told the dogs, now speaking out loud to be sure I had their attention, "every time Nancy's daughter needed a gown to wear for one of her dance recitals, I gave her one of Jenny's. And did Nancy ever thank me? No, she did not. As a matter of fact, after a while she began to take my generosity for granted. I even remember one time she actually commented that a dress Jenny was wearing would look better on Terry. That's her daughter's name in case you've forgotten."

Lucy yawned. I could sense that even sweet Ethel was beginning to lose interest.

Well, those generous days were over right now. And I knew that our closest friends, Claire and Mary Alice, would agree that Nancy had been taking advantage of my good nature ever since we were all kids.

I nodded my head. This was war. It was time for my posse to choose sides. Who were they with—selfish, self-centered, egotistical Nancy, or sweet, caring, selfless me?

And what are you going to do if Mary Alice and Claire choose Nancy? Are you prepared to take that risk and break up the circle of four after all these years?

I smiled. No way would they side with Nancy, especially when I told them what just happened before Nancy did.

I had a pang of self-doubt.

Remember all the times Claire's criticized you? She's always telling you that you take forever to get to the point of a story, jump to conclusions all the time, and are much more emotional than a normal, rational adult should be. She'd definitely be Team Nancy.

Good riddance. Claire had been getting on my nerves for years. Yes, this was definitely a good thing. It was way past time for me to do some house-cleaning in the so-called "friends" department. I knew Mary Alice was sure to see things my way. She's the sweetest person ever born. Sure, she carries on too much about health issues, like osteoporosis and heart disease, but that's because she's a retired nurse and she only wants what's best for all of us. She's never said a bad thing about anyone in her whole life, and she bends over backward not to offend anyone.

All of a sudden, I realized that if Nancy and I stopped speaking, I'd be putting Mary Alice in a terrible position. Was I forcing one of my very best friends in the whole world to sneak around, meeting Team Nancy for lunch in secret on Tuesdays and Team Carol for lunch on Fridays? "I can't do that to Mary Alice," I said; my eyes filled with tears.

"Can't do what to Mary Alice?" Jim asked, ambling into the kitchen wearing his favorite stretched-out tee shirt and chino pants. "Why are you crying?" He put his arms around me and stroked my back, which made me cry even harder.

"You know I can't help you if you don't tell me what's gotten you so upset. Is something wrong with Mary Alice? I know you'd never do anything to hurt her. Stop blaming yourself for whatever happened. I'm sure whatever's wrong is something that can be fixed." He pulled a handkerchief from his pocket and pressed it into my hand.

Even though the handkerchief looked like it hadn't been washed since Mike was born, I knew Jim was just trying to help. I pulled myself together and waved his hand away. "Thanks anyway, but I don't need this. I'm feeling better. My getting upset is all Nancy's fault. She said some terrible things to me. We had a big fight."

"Oh, now I get it," Jim said. "Was Mary Alice involved in the argument, too? I find that hard to believe. She's the kindest person I've ever known."

"No. Mary Alice doesn't even know about it."

"You've completely lost me," Jim admitted.

"I know. I'm just being too emotional and stupid, the way I usually am." I waited a beat, then added, "This is the part of the conversation where you're supposed to tell me I'm never too emotional and stupid."

"Stupid, no. But as far as being emotional is concerned, well...." Jim left the end of that sentence unfinished. Smart man.

"How about changing the subject?" I suggested.

"Fine with me. Especially since I still have no idea what the subject was."

"I know, dear. And believe me, it's better that you don't. Now, how was your day? Did you finish your State of the Town column for the *Fairport News*? I know you were at the paper for a few hours this morning." Thank God. I love my husband, but since that fateful day when he retired from his PR job in the Big Apple, my life has never been the same. If it wasn't for his part-time writing job for the local paper, which takes him out of the house most days, I'd never have any time to myself.

"I finished writing it at the paper," Jim said. "I think it's one of my best. I couldn't have done it without Mark's help, though. Having a son-in-law on the police force comes in very handy." He gave me a look. "As you know."

I knew he was teasing me, so I ignored him. I'm a helpful person, and because I've stumbled across an occasional dead body (not my fault, I assure you), I've been able to "help" the police figure out what happened. I always give the authorities all the credit for cracking the case, however. I am a very modest person. Mark is (occasionally) grateful for my help, unlike his annoying partner, Detective Paul Wheeler, who thinks I'm an interfering busybody with far too much time on her hands.

"It's nice that Mark was helpful," I said, resisting the urge to ask exactly what he was helpful with. I looked at the kitchen clock and sighed. "I suppose it's time to start dinner."

"You used to enjoy cooking. Now it seems like nothing but a chore for you."

That's because, back in the good old days, you weren't around when I was cooking, so I was free to put meals together without any "extra help." I didn't really say that out loud, of course.

"Mark also mentioned that they're hosting Christmas this year. I bet you're thrilled to finally be off the hook for cooking that big dinner. I know how you always hated it."

I had just found a large container of frozen chili in the deep recesses of the freezer. To tell you the honest truth, when I heard Jim's comment about my relationship to our family's time-honored, sacred Christmas celebration, I almost hit him over the head with it. I hope I get points for restraint. I slammed the container on my granite countertop and faced my husband. I was so mad I was sure I had smoke coming out of my ears.

My clueless husband then added the *coup de grace.* "I hope Jenny cooks enough for dinner so we have leftovers to take home. That was one good thing about having Christmas here every year."

Lucy and Ethel, always sensitive to my emotional temperature, immediately moved from their usual spot under the kitchen table toward the safety of the master bedroom.

"What?" Jim asked, looking at my face. "Did I say something wrong?"

"Let me count the ways," I said. "As a point of clarification, I love having Christmas here every year. It's my very favorite holiday, and I *never* hate cooking for it. I cook out of love, as a way to show the people who are the most important to me how much I care about them. Why do I have to tell you that? It should be crystal clear after all these years. What's the matter with you?"

Jim looked contrite. It was a good look for him, but it was gone in a skinny second before I had a chance to enjoy it.

"If you like cooking for the holiday so much, why do you complain when you have to do it?" Jim challenged. "I've heard you muttering under your breath that nobody ever appreciates all the effort you put in to make every holiday meal wonderful. And don't get me started about all the times you've complained about everything else you had to do to make Christmas perfect. Like shopping for presents, wrapping, baking cookies—"

"I never complained about shopping for presents." Oops. I realized, too late, that I shouldn't have brought up shopping.

"Humph. Your love of shopping is a subject for a totally different conversation," Jim said. "We're talking about everything else that's part of the holiday, especially cooking. I've offered to help you countless times, and you always refuse. I could at least peel the potatoes. You have to admit that even *I* can't screw that up. I think you enjoy playing the role of the cooking martyr. It feeds your ego."

Whoa. This argument was getting way out of control. And I thought Nancy's criticisms were bad. Now I was getting slammed by my own husband.

I will not cry. I will not cry. I will not cry. Naturally, my eyes paid no attention and filled with tears anyway.

"I've gone way over the line here, and I'm sorry," Jim said. "But before you haul off and slug me, just think about what I'm saying for half a second. Maybe I'm exaggerating, but there's also a tiny kernel of truth. Personally, I think it's wonderful that Jenny and Mark want to create a new family tradition by hosting Christmas this year. Why don't you talk to her and share the jobs? Like cooking something here to bring with us."

I just hate it when Jim's being rational. I never know how to respond without sounding like a complete idiot. Especially the few times when I agree with him. Like right now.

I took a deep breath. *Suck it up, Carol. It's a good compromise.*

"I'm sure Jenny will be grateful for your help," Jim added. "Maybe we can also bring the Spode Christmas china you always use. What do you say?"

"I suppose it's time for me to pass my apron to the next generation. I guess I'm being selfish. Jenny texted me earlier today about Christmas and I haven't responded yet. I was so shocked I didn't know what to say, to tell you the truth." I gave Jim a peck on the cheek. "Thanks to you, now I do. As long as we still decorate the house and put up a Christmas tree, I'm okay with the new plan."

The look on my husband's face spoke volumes. I knew Jim was thinking about how he could save a few bucks by not buying a tree, and save himself from the arduous task—the only one he does to contribute to the Andrews family holiday festivities—of putting it up in our family room. "Don't even think about it, Jim. Just because we're not hosting Christmas here doesn't mean we're not going to make the house festive. And we're still buying a real tree and lots of mistletoe, just like we do every year."

Jim sighed and nodded. He sometimes knew when he should surrender.

I wasn't quite through with him yet. "You need to make it up to me for the mean things you said, so you're making dinner tonight. I think you can handle heating up the leftover chili. I'll be in front of the television, channel surfing, waiting for you to call me." I smiled sweetly and scurried away before he could say no.

You didn't think I was going to let him have the last word, did you?

Chapter 3

When someone asks what I did over the weekend, I squint and ask, "Why? What did you hear?"

I was cleaning up the kitchen after dinner—Jim had done an awesome job reheating the chili I'd made two weeks ago, but, alas, cleanup fell on me—when my phone announced an incoming text.

Jenny: *Haven't heard back from u about Christmas. R u mad at me?*

Since there was no need to share my knee-jerk negative reaction—emphasis on "jerk"—with my daughter, I responded immediately with a smiley emoji.

Me: *Don't be silly! I'm not mad. But if you need help, I'm available.*

Jenny: *U bet! None better than u.*

Me: *Get together soon to plan?*

Jenny: *How about now? I'm already nervous just thinking about everything I have to do.*

Me: *Sure. Where?*

Jenny: *Fairport Diner? Half hour?*

Me: *Perfect. C u then.*

My heart swelled. Jenny needs me! She really needs me! For a split second, I thought about texting Nancy to brag a little, then decided against it. I couldn't resist doing the Happy Dance around my kitchen, though. Thank goodness Jim didn't see me. He'd think I was crazy. And maybe this time, he'd be right. I sent him a quick text, which was far more efficient and far less annoying than having to track him down somewhere in the house and tell him I was going out, which he wouldn't hear, anyway.

Me: *Meeting Jenny. Be back soon.*

Jim: *K.*

I was proud of myself for having undeniable proof on my phone and his response, when he insisted later (as I was sure he would) that I never told him I was leaving.

"Thanks for meeting me, Mom." Jenny jumped up and gave me a kiss. "I already ordered you hot tea and a piece of lemon meringue pie for us to share. I hope that's okay."

"It's perfect," I said. "You know that's my favorite."

"And this is my treat," Jenny stated.

"Oh, no, sweetheart. Let's at least split the check."

"Don't be silly. The whole thing will probably come to ten dollars. Believe me, I can afford it. Besides, since I invited you, technically I'm the host and should pay. So, no arguments, Mother dear. Besides, I have a huge favor to ask, and I'm shamelessly buttering you up so you'll agree. In other words, I'm taking a cue from the Carol Andrews method of how to get your loved ones to do what you want by using bribery."

"It always works on your father," I said, laughing.

Our waitress arrived with our beverages and two generous slices of pie, which she assured us was only a single piece cut in half. I ignored the fact that she winked when she said it and dug right in.

"That was yummy," I said, sad to see that only a few lonely crumbs now remained on my plate. "What a treat. My elastic waistband thanks you. Consider me sufficiently bribed to do your bidding. What's your huge favor? I already agreed to help you with Christmas."

"I know you did, Mom. I appreciate it so much."

"Let's start with who does what," I suggested. "I'd be glad to cook a turkey at home and bring it to your condo while it's still warm. I can make the gravy, too. Dad can peel the potatoes. That's not a huge favor. We're glad to do it."

I started to make a few notes on my phone. When I looked up, I realized Jenny was toying with a few leftover pie crumbs on her plate. She looked troubled, and I immediately knew why.

"I've overstepped, haven't I? You wanted to do Christmas at your house, and I'm taking it over completely."

"No, Mom. That's not it. The favor I'm going to ask you is a lot more complicated than that. I was afraid you'd be mad when I asked you, so that's why I asked you to meet me here, in a public place, instead of at home." She took a deep breath, then continued, "Guess who's coming for Christmas?"

"Well, I guess I have to rule out Spencer Tracy and Katharine Hepburn," I said, referring to the two celebrated actors who played leading roles in a 1967 movie with a similar title. "They passed on years ago."

Jenny was now fiddling with her fork. I reached over, grabbed the fork out of her hand and put it on my plate. "Out with it. Right now."

"This isn't easy," she said.

"I can tell," I said. "So quit stalling and just tell me."

"Okay. Here goes." She grabbed my hands and held them tight. "You have to promise me you won't overreact."

"Oh, for Pete's sake. Just tell me."

"Mark's mother."

Chapter 4

When I first met you, I didn't know you, so I didn't like you. Now I know you, and I still don't like you.

Have you ever met someone and immediately had a deep down, unexplainable negative reaction? I'm talking about the kind that starts at the top of your head and travels right through your whole body to the tips of your toes. An instantaneous non-attraction. Instead of love at first sight, this was loathing at first sight.

That pretty much sums up how I felt the first time I set eyes on Margo Anderson. And I think I was justified. How would you feel if you were cuddling your just-born first grandchild in your arms and some strange woman rushes into your daughter's hospital room and snatches the baby from you?

Don't give me that baloney about how CJ is Margo's grandson just as much as he is mine. (And Jim's, naturally.) On a conscious level, I know that already! This same woman deserted her family and left Fairport years ago, and couldn't even bother to come to her own son's wedding. So I hope you'll forgive me if I wasn't exactly overjoyed to see her when the baby was born. Neither was her son, to tell you the truth.

Are you shaking your head and tsking at my negative reaction?

Then may I remind you that, out of the goodness of my heart, I took Margo into my home for several stress-filled days after CJ's birth, to try and ease the tension between her and Mark, and almost didn't survive the experience. She was the most annoying, demanding, horrible guest we've ever had. Plus, she informed me the moment she arrived that I had to keep Lucy and Ethel locked up while she was there because she was allergic to dog.

All these negative, knee-jerk memories flooded my brain without any prompting from me the instant I heard Jenny's news. I knew what was coming next. The huge favor she was about to ask me was to provide room and board for Margo once again during her hopefully brief stay over Christmas. No wonder she wanted to ask me in a public place. If we were having this conversation in my own home right now, it wouldn't be a pretty scene.

Courage, Carol. Instead of focusing on your own problems with Margo, just think about what your poor daughter will have to deal with. The mother-in-law from hell. Jenny needs you, and you can't let her down.

I released my hands from her death grip and gave Jenny a tender look. "Sweetheart, I understand how difficult it was for you to tell me this. But don't worry. Dad and I will host Margo for Christmas, if that'll make things easier for you and Mark. We'll make it work somehow."

Jenny let out a deep breath. "Thanks, Mom. I hoped I could count on you. But relax. She's staying at the Fairport Inn and Suites, so you and Daddy are off the hook."

"I've never heard of that place," I said. "Is it new? Not that it matters, but you know how I hate to miss anything that's going on in town."

"It's where the old Harborview Motel used to be," Jenny clarified. "The inn just opened a few weeks ago. I've heard it's very nice."

Just between you and me, I didn't care if the place was nice or not. The only thing that mattered was the fact that Margo would be staying there, and not with us.

"Since you're assuring me that we won't have to entertain Margo, I promise I'll do anything else you ask. No matter what."

I made a big show out of raising my hand and crossing my heart. The server magically appeared with our check, and Jenny grabbed it.

"Not so fast, young lady," I said. "We're not leaving until you give me all the gory details about this huge favor I've agreed to do for you. I love you, but I'm not crazy. I need details, especially if I have to involve your father. You know how he is. He hates to miss anything these days."

"You already volunteered him," Jenny said. "He's going to peel the potatoes."

"Aha. The light has dawned. You mean the huge favor is about helping you with Christmas dinner, right? I already said yes."

"No, that's not it, exactly. I want you to decorate our condo for Christmas. You're so good at decorating. You really have a magic touch."

I was flattered. But a little suspicious. "That's easy. We have plenty of extra decorations up in the attic I can use. I'd love to do that."

"There's more," Jenny said, looking uncomfortable. "Would you also cook the whole dinner and sneak it into our condo and give me the credit, even if all I did was open a bag of chips and put them in a bowl? I need to impress Mark's mother, and this is the only way I can think of to do it. Please, Mom. When Margo was here for CJ's birth, I felt like she was always judging me and I wasn't measuring up to her idea of an ideal daughter-in-law."

"That's silly," I said. "Mark was angry that she'd just shown up out of the blue after being AWOL from his life for years. You barely saw the woman."

If Margo was judging anyone, it was me. Her stay at my house almost stretched my usually impeccable hostess skills to the breaking point. I didn't share that with my daughter. I didn't need to. She already knew.

"I'm talking about the end of her trip, when everything had been worked out," Jenny clarified. "I know this is a lot of work for you. I promise I'll make it up to you, somehow. I realize it's also underhanded and sneaky, and I wouldn't ask you for help, but...."

Just between you and me, Jenny's huge favor was a no brainer for me. I've been known to be "creative" in my thought process—lying is such a harsh word, don't you think?—when the situation demanded it. And keeping secrets is my specialty.

"I'm glad to do this for you. I'm sure the two of us can pull the whole thing off without anyone catching on."

Uh oh.

I considered what I'd just said. There was a big flaw in Jenny's plan, and it had just come crashing into my conscious mind with all the power of an incoming tsunami. "Except there are four of us involved, not two. I'm not worried about Dad; I'll figure out something to keep him in line. The decorating part is easy. But Mark's bound to figure it out if he sees me sneaking into your kitchen with the entire dinner. How are you going to keep this scheme a secret from him? Or are you?" I was having cold feet, and I hadn't even shopped for the darn turkey yet.

Jenny gave me a wicked grin. "Hey, give me a little credit, please. I'm your daughter, remember? I've been watching you pull the wool over Daddy's eyes for years. I'm going to tell Mark that you're letting me do all the cooking ahead of time at your house, because you have the bigger kitchen. And you'll bring it over as we need it."

My culinary wheels were starting to turn. "We can have lasagna for Christmas Eve, because that can be put together in advance and baked at my house. You'll just have to reheat it a little in your kitchen right before you serve it. But a traditional Christmas Day dinner can't be cooked ahead. Except the desserts. They can be made ahead of time." I had a sudden memory of the first Christmas after Jim and I were married. And how I screwed up bigtime when I was trying to impress my own new mother-in-law with my baking skills, which turned out to be non-existent. I had decided to make an apple pie from scratch, including the crust, and it turned out that I didn't own a rolling pin. Have any of you tried to use a soda bottle to roll out pie crust dough? Believe me, it doesn't work well.

"You've got a funny look on your face," Jenny said. "Are you remembering the time you were baking Mrs. Smith's pies on

Christmas Eve and you dropped the pumpkin pie on the floor when you took it out of the oven? You drove to the market to pick up another one, so it all worked out fine. At least you didn't scrape it off the floor and serve it."

"That wasn't the Christmas I was thinking about, smarty-pants," I said, smiling at the memory. "Although I remember racing into the store right before closing time, terrified that I wouldn't be able to find a pie to replace the one I'd ruined. The registers were all closing, and I had to pay in cash. I barely had enough with me to cover it. I avoided shopping there for months."

"So, what were you thinking about?"

I wasn't sure I should share the rest of that story with Jenny, since it pointed out how stupid I could be when I was desperate to impress someone. Especially since she was now counting on me to help her do the exact same thing. I looked at my watch, then at our server, who was now hovering near the exit and giving us dirty looks. It looked like we'd overstayed our welcome, as far as she was concerned.

"I'll tell you another time," I said. "Right now, we have to leave." I gestured toward the server, who was now glaring. "I think her shift is over and she's ready to go home." I slapped an extra $5 tip on the table and grabbed my coat. "For your trouble," I said over my shoulder as we made a speedy exit. I resisted pointing out that the diner was open 24 hours, so staying an extra few minutes wouldn't have killed her. Figuratively speaking, of course. If I'd had to stand on my feet for hours, I'd be grumpy too.

After promising to text each other early the next morning to plan more of our menu, Jenny and I headed back to our respective spouses. It wasn't until I was lying in bed, wedged between a snoring Jim on one side and two snoring canines on the other, that I thought about the part of the pumpkin pie debacle that I didn't tell Jenny. In the spirit of being a good neighbor, I had invited Phyllis and Bill Stevens, a childless couple who live across the street, to Christmas dinner that year. Phyllis always bragged about her culinary skills, so I was determined to impress her. Not being blessed with the baking gene (see above), I'd decided to buy some frozen pies, jazz them up a little, and pass them off as homemade. But the universe had other ideas, obviously. When I raced into the grocery store at the last minute on Christmas Eve, who did I also run into in one of the aisles while I was holding a frozen pumpkin pie? That's right. Phyllis Stevens. The jig was definitely up, and defrosting in my hands.

I decided right then that I better not handle the dessert course this year.

Chapter 5

I don't need anger management. I need people to stop ticking me off.

I woke at a disgustingly early hour the next morning to the sound of someone pounding on my front door. I rolled over on my side, intending to shake Jim awake and insist he deal with whoever the rude person was, but his side of the bed was empty. I heard the shower running, and Jim's tenor voice warbling, "Oh, What A Beautiful Morning." Humph. Not by my standards.

Grabbing my ratty flannel robe, I tied the sash tightly around my middle and climbed over Lucy and Ethel, neither of whom had even twitched in response to my movement or the noise from outside. Maybe Jim wasn't the only one in the Andrews family whose hearing was going. Then, as if reading my mind, Lucy raised her head and growled, annoyed at being disturbed.

"I agree, Your Majesty. Whoever's outside has a lot to answer for. Feel free to come with me and express your displeasure." I was surprised that she and her trusty shadow, Ethel, didn't hop off the bed to follow me and demand their breakfast.

"Save my spot," I instructed her. "I'll be right back."

I padded through the kitchen on my bare feet, hoping that it was a delivery person or someone else I could get rid of quickly. I figured our visitor was someone who didn't know us, because all our friends and family use the side door. They also know that the sight of me first thing in the morning would make any normal person run for the Fairport town line ASAP.

Pulling open the antique, squeaky front door, I was greeted by one of my least favorite people—our across-the-street neighbor, Phyllis Stevens. For a split second, I was afraid she knew I'd been reliving the pumpkin pie debacle from years past, then dismissed that idea as totally ridiculous, even for me.

Judging by her appearance, Phyllis had been up for hours and completed her morning walk around our neighborhood, no doubt checking to be sure everyone's garbage cans were already back in their proper place behind their houses. Except ours, which was glaringly visible in front of our white picket fence. Oh, no. I was about to get a lecture about the importance of keeping Old Fairport Turnpike beautiful.

I pasted on a phony smile. "Good morning, Phyllis. My, aren't you the early bird today? I'm sorry about our garbage can. Jim's in the shower, but I'll be sure he takes care of it as soon as he dries off."

Phyllis blushed a little. Perhaps the reference to my husband's bathing routine was too personal for her to handle. "Not to worry, Carol," she said. "I know you and Jim can always be counted on to keep Old Fairport Turnpike looking its best. Which brings me to why I'm here."

She thrust an envelope into my hand. "We are about to have new neighbors, Dr. Ellen and Dr. Frank Adams. They're buying the Old Parsonage, and plan to fully restore it to its former historic glory. Isn't that wonderful?"

"Wonderful," I mumbled, trying to look enthused. I didn't share the obsession Phyllis had with the various historical buildings in our neighborhood. (Just between us, I don't think anyone could.)

The history buffs among you may be interested to learn that the original Old Parsonage dated back to pre-revolutionary days. It's gone through several metamorphoses and structural additions since then, and was most recently a bed and breakfast which went bust five years ago. Since then, the eight-bedroom structure had been neglected and fallen into disrepair. I hoped the new owners weren't planning on turning it into condos, not that I'd dare mention that possibility to Phyllis. She'd have an absolute fit.

"What's this you've handed me?" For a split second, I was afraid it was a notice for some unknown infraction I'd committed. Although Phyllis thinks the sun rises and sets on Jim and our kids, she doesn't always think that highly of me.

"I'm sure they'll be an excellent addition to Old Fairport Turnpike," Phyllis continued, ignoring my question. "Just imagine, two doctors in the same family."

I had a sudden image of Phyllis hatching a plan to corner the two doctors sometime and share her personal medical problems, which would shock the heck out of them if they happened to be history professors, for example. "Not everyone who's a doctor is a medical one, Phyllis."

Ignoring me again, Phyllis said, "My first idea was to welcome Dr. Ellen and Dr. Frank to our neighborhood by doing a progressive dinner, like we used to do at the holidays." Her eyes misted over. "Those were great times. We saw the different ways our homes were decorated and shared a communal gourmet feast, too. Remember those, Carol?"

My memories of those days were not the same positive ones Phyllis had. I remember panicking the morning of the dinner every year, when it suddenly dawned on me that the meal was that same night and I hadn't done a thing to prepare. No decorating, no food shopping, no house cleaning—zippo. Panic city at the Andrews house. I used to dread that dinner, but there was no way we could get out of being involved. It was a huge relief when attendance started dwindling as the "core group" of neighbors started to move away and none of the new neighbors had any interest in continuing the tradition. Thank God.

I immediately tried to think of a creative excuse to bow out of this before Phyllis asked me to be part of it. Unfortunately, without my usual day-starter of a huge jolt of caffeine, I couldn't come up with much.

"Jim and I already have several holiday commitments. It's our grandson CJ's first Christmas, so it's going to be a lot different for our family this year. We can't participate in a progressive dinner. There's just not enough time."

Phyllis looked at me like I was an idiot. "You misunderstand, Carol. I'm not suggesting another progressive dinner. I know how busy everyone's lives are these days, and an event that size is much too complicated. Bill and I, having no family, will host the dinner to welcome our new neighbors, and each neighbor will be assigned a specific part of the meal to cook and bring to our home. I've already planned the menu. The envelope contains your assignment. The dinner is next Sunday. I've simplified the assignments for each neighbor by dividing the list alphabetically, according to last name and course. Since your last name begins with 'A,' you will provide an appetizer course."

"I don't think I can...."

"Don't be silly, Carol. Appetizers are the easiest course. Even you can't fail with that one. You're fortunate your last name doesn't begin with a 'D.' Then you'd have to make a dessert." And then she made a speedy exit—no doubt to inflict her invitation on another unsuspecting neighbor—before I had a chance to respond.

Chapter 6

Men wake up in the morning as good-looking as when they went to bed the night before. Women, on the other hand, seem to deteriorate overnight.

Muttering to myself, I stormed into the kitchen. "Who does she think she is, anyway? Like she's so perfect? I bet there are loads of times that she foisted a casserole off on one of the neighbors and pretended it was made from scratch, when it was really a Stouffer's frozen meal that she'd just defrosted and heated up."

"Is that what we're having for supper tonight?" Jim asked, unaware that he'd just stepped into a culinary minefield. "Stouffer's lasagna isn't bad, but it's not nearly as good as yours."

I gave Jim a big smooch. "You've said exactly the right thing. And I love you for it. Thank you."

"I have absolutely no idea why what I said made you so happy, but you're welcome. I love you, too."

"And you saved me some coffee," I said, pouring a cup and sitting down at the kitchen table. "You're well on the way to sainthood this morning. I shouldn't let her get to me so much. But I didn't expect to start my day with a visit from Phyllis Stevens. This holiday season is going to be one for the books. In a bad way."

"You've completely lost me," Jim said, rummaging in the refrigerator and rearranging all the food I had so carefully organized so I could find it. "Where are the eggs?"

"They're on the right side of the bottom shelf," I said. "That's where they *always* are, as you should know by now."

Knock it off, Carol. Just because you're mad at Phyllis, don't take it out on him.

"What did Phyllis do that's gotten you all riled up?" Jim asked, cracking an egg into a cup, mixing it thoroughly, and popping it in the microwave for one minute, just the way I taught him.

"I guess it's really no big deal," I said. "She stopped by with an invitation to a party she and Bill are giving to welcome some new neighbors. They've bought the Old Parsonage, which is a good thing. That house has been in sad shape for years. Phyllis claims the new owners are planning to give it some love and renovate it back to its former glory."

"Meaning, done entirely to the Old Fairport Turnpike Historic District specifications as interpreted by her, no doubt," he said with a smile.

"No doubt." The light dawned. "I bet that's why she decided to give this welcome party. It's a command performance, so don't get any bright ideas about not showing up. She wants to be sure the new neighbors are properly schooled in the association's rules and regulations as soon as possible."

"That does make sense," Jim said, "especially since she and Bill never entertain. You know that she lives and breathes for this neighborhood." He put the perfectly scrambled egg and a single piece of low-calorie (no taste) whole wheat toast in front of me, then joined me at the table. "Here. I made this for you. I had breakfast before I took my shower."

I suspected that Jim had breakfast before me because he didn't want me to see his breakfast choice, which was probably two jelly donuts or an everything bagel slathered with high-calorie, high-fat cream cheese. But I had other issues on my mind this morning, so I didn't call him out on it. Instead, I smiled sweetly and said, "Thank you, honey."

As I ate my high-protein breakfast like a good little girl, I began to feel guilty about my conversation with Phyllis. So what if she was a complete control freak? Or if she didn't trust any of her neighbors to decide on their own what to bring to "her" dinner party? At heart, she was a good person, and everything she did improved our property values. Old Fairport Turnpike was a beautiful street with one eyesore, the Old Parsonage. Even Nancy, who's the best real estate agent in town, gave up on trying to sell it. And now, someone had finally bought it. I should be happy to join in a neighborly welcome. I just didn't like being forced into it.

"The party's next Sunday," I said, shoving the invitation in his direction. "Put it on your calendar. I've been ordered to bring an appetizer."

"Dutifully noted," he said, making a note on his phone. "Bring your famous Carol's Killer Meatballs."

Carol's Killer Meatballs have never (to my knowledge) killed anybody. And they're so easy that CJ could probably manage to make them, even if he's only four months old. (He's very advanced for his age.) Jim calls them "killer meatballs" for two reasons. First, because the original recipe came from a former neighbor of ours who's currently serving jail time for bopping her son-in-law over the head and killing him with some frozen beef. And second, he thinks it's funny and is guaranteed to get a rise out of me. Humph.

Then I remembered all the other things I had to deal with to get ready for Christmas, and realized it was the perfect solution, especially since nobody's ever been able to figure out the exact recipe. If I decide I can trust you, I may share it. But don't count on it.

"That's not a bad idea," I said, agreeing while trying to figure out the best way to start another Christmas conversation. I had to be very careful, because I needed him on Jenny's side right away, even if what she was asking of her parents was underhanded and sneaky. (A chip off the old mom block, so to speak.) Although, since Mark and Jim were really good buddies, it was possible our son-in-law had already brought Jim up to speed on his mother's surprise Christmas appearance.

"Anything new with Mike?" I asked. Our Florida son has a habit of surprising us with visits, and I was hopeful that there might be another one around the holidays.

Jim shook his head. "I haven't heard from him," he said. "Mark told me Mike called them recently, though. He wanted to see how CJ was. He's really excited to be an uncle."

I congratulated myself on stumbling into the perfect segue to inquire about Mark. "I think it's wonderful that Mike wants to be more involved with the family," I said. "Maybe we'll see him more often." I took a sip of coffee, then asked, "What else did Mark have to say? Anything new?"

"No, except he's up to his eyeballs with work, as usual. He's especially looking forward to a break around Christmas, even though it'll only be two days."

"Speaking of Christmas," I began.

Jim interrupted me. "Please don't tell me you're still going off the deep end about Jenny wanting to host it. I thought we'd come up with the perfect solution."

"Don't worry. Jenny and I talked last night and all is well. We divvied up the assignments, and decided to do most of the cooking here, because we have a bigger kitchen, then bring all the food to the kids' condo when it's ready to serve. You're in charge of potatoes. I'm giving her some of the tree decorations we never use and helping her decorate."

"It sounds more complicated than necessary, but if that's what you two decided, we'll make it work," Jim said.

Amazing. I never figured this would be such an easy sell.

Then Jim scowled, and I could tell he was having second thoughts about the plan. "Transporting hot food from one house to another isn't going to be easy. We're taking a chance that dinner will get cold on the way."

Oh, no. I was losing him. I had to come up with something else, and quick. Thank goodness, the memory of another holiday debacle popped into my head. Not one I thought I'd ever want to talk about again, but I was desperate. And I hadn't even told him about Margo yet.

"It's not as complicated as the first year we hosted your parents," I said. "In case you've forgotten that disaster, allow me to remind you. The apartment we were in then had a kitchen that was bigger than Jenny's, but there still wasn't enough room to cook all the courses for Christmas dinner. So we borrowed the keys from three neighbors who weren't home for the holidays and did some of the cooking in each apartment. We had to run around all day checking on the courses, and then we locked ourselves out of the apartment that had the turkey cooking. We had to call the super to unlock the unit, and he was not happy. And all this happened while your parents were sitting in our living room."

Jim laughed so hard he almost choked on his coffee. "Don't say things like that when you can see I'm drinking something," he said. "What are you trying to do, kill me?"

"Of course not, Jim. But why do you think that story is so funny? I was so embarrassed when it happened that I wanted to run away and never come back."

"I apologize. I didn't realize how upset you were. My parents got a big kick out of it. I think my mom even pitched in to help and ran to a neighbor's apartment to pick up the stuffing. And you were the one who brought the subject up, not me."

"I was trying to make a point about why it's so important to help Jenny this Christmas. She wants everything to be perfect. Especially because...."

I knew Margo Anderson was not one of Jim's favorite people, either. In fact, after she left Fairport, Jim referred to her as the Houseguest from Hell. *Just tell him and get it over with.*

"There'll be an extra person for Christmas this year, and our daughter needs our help to impress her." I took a deep breath. "Guess who it is."

Jim had the oddest look on his face. It was a combination of guilt and fear. "I think I already know what you're going to say."

"There's no way you could possibly know," I said. "It's Margo Anderson." I sat there, waiting for the explosion.

"I know, Carol," he said. "She called on the house phone last night and asked for our help smoothing the way with Mark. She'd tried to reach you on your cell, but you didn't pick up." I'd turned my phone ringer off while I was having coffee with Jenny so we wouldn't be interrupted. Thank goodness I did.

"Margo called and asked for our help? You mean she hasn't told her own son that she's coming for Christmas? That doesn't make any sense."

"Mark knows she's coming. But Margo hasn't told him she's bringing her new boyfriend." It took me a minute to digest this bombshell. Then the implications for us hit like a bolt of lightning.

"Are you saying that Margo asked us to give Mark the happy news that she's showing up for Christmas with a guy? What the heck is she thinking? She and Mark are finally rebuilding their relationship after being estranged for years. This could slam the brakes on that possibility. No way are we going to be the bad guys and put ourselves in the middle of her latest drama. How *dare* she put us in such a terrible position!"

Be rational about this, Carol. This situation isn't Jim's fault. He's just the unlucky guy who answered the phone when she called.

"Whoa, Carol. Hold on and let me clarify. Margo's going to call Mark herself and tell him in advance about her...guest. She's just asking us to help smooth things over if he doesn't react well. She pointed out that he thinks of us more as parents than in-laws, which you know is true."

"I know he does," I said. "And I love him as much as if he was our own son. But still, this is asking a lot." And I resent it.

"How did you leave it with her?" I asked, dreading his answer.

"I told her I'd discuss it with you, of course."

"Oh, great. She'll probably call again today. I don't want to deal with her."

"Maybe you can find one of your special patron saints to intercede," Jim said, grinning. "How about St. Jude? He's the patron saint of hopeless causes, right?"

"Very funny."

"There is a bright side to all this, you know," my husband said.

"Oh, really? And what exactly would that be, Mr. Know-It-All?"

"It's pretty obvious to me. If Margo is preoccupied with this new boyfriend, she won't usurp your position as Grandmother

Number One while she's here. And if we all get really lucky, she'll be so busy with her new guy that she'll leave Fairport after the holidays and won't come back again for a long, long time."

Honestly, that Jim.

Chapter 7

This morning I saw a neighbor talking to her cat. It was obvious she thought her cat understood her. I came into the house and told my dogs. We laughed a lot.

"Jim sometimes comes up with good suggestions," I said to the dogs as I shook generous amounts of kibble into their bowls. Lucy gave me one of her famous "I'll agree with anything you say just as long as you feed me" looks. Ethel, of course, agreed with me. She always does.

It's true that, no matter how outlandish a situation might be, I can usually find a patron saint who's been assigned to it and call on him—or her—for help. For those of you who haven't had the benefit of a Catholic education like mine, a patron saint is someone who's been assigned to be the heavenly advocate of a nation, place, craft, activity, class, family, or person. In other words, the go-to guy (or girl) for specific occasions or needs.

One of my all-time favorites is St. Genesius, the patron saint of sarcasm. His major shrine is the Church of Santa Susanna in Rome. He's a very handy guy to know, and he's also the patron saint of actors, clowns, comedians, dancers, musicians, lawyers, thieves and torture victims. When a sarcastic reply to one of my husband's frequent—and unasked for—observations pops into my head, I know it's St. Genesius giving me the perfect reply. I suddenly realized I had nothing to worry about. If Margo had the nerve to contact me, I'd just rely on St. Genesius to come up with my perfect response.

"Okay, first things first. And don't you dare give me that pleading, 'I'm still hungry' look," I said to the dogs.

"What makes you think I'm still hungry?" Jim asked, walking into the kitchen carrying his laptop.

"I was talking to the dogs," I admitted. "And if you want to work at the kitchen table, let me clean it off first."

"I'm on my way to the town hall," Jim said. "There's a meeting there about possible revisions to the town charter. I may decide to use that as the subject for a future column, and I'm bringing my laptop to take notes. I have no idea how long the meeting will last. You know how these politicians love to talk."

No response was necessary. I knew Jim got a real kick out of discovering what was going on behind the scenes in town government and would stay until the bitter end of whatever issue the powers-that-be were hashing over this time.

"In that case, I won't expect you back until dark," I said, laughing.

Jim rolled his eyes. "I may go from the meeting to the paper to kick around more ideas for next week's column with my editor. Jeff always has good suggestions. I'll let you know, so you won't worry about me."

"I won't worry," I said, giving him a farewell smooch and opening the kitchen door. "Have a good day."

I never worry about where Jim is, but he constantly frets about where I am, who I'm with, and what I'm doing. He has an overwhelming need to be able to contact me at any time, no matter what. And if for some reason I don't return his text or call immediately, he goes ballistic and assumes I've either been in a serious accident or I'm up to something I don't want him to know about. Thank goodness it's never been the former situation. As to the frequency of the latter, I reserve the right to remain silent because anything I say could be used against me in the future.

Jim reached the open door, then stopped. "I think I left my cell phone in the bedroom."

Sheesh. When was the guy going to leave so I could get on with my own day? He was acting just like Mike used to when he didn't want to go to school.

"It's here on the kitchen table," I said, waving it in his face. "Here. Now go, or you'll be late."

"Thanks, Carol," Jim said, taking his phone, and heading out the door. In a few seconds, I heard the welcome sound of his car roaring out the driveway. Finally!

"So, what do you want to do today?" I asked Lucy and Ethel. "Besides the usual things, which involve me catering to your every need. We probably have time to ourselves till at least 2:00. Let's not waste a second."

The dogs responded by flopping down in front of a sunbeam that was making its way through the large kitchen window. Which needed to be cleaned, as Lucy pointed out by raising her head, giving me a stare, then looking at the window again.

"You must be kidding," I said. "No way am I cleaning any windows today. If this one bothers you, I'll give you the Windex and you can do it."

I had two top priorities for the day—making up with Nancy and avoiding Margo Anderson for as long as possible.

I checked the time on my phone: 8:45. Since I'd been on the receiving end of Nancy's last unfair comment, I figured she'd be contacting me any minute to apologize. In fact, I was sure she'd feel so bad that she'd want to have lunch, and maybe even do some Christmas shopping if her schedule allowed. Which reminded me that I had yet to buy her gift. I made a note on my phone to start that search ASAP. I couldn't wait to tell her about my talk with Jenny last night.

I knew Nancy's schedule better than my own. She'd been up for hours, had already finished her daily workout at our local gym doing all those heinous exercises that she thinks are fun, and was home now, freshly showered and made up, having her usual low-carb, no-taste breakfast. This ritual would be followed by a trip through her enormous walk-in closet where she would choose which of her high fashion ensembles she'd wear for the day. This ritual was always completed by 9:00, then followed by a flurry of texts and calls to finalize her schedule for the day. And after all that, she was sure to contact me, begging for forgiveness.

I needed to be ready for whatever she had in mind to make up for being so mean to me. I raced to the bathroom, cell phone in hand, and turned the ringer to its highest decibel so I wouldn't miss her text. A quick shower later, after blow-drying my blondish locks (which badly needed a touchup and cut before the holidays), I checked my phone for messages.

None. Zip. Nada.

Nancy probably had an emergency with one of her real estate clients this morning. She'll be in touch soon.

But she wasn't. Not a peep. By 10:00, I was so mad at her I decided I wouldn't forgive her when she did finally apologize. By 10:30, I began to worry that she was still mad at me, and that's why I hadn't heard from her.

By 11:00, I decided that, even though Nancy was clearly in the wrong, I would be the bigger person and reach out to her.

At 11:05, just as I was struggling with the perfect words to end this stupid argument with Nancy, my phone rang. At last!

"Hello? Can you hear me?"

I was confused. This wasn't Nancy's voice. "Yes, I can hear you," I said. "Who's this? Hello? Hello?" But the caller had hung up.

"How rude," I said to the dogs. "Why didn't the person just apologize for calling a wrong number, instead of hanging up in my ear without saying another word?"

If this was Nancy, trying to get me madder, she was doing a great job.

The phone immediately rang again.

"Okay, Nancy. Knock it off. You're not being funny. If we get together for lunch today, it's definitely your treat," I said. "And I'm pretty hungry, just so you know that in advance."

"Hi, Carol. It's Margo Anderson, not Nancy, and lunch today

is fine with me. I'm back in Fairport and looking forward to catching up. Name the place and time and I'll be there."

Oh, Lord, no. This'll teach me to always check my caller i.d. first. I resisted what I really wanted to say, and I won't repeat it to you because it involves several colorful words I didn't learn at Mount Saint Francis Academy. And Margo was already in town. Rats.

Think, Carol. Use those creative brain cells of yours to wiggle out of this. You can do it.

I mustered up the cheeriest fake tone of voice I could and decided to stall her. "Hi, Margo. Jenny told me that you were coming for Christmas. She and Mark are very excited about hosting the holiday for the first time. It will be so nice to have both sides of the family represented. And, yes, we certainly do have lots to catch up on. Although it just seems like only yesterday since you headed back home."

Oops, stupid. You shouldn't have said that. Even by my desperate standards, that was pretty insulting. This time, my pal St. Genesius had gone a little too far. I realized I'd overplayed my hand and hastened to backpedal. "I don't know about you, but the older I am, the quicker time seems to pass. At least, that's what Jim always says."

"You're absolutely right, Carol. Time does seem to pass more quickly the older we get. That's one of the reasons why I wanted to come back to Fairport for Christmas. I don't want to miss a single minute of being with my precious grandson."

I felt the familiar stab of jealousy. Even though I have the "home team grandma" advantage, it's hard for me to admit that CJ has more than one grandmother, much less have it waved in my face. *My* precious grandson, indeed. We'll just see about that. A lunch date with Margo was looking less attractive by the minute.

"I totally understand," I said through gritted teeth. "Every time I take care of him, it's so hard to leave. Even though I know I'll be back at least three more times the same week." Score one for Carol. And call me petty. Go ahead, I dare you.

This brief conversation had made me realize that there was

no way I could get through a private lunch with Margo without having the urge to deck her. Lord knows, I am the soul of good taste under most circumstances. I never lose my cool. But this... this person...had the ability to get under my skin like nobody else. Even more than Phyllis Stevens, although she certainly came close this morning.

"I have something very important I want to talk to you about, woman to woman," Margo said. "I have a huge favor to ask, and I'm hoping you'll be understanding and supportive." Her voice quavered. "I have a problem. Or, I may have a problem. I don't know how to begin."

I knew exactly what she was talking about, but there was no way I was going to admit it. So I clamped my lips shut and waited for her to continue.

"Did Jim tell you that I called last night?"

"He mentioned something about it when he was on his way to a meeting this morning," I said. "But he was in a hurry, so he didn't give me any specifics."

"That's why I want to talk to you," Margo continued. "To explain, and ask for your advice. But I've just had a better idea. How about, instead of lunch, we get together for a quiet dinner tonight? Our hotel has a nice restaurant. We went there last night and really enjoyed it. The menu is wonderful."

Okay, so do I respond to her use of the pronoun "we" now? Or let it slide and let her keep talking? Hmm. Tough choice. I went with option two.

"I don't know if Jim has any plans for us tonight," I said. (Unless falling asleep in front of the television counts.) "I'd have to check with him first. And when you say the restaurant has a wonderful menu, what do you mean? When you stayed with us before, you didn't like my food, so you went out and bought your own. We're basic meat, potatoes and pasta kind of people, in case you don't remember." *And I'm still angry about your rude and ungrateful attitude when I let you stay here, out of the goodness of my heart, because you had no place else to go.* I didn't really say that last part out loud, but I sure wanted to.

51

"You're absolutely right, Carol, and I'm sorry. But in the last few months, thanks to Jeremy, my palate has really expanded. He's changed my life. I can't wait for you and Jim to meet him. And dinner tonight will be our treat. He's what I want to talk to you about. But it'll be even better if you both meet him. You'll understand then how amazing he is."

I waited a beat. Then, what the heck, I waited for another one.

"Jeremy," I repeated. "You want us to meet Jeremy. Is he a new friend?"

"He's a lot more than that," Margo said. "I've finally found my soulmate, after all these years. Please say you'll come."

No way was I going to let this opportunity pass by. "I'll do my best to work things out with Jim. What time?"

"Thank you, Carol. You won't regret it. This is going to be wonderful. A double date! Will 6:30 work for you both?"

"I think so. If there's a problem, I'll text you at this number. Okay?"

"That's fine. We'll see you in the Fairport Inn and Suites lobby at 6:30 tonight." And she clicked off.

I sat there, in shock. I already regretted it. I had no idea how to handle a delicate situation like this. At its best, this dinner would be awkward. And at its worst, well...I didn't dare think about that possibility. Although if I closed my eyes, I could picture the veins on my son-in-law's neck pulsating as he accused me of treachery, treason, or conduct unbecoming CJ's Number One Grandmother.

I needed advice, pronto. And I knew exactly who would have it. In a flash, I texted Nancy.

Me: *I need help. Margo's back in town with her new boyfriend!*

In a heartbeat, there was a return text. I smiled. I knew Nancy would always be there for me when I needed her. I squinted at the screen and saw there was a photo included.

Nancy: *I know! Bob and I saw the happy couple at the Fairport Inn and Suites last night.*

I grabbed my glasses and checked out the picture. If this was Jeremy, Margo was either the luckiest woman in the world, or the stupidest. He was young, tall, with sandy blond hair and a smile to die for. He was gazing at Margo like she was a piece of chocolate cake and he was ready for dessert. OMG. Mark was going to freak out, for sure, when he saw his mother's new boyfriend.

Chapter 8

Sometimes, it takes me all day to get nothing done.

I'm not going to lie. I was jealous as heck that a woman my age—and I'm not going to tell you what that is, so save your breath and don't ask me—had somehow managed to attract the attention of someone so gorgeous.

"What the heck does Margo Anderson have that I don't?" I muttered. I was determined to find out at dinner tonight.

For all I knew, Jeremy was a paid escort. Not that any of my friends would stoop to such unsavory methods. Even Mary Alice, who's been a widow for years and has told me that everyone she's met on online dating sites has been a real loser.

I gave myself a mental slap for even considering such an outrageous idea. But still....

I was lost in a fantasy world where Jeremy would take one look at me at dinner, immediately ditch Margo, kiss my hand and say, "At last, I have met the woman of my dreams." I would be embarrassed, of course, blush and snatch my hand away. Margo would burst into tears. And Jim...yikes! What about Jim? I couldn't leave my husband of almost forty years for a young stud, could I?

Suddenly I became conscious of loud banging on the kitchen door and a screechy voice. "Carol, let me in. I know you're home.

I can see you through the window."

I jumped up like I'd been shot out of a cannon and let Nancy in.

"I thought I'd have to break a window to get your attention," Nancy scolded. "What the heck took you so long? I hope you're not still mad at me."

"Mad at you? Why would I be mad at you?" Then I remembered our quarrel yesterday, the one I was so upset about until Margo's phone call turned my day, life, and dinner plans, upside down. "Don't be silly," I said, pulling her inside before the dogs made a break for the outside world. "We both said some things we didn't mean. Let's forgive each other so you can tell me about this picture!" I waved my phone around. "You almost gave me a heart attack when I saw it."

"How do you think I felt when I saw them in person?" Nancy asked, making herself comfortable and giving each dog a cursory head scratch. "Why didn't you tell me Margo was back in town? Or did you just decide to withhold that tidbit because you were mad at me?"

"Don't be ridiculous. Margo just called me a few minutes ago to tell me she was here."

Nancy raised her eyebrows, then realized that her expression might cause a new wrinkle and relaxed her face. "I believe you. Sorry I jumped to an unfair conclusion. I didn't get much sleep last night." She yawned, then grinned. "Not that I'm complaining."

I gave her a swat. "You know I'm not going to ask you to elaborate. I think I can guess that you and your on-again/off-again husband had a 'date' last night. Am I right?"

Nancy nodded. "Our marriage is so much more fun now that we're only dating instead of living together 24-7. You and Jim should try it sometime."

"No way," I said. "I'm finally getting him trained the way I've always wanted. I'm not risking any backsliding now." I pointed to the picture. "Don't make me beg. For Pete's sake, tell me about this photo and don't leave out a single detail."

"Oh, all right. Bob called about 5:00 last night and offered to take me to dinner. When he came to pick me up, we had an argument about where to go. I wanted to go to Maria's Trattoria, of course, and he wanted to go to the restaurant at the new Fairport Inn and Suites." She made a sour face. "I just hate hotel food. It's always so terrible."

Good heavens. And some people say *I* take too long to get to the point.

"Anyway, I let him win, so off we went in his—"

"Nancy! For heaven's sake, I don't care what car Bob was driving! Get to the part about Margo!"

"Oh, all right. When did you get so impatient? It's not an attractive quality, Carol. You need to practice patience more, like Sister Rose always told us in high school."

I gritted my teeth. "I promise I'll work on it, right after you tell me about Margo."

"We walked into the restaurant, and it wasn't crowded at all. We were seated right away. All of a sudden, I heard someone calling my name from across the room. I looked up and saw it was Margo and a man. It's a good thing I was already sitting down at the time, I was that surprised. I waved because I didn't know what else to do. And the next thing I knew, a server came and told us we'd been invited to join them."

"Are you telling me that you actually had dinner with them?"

"We had no choice. Margo was standing up and waving us over to their table. Unless we wanted to make a quick break for the door, we had to join them. Bob was very reluctant to go. I had to practically drag him over. It wasn't until we sat down that I got a really close look at the guy with Margo. And then I couldn't take my eyes off him for most of the meal."

"Ooooh, now we're getting to the good stuff. What's his full name? Is he as young as he looks in the photo? How did Margo meet him?"

Nancy raised her hand to stop my tirade of questions. "Whoa, Carol. Slow down. We were their guests for dinner. I couldn't exactly cross-examine him without being rude. Or obvious. I was dying to put my phone on speaker, so you could hear our conversation, but I couldn't figure out how to do it without being obvious."

"That wouldn't work. You'd have to call me first."

"I did my best to remember everything we talked about. Aside from the usual small talk."

"So...come on, tell me what you remember. And don't skip the small talk. That may be very useful. You never know."

"Okay. His name is Jeremy Dixon, and he's originally from some place in the Midwest near Chicago. He didn't mention the name of his hometown. I would guess he's in his early forties, but he could be older." Nancy wrinkled her brow again. "Or he could be younger. I never am very good figuring out a person's age. Especially since I look so much younger than my actual age. Nobody ever guesses mine. They think I'm years younger than I really am."

I nodded impatiently. As usual, Nancy was getting way off track.

"No matter what, Jeremy's decades younger than Margo, right?"

"He's definitely younger, but from what I saw last night, that fact doesn't matter at all in their relationship. Unless they were both putting on a pretty good act for our benefit, they're bonkers about each other."

"Did the subject of how you and Margo know each other come up?"

"Carol, for heaven's sake, be serious. Do you think Margo would casually mention that she used to be romantically involved with a drug dealer, who coincidentally became my real estate client, and whose murdered body I just happened to find? Of course we didn't talk about that!"

"Okay," I said, chastened. "I was just wondering. Don't get mad at me. So, back to Jeremy. What does he do for a living? I assume he's employed." *At least, I hope he is, and he's not one of those gigolos I've heard about who attaches himself to an older woman for her money.*

"The subject didn't come up," Nancy said. "Now that you

mention it, I think at one point Bob asked him and Jeremy sort of deflected the question." She checked the time on her phone. "I have to leave. I'm showing a house to a prospective buyer in fifteen minutes."

"That's it? That's all you have to tell me?" I asked.

"Don't be critical, Carol. Under the circumstances, I think I did a pretty good job. Jeremy seems very nice, and he and Margo seem very happy together. And the inn is gorgeous. It's all decorated for the holidays. Lots of mistletoe." She grinned, then gave me a quick peck on the cheek and disappeared before I had the chance to tell her that Jenny begged me to help her with Christmas. Oh, well. Another time.

Chapter 9

One minute, you're young and fun. The next minute, you're turning down the car stereo so you can see better.

"Explain to me again why we're doing this," Jim said, giving me a disgusted look. "It's absolutely ridiculous to be driving during rush hour on the worst highway in the entire United States to meet a woman we don't even like and her new...whatever the heck he is. I don't know why I let you talk me into this. This is all your fault, Carol. You have to learn how to say no to people." As added emphasis, he leaned on the horn, startling the poor driver who was crawling along Route 95 ahead of us, who responded with a one-finger salute.

It was early evening, and Jim was in a real snit. First, he gave me grief about going to dinner when I sprang it on him after a particularly nice and surprising afternoon's activities. And now, he was complaining about the traffic.

I gritted my teeth. No way was any of this my fault. *You know how he hates driving in heavy traffic. It brings out the worst in him, and he's taking his frustration out on you. He doesn't really mean it.*

"I suggested we stay on Fairport Turnpike," I reminded him. "But you thought the highway would be quicker, because there'd been an accident on that road earlier today and traffic was still slow."

"We don't even like Margo," Jim reiterated.

"True, but she's family, so whether we like her or not, we're stuck with her. Besides, I don't know about you, but I've never met anyone's soulmate before. It should be an interesting experience."

Jim reached over and gave my gloved hand a quick pat. "Yes, you have. You've met yours. Aren't we soulmates?"

"I guess we are," I said slowly. "I never thought about us that way before. And this is the hotel exit," I said, pointing out the sign.

"I know, Carol. I see it," Jim snapped. "And not a minute too soon."

If the drive to dinner was this bad, dinner was going to be a disaster.

After the usual argument about valet parking, which Jim refuses to do under any circumstances, we ended up parking on an icy side street and walking—or, in my case, slipping and sliding—the three blocks to the hotel. At least my husband held my arm to prevent me from falling. Or maybe it was to hold himself up. Who knows?

I am going to enjoy this dinner. I am going enjoy this dinner. I am going to enjoy this dinner. I shook my head. It didn't matter how many times I said it to myself, I still wasn't convinced.

But once I walked into the hotel, my bad mood evaporated. Even I couldn't be crabby when I saw the beautiful holiday decorations in the lobby, especially the largest gingerbread house I'd ever seen. I swear, it had to be over fifteen feet tall, and it was laden with ornaments that looked good enough to eat. I looked closer, and gasped. Was I crazy? Or were all the ornaments made out of chocolate?

Leaving Jim gazing at the gingerbread house in amazement, I hustled to the front desk. I just had to know more about that display.

"Checking in?" asked the young woman behind the counter, whose name badge identified her as April.

"I wish," I said, smiling. "My husband and I are meeting some people here for dinner. It's our first time at your hotel. I cannot believe that gingerbread house. Are the ornaments all chocolate?"

"Everyone is impressed with that display," April said. "And, yes, the ornaments are chocolate. We have an amazing pastry chef, and he designed it from scratch. It's our first holiday season here in Connecticut, and we wanted to make a good impression.

"Here, take this brochure about the Inn. We really strive to make every guest's experience here just like home."

"Let me tell you," I said, "so far, this is a lot better than what we have at home."

"We're pet friendly, too," April added, turning over the brochure to the back.

Fairport Inn and Suites pet policy: Dogs are welcome here. We've never had a dog that smoked in bed and set fire to the blankets. We've never had a dog that stole our towels or played the T.V. too loud, or had a noisy fight with his traveling companion. We've never had a dog that got drunk and broke up the furniture. So if your dog can vouch for you, you're welcome here, too.

The Management

"I'm definitely keeping this," I said. "Your hotel sounds like the place of my dreams."

"Come back and see us anytime. And enjoy your dinner." April pointed over my right shoulder. "I think the people you're meeting are waiting for you."

Rats. Just when I was in such a good mood, I remembered why we were here. I set my mouth into the smile I'd practiced in front of the bathroom mirror right before we left, turned around, and was surprised to see Sister Rose, my former high school English teacher. Sister Rose is now the director of a program to assist women in crisis, and the manager of its local fund-raising thrift shop, Sally's Closet. She and I now have what could be called a friendship, although to tell the truth, she still has the same ability to scare the living daylights out of me like she could in school.

"Hello, Sister," I said, recovering as quickly as I could. "What a nice surprise."

Sister Rose leaned forward and gave me a quick kiss on the cheek, which was a novelty in our relationship, believe me. "It's always lovely to see you, dear," she said. "I'd like you to meet two people who, I hope, will become very good friends and supporters of Sally's Closet, Dr. Frank Adams and his wife, Dr. Ellen Adams." Turning to the couple, she added, "Carol was a student of mine at Mount Saint Francis Academy many years ago, and she is one of our most faithful thrift shop volunteers." That introduction really threw me, because the good Sister knew that I hadn't been in to do any volunteer work in months.

She gave me a look which told me, loud and clear, to go along with her. I figured that she must have her reasons for this deception and, knowing her, she'd already worked it out with the Good Lord and received a dispensation for her transgression. Either that, or she was laying a massive guilt trip on me.

"I'm so glad to meet you, Carol," the woman said, shaking my hand with an iron grip. "And I know Frank is as well." She poked her husband, who looked like he was a million miles away.

"Sorry, I was wool-gathering," he said, embarrassed. "Yes, it's a pleasure. Sister Rose has been filling us in on all the wonderful work the volunteers do to keep the thrift shop going."

I was trying to pick up just a tiny hint from Sister Rose on what exactly this conversation was all about. None was forthcoming, and we were just standing there, so I said, "Are you both thinking of volunteering at Sally's Closet? We can always use more help."

"Frank and Ellen are new in the area and looking for a worthy nonprofit to support financially," Sister Rose clarified. "Although, as Carol said, we're always looking for some extra help in the shop as well."

"The program for women in crisis is wonderful," I said. I'd done my duty, to the best of my ability, and now it was time to get away from this increasingly uncomfortable situation and dive into another one. "I'd love to stay and talk more, but Jim and I are meeting people for dinner here."

"We were just leaving," Sister Rose said, putting me out of my misery at last. "And I believe Jim is waiting for you in the restaurant. Don't forget the volunteer appreciation reception at the shop."

"It's on my calendar," I said, lying with a straight face. I hoped her dispensation from the Good Lord was broad enough to cover me, too.

Chapter 10

Don't bother walking a mile in my shoes. That would be boring. Spend 30 seconds in my head. That'll freak you right out.

"It's lovely to see you again, Carol," Margo said. I noted that it wasn't lovely enough for her to stand and greet me, but, as you know, I'm never petty.

"You, too," I said, sinking gratefully into the chair Jim had pulled out for me. "Sorry I was delayed. I ran into someone I know in the lobby and it was hard for me to break away without being rude." I turned to Jim and said, "Sister Rose."

Jim raised his eyebrows. He's heard my ranting and raving about her for years and knows he shouldn't ask me for details on any encounters with the good sister.

I caught my breath and looked around the table. There was one empty chair. Where was Margo's soulmate? Was I supposed to ask about Jeremy's whereabouts or ignore the fact that he wasn't here? Lacking anything meaningful to say, I blurted out the first thing that popped into my head. "This is going to be such a memorable Christmas. Last year at this time, Jim and I had no idea we were going to be grandparents. Did we, Jim?" *Help me out here, for heaven's sake. Say something.*

Jim was busy pretending to peruse the menu and ignored

me. The rat.

"Yes, it's certainly going to be a memorable one," Margo agreed, "although at CJ's tender age, he won't remember it. I hope it will be a very happy one, too."

"Yes," I said. "Happy for all of us." *Just take a gun and shoot me now. That'd put me out of my misery and make me happy.*

"When did you arrive?" I already knew the answer because she'd told me on the phone. But I was grasping at conversational straws here.

"We checked in yesterday," Margo said. "Jeremy had to take a phone call and he didn't want to disturb the other diners. I can't wait for you both to meet him." She patted the empty chair. "He'll be along in a minute, I'm sure."

Oooh. I realized I had a golden opportunity for a quick interrogation, and I didn't want to waste a single second. I leaned across the table so I didn't have to raise my voice. "Margo, let's stop beating around the bush here. Who is this guy and did you tell your son about him yet?"

Margo flushed. "I'd forgotten how direct you can be, Carol."

"If you mean rude, I suppose I am in this instance. I apologize in advance, but you've landed Jim and me in the middle of what could be an extremely volatile family situation and I think we have a right to know what's going on. Right, Jim?"

I turned, expecting some spousal support, but my husband had vamoosed. Boy, was he going to get an earful from me when we got home.

Margo's eyes filled up, and I immediately felt guilty. "I don't mean to upset you, but can you see the situation from my point of view? I'm glad you're so happy with this guy, but you have to understand what a complete surprise it is to the rest of us. And you've made Jim and me part of it."

"You're right. I'm sorry, but I needed an ally, and since we share our darling grandson, I reached out to you. I hoped that because you have such a loving relationship with your husband, you'd be supportive and happy for me. I'm very lucky to have found someone so wonderful at my age."

Food for thought, which I resolved to think about later. Much later.

Jim's voice interrupted my musing. "Look who I met while I was getting our drinks at the bar." Margo's face lit up like the proverbial Christmas tree. "You must be Carol," said the man, holding a glass of red wine in each hand. He carefully placed one glass in front of Margo. I was impressed that he didn't spill a drop. "I took the liberty of ordering you a Merlot. I hope that's all right."

Margo beamed even brighter, if that was possible. "Perfect. As always. Thank you."

"I'm Jeremy Dixon," he said, leaning down and shaking my hand. "This is a real pleasure. Margo's told me so much about you that I feel I know you already."

She's told us nothing about you. I didn't really say that out loud, of course.

"I apologize for keeping you all waiting," Jeremy continued. "The phone call took a lot more time than I expected. But now," he raised his glass, "I think this happy occasion deserves a toast. To family. And Merry Christmas."

"Merry Christmas," Jim echoed, clinking glasses with Margo, Jeremy, and lastly, me.

I raised my glass of chardonnay in a half-hearted effort to follow Jim's example. My darling husband, the same man who had just been complaining a short time ago about being dragged to this dinner, had completely gotten into the holiday spirit. Or maybe he'd snuck in an extra glass of wine when I wasn't looking.

Here's the problem with me. When I'm in a bad mood, I can't hide it. My face betrays me every single time. And right now, for completely petty reasons, I was well on my way to a humdinger of a bad mood.

Give Jeremy a chance. And for Pete's sake, don't be rude to Margo. For better or for worse, you're going to be stuck with these two for the holidays, so suck it up. And for heaven's sake, don't stare at Jeremy. You look like an idiot.

I had to admit, the guy was every bit as good-looking in person as he was in Nancy's photo. His blond hair was longer than I prefer on a man, but it was certainly thick and neatly trimmed. His expression was open and friendly when he was looking at me. But when he focused on Margo, I could see the love he had for her, no matter what their age difference was. He was either totally in love with her or the best actor I'd ever met outside of a Broadway theater. When I snuck another surreptitious look, I realized he had to be in his late forties, even though his boyish good looks made him appear younger. He'd definitely be one of those men who'd grow older but never show his age.

I took a ladylike sip of wine and looked around me. The dining room was beautifully decorated, just like the lobby was. And it appeared that the Christmas tree tucked in a corner of the room was filled with a variety of colorful ornaments.

Jeremy noticed me gazing at the tree. "Isn't that display something? In case you're wondering, those ornaments would all be edible if they hadn't been sprayed with a preservative first so they'd last through the whole season."

"It's amazing," I agreed.

"And on the other side of the dining room, there's one just for kids," Jeremy continued, pointing to a taller tree filled with toys. I grinned when I saw how many teddy bears there were hiding among all the branches. "CJ would love this," I said. "Well, he's only four months old, but he's very advanced for his age."

"I can't wait to meet him. Margo's shown me lots of pictures. He looks adorable. I couldn't believe it when she told me CJ was her grandson."

"Mine, too," I said, immediately staking my claim just in case it wasn't crystal clear. "I mean, Jim's and mine."

Margo and Jim were now chatting away, and it seemed like this was a golden opportunity for me to play Twenty Questions with Jeremy.

"You might as well know right now that being inquisitive is one of my signature character traits, Jeremy," I said with a smile.

Jeremy burst out laughing.

"I warned him already," Margo said, squeezing his hand. "He said he was up to the challenge."

"I bet you want to know how Margo and I met," he said, his eyes twinkling. "It happened one enchanted evening, across a crowded room." And he started to hum the song from the famous musical, *South Pacific*.

"That's not how we met and you know it," Margo said, blushing. "He's just teasing you. The truth is, Jeremy saved my life a few months ago, right after I left Fairport, and one thing led to another."

"She's exaggerating," Jeremy said. "I did not save her life. I just happened to be in the right place at the right time. Any other man would have done exactly the same thing and helped a lovely lady in distress. Am I right, Jim?"

I could tell from Jim's expression that he wasn't sure how to respond to Jeremy's question. So in the interests of preserving marital harmony, and to ensure a stress-free drive home, I jumped in to help him. "Jim and I have been married for almost forty years," I said. "Whenever I need him, he's always there for me without question. So I can say with absolute certainty that, whatever you did, Jeremy, Jim has already done the same thing and more for me." I patted his hand for emphasis. (Jim's hand, not Jeremy's, in case you were confused.)

"Jeremy and I met the night I arrived back home from my trip here," Margo clarified. "I'd taken a late flight that didn't arrive until after midnight. When I got to my car in the long-term parking lot, it wouldn't start. Which is understandable, I found out later, because it had been sitting there for so long. Anyway, I panicked. I tried to call Triple A, but I was put on hold for what seemed like an eternity. I got out of the car and tried to raise the hood so I could see if I could figure out what was wrong." She looked at me. "I don't know about you, Carol, but I am totally clueless about how a car works."

I nodded in female solidarity. "Me, too. And I'd be scared to death if I had to deal with car trouble in the middle of the night all by myself."

"I was terrified. Then another car pulled up beside mine. The driver asked if I needed help. Boy, did I ever." She beamed at

Jeremy. "Not only was he able to start my car with jumper cables, he followed me all the way to my condo to be sure I got home safely. I was nervous when I realized I'd allowed a strange man to follow me home, in case he wasn't trustworthy, but he turned out to be a perfect gentleman. Without him, I'd probably still be sitting in that airport parking lot. He even came with me to the repair shop the next day, to be sure I was treated fairly."

"I can see now why you say Jeremy saved your life," I said. "And, yes, Jim would do the same thing for me." *Right after he interrogated me for at least 15 minutes about how I got myself into such a stupid mess in the first place.* I didn't add that last part, of course.

"I certainly would," Jim said. "And feel free to remind me about that, should I forget."

"Don't worry, I will."

"How did you and Jim meet?" Margo asked. "I don't think you ever said."

That launched Jim off into telling the story of our chance meeting in college, with me interrupting him every other minute with so many additions and corrections that he finally threw up his hands and said, "I give up. You tell the story, Carol."

By that time Margo and Jeremy were laughing so hard that they had tears running down their cheeks. "How long did it take you to perfect a comedy routine like that?" Jeremy asked, wiping his eyes. "You two are a riot."

"I refuse to answer on the grounds that I will be interrupted again," Jim said, sending the rest of us—including me—into another laughing fit.

"How about we order now?" Jeremy suggested. "The restaurant's starting to fill up with other customers."

The rest of the dinner was pleasant until I made the mistake of asking Margo if she'd seen CJ yet. Her eyes filled up, and I realized that I had brought up a touchy subject.

"Let's just say that I saw CJ, then Mark and I talked, and it did not go well. I don't want to ruin a wonderful evening, so I'll tell you another time." She was clearly upset, so I didn't pursue it. But I wasn't looking forward to the phone calls or texts I was sure were heading my way later tonight or tomorrow.

The meal ended abruptly when Jeremy got a text and said, "I have to answer this right away. Please excuse me. I've asked the server to put this dinner on our bill. It's been a pleasure, and I'm looking forward to seeing you both again."

Jim started to protest that we should share the tab, but Jeremy was already gone.

"This dinner was on us because we invited you," Margo said. "Just between us, he can afford it. Money's no problem for him. He treats me like a queen. Everything is first-class, all the way."

Naturally, I wanted to know more. "What does Jeremy do for a living?" I asked, as Jim was helping me with my coat.

"Jeremy's a consultant for one of the alphabet agencies in DC. I'm not sure which one, but they give him a huge expense account. He's frequently flying off somewhere on business. He's even gone to Europe twice since we've been seeing each other."

"What does he consult about?" Jim asked. "Is he a lobbyist?"

"I have no idea. I've never asked him."

Chapter 11

I run like the winded.

"Go ahead, admit it," I said, clinging to Jim's arm tightly so I wouldn't slip and fall on the icy sidewalk. "You had a good time. I know I did. And I liked Jeremy. He's a nice guy, and he seems to really care about Margo."

"It was a lot more enjoyable than I expected it to be. But I'm bushed. I'm not used to staying out this late."

"Neither am I," I said. I stopped walking so quickly that Jim almost fell.

"What the hell? Come on, Carol, keep going. You can make it to the car. It's only one more block."

"That's not it, Jim. I thought I heard someone calling for help." I pointed to my right. "Over there, near that hedge. Be quiet and listen."

This time, the voice was unmistakable. Even Jim, with his bad hearing, couldn't deny that someone was in trouble.

"Help me. Please. Is someone there? I need help."

I took a few tenuous steps in the direction of the cries, using the light on my cell phone to show me the way. Jim followed close behind me.

A young woman was lying on her side in a crumpled heap. "Oh, thank God someone heard me. I can't get up. I think I may have broken my ankle." Jim helped her sit up and I realized it was April, the front desk clerk at the inn. Her face was swollen and bleeding, and her right eye looked like she'd have a doozy of a shiner before too long.

"Can you stand if I help you?" Jim asked.

"What the heck happened to you?" I blurted out. "Were you attacked?"

Note to self: Be sure to tell Jim that under no circumstances was he allowed to skip a valet parking service just to save a few bucks any more. It could have just as easily been us who'd been attacked. Our safety was much more important than saving a few dollars.

"Nothing that dramatic, thank goodness," April assured us as she leaned on Jim and stood up. I noticed she wasn't putting much weight on her left foot. "It was my own stupid fault. I work at the Fairport Inn and Suites, and the staff uses this path all the time to walk from the building to the separate lot where we all park. It's much quicker than walking all the way around the building. I came out on my break to grab an extra pair of shoes I keep for emergencies. I've been standing all night, and my feet are killing me." She tried to stand on her own and winced. "I don't know what really happened. It was all so fast. I must have slipped on some ice and fallen."

"How long have you been lying there? You look like you're freezing," I said. My gallant Jim immediately took the hint and offered his coat to warm the girl up, earning extra good points from me.

"I don't know," April said. "It seemed like a long time, but it probably wasn't more than fifteen minutes."

"You should get your ankle checked," I said. "You may need an x-ray to be sure it's not broken." I rooted around in my purse and found the clean handkerchief I occasionally remember to bring with me. "This is probably going to sting, but you're bleeding, and your eye is all puffy. Maybe this will help."

April took the handkerchief and applied it to her face. "Ouch. That really hurts."

"You need to go to an Urgent Care facility or the hospital emergency room," I pronounced.

"That's not necessary," April said. "If you two kind people can help me get back to the Inn, we have a physician on call 24 hours a day. I can text him when I get there and he'll come right over."

I whipped out my cell phone. "Even better, give me his number and I'll text him now. It'll save time and he can meet you there."

"Lean on me for support," Jim said. "We'll get you back there as quickly and painlessly as possible." So that's what we did.

Naturally, by the time we finally got home, took care of the dogs, and collapsed into bed, Jim had no trouble getting to sleep. Not me. I lay there, exhausted but wide awake, reviewing the evening's events like I was watching a movie. There was something at the back of my mind that I was having trouble remembering. I hate when that happens almost as much as I hate it when I can't get to sleep. It suddenly dawned on me that one problem was the reason for the other. What the heck was I trying to remember?

All of a sudden, I had it. The wealthy couple Sister Rose introduced me to were our new neighbors, the people Phyllis Stevens said were moving into the Old Parsonage. I couldn't wait to tell Phyllis I'd actually met them. Maybe she'd let me off the hook for the holiday party. With that happy thought, I finally drifted off to sleep.

Chapter 12

Life is what happens when you're making other plans.

The next morning, I woke up later than usual, groggy and feeling like I hadn't slept at all. I turned off the electric blanket, forcing myself to abandon the cozy cocoon of warmth I'd been wrapped in, sat up in bed, and stretched carefully, so as not to throw out my back like I'd done so many times before.

Satisfied that I wasn't going to be in excruciating pain today, I noted that my three usual slumber-time companions—Jim, Lucy, and Ethel—were absent. I smiled. With any luck at all, Jim had already exercised and fed the dogs and made the coffee, one of the few perks (my apologies!) of having him retire. I was in a good mood, despite my lack of shut-eye, because today was the day we were finally going to buy our Christmas tree. Jim had been finding excuses to put off the purchase for days, no doubt hoping that prices would come down, which was ridiculous. As the tree inventory shrank, prices were bound to go up, but I'd been unable to convince him of that. Thank goodness the beautiful decorations at the Fairport Inn and Suites had inspired him.

As soon as my bare feet hit the floor, I realized I was in trouble. The room was cold. No, not just cold; the room was freezing. And I knew why. I've never admitted this to anyone before, but Jim and I are temperature-incompatible. During the summer, when it's blazing hot and disgustingly humid in Connecticut, I have to fight with Jim to turn on our central air conditioning. When I ask him why the heck we paid all that money to install it and not use it, he always replies, "It adds to the house's resale value." Ha! Like I care about that when I'm sitting in a hot house sweating my buns off.

In the winter, when I'm chilly most of the time because Jim keeps the thermostat so low, there are only so many layers of clothing I can add before I can't bend my arms or sit down comfortably. No way was I letting him get away with keeping the thermostat low today.

I threw a sweatsuit on over my flannel pajamas, checked to be sure I could move my arms (I could), added woolen knee socks to keep my feet warm, pulled on a pair of Ugg boots, and after rummaging in a dresser drawer, completed the look with warm mittens. Satisfied that I'd at least make it through the time until the furnace finally warmed my antique house, I marched into the front hall, ready to do battle with the thermostat and Jim. To my complete shock, the thermostat was set at 72 degrees. But the house was cold. What the heck was going on? Apparently, not the furnace.

I heard Jim's footsteps coming up the cellar stairs. My hero. I was sure he'd found the problem and fixed it. *Relax, Carol. You'll be toasty warm soon.*

One look at my husband's face and my heart sank down to the Ugg boots. "We have a big problem. I can't get the furnace to go on. I've been down there fiddling with it for over an hour, but it's just not working." He looked like he was close to tears.

Be supportive, Carol. The poor guy's doing his best. Don't lash out and accuse him of making the problem worse. Even though he probably did.

"We'll call someone to come and fix it," I said. "Reliable Fuel delivers our heating oil, and they have a service department."

Jim's face darkened. "Those robbers? No way. They're way overpriced. And besides, we don't have a service contract with them."

That's because you didn't want to pay extra for one. I didn't really say that out loud, of course.

"Jim, we have no choice." I padded back into the kitchen, picked up the house phone, and waved it in front of my husband. "Do you want to call them, or should I?"

Jim grabbed the phone. "Okay, okay. I'll do it." He stomped into the family room and I heard him making the call.

After pouring myself a cup of coffee to jumpstart my brain, I tried to wrap Lucy and Ethel with quilts to be sure they didn't freeze. It was probably my imagination but I think they looked grateful.

After a few minutes, Jim stomped back into the kitchen, looking relieved. "Good news, Carol," he said. "The dispatcher said there was a repairman just finishing a service call one block over. He'll be here in five minutes."

I gave him 'The Look.' "It's a good thing you called when you did," I said, a subtle reminder of whose idea *that* was.

"Yeah, yeah. I know. Thanks to you. I'm going to stand outside to be sure he comes to the right house. We don't want him to drive right by without stopping."

I didn't comment. I merely smiled sweetly and wrapped my hands around my coffee mug. At least a small part of me would be warm.

Both dogs started barking furiously, and then I heard an unfamiliar male voice, Jim, and the sound of footsteps on the stairs to the cellar. I crossed my fingers that this was an easy, quick, and—even more important—cheap fix, and waited for the next update.

I heard Jim's voice again, and he didn't sound happy. "Replace the whole unit? Are you kidding me? How much is that going to cost me?" This outburst was followed by the sound of footsteps ascending the stairs, then the appearance of my irate husband and the repairman in our kitchen. "This is my wife," Jim said. "Tell her what you just told me."

"I'm really sorry, ma'am, but your furnace is a goner. It's so old that I'm surprised it's lasted as long as it has. We may have to rip out some pipes, too, in order to get the job done."

My eyes filled with tears. This was much worse than I'd expected. "But it's Christmas," I blurted out without thinking. "This can't be happening. Not now."

The repairman looked like he was ready to burst into tears himself. "I know, ma'am and I'm really sorry about that. But there's a bright spot to this because of the holiday's being so close, lots of our customers have decided to postpone regular maintenance work until after the first of next year. So we have an opening in our workload. We can start the job as soon as you and your husband move out."

"Move out?" I repeated. "Are you saying we have to leave our house while you're doing the work? Oh, my God. This can't be happening."

"We can still come back here to sleep at night, right?" Jim said. "We just have to vacate while you're working."

"No, sir. I'm afraid you'll have to move out completely while the job's going on. We may have to work late at night to get it all done. And we'll probably have to turn off the water and the power at times, too."

"I don't know how we're going to pay for all this," Jim said, looking like a defeated man. "I suppose you think I was wrong to ask the guy to give us a little time to process all this and figure out a plan."

"He was very nice, all things considered. He knew he'd shocked the heck out of us. At least we're on their schedule. But we can't move out until we figure out where we're going to go."

"Yeah, and who's going to pay for that, on top of a new furnace." My husband just shook his head. "This is a disaster."

Sometimes, I'm smart. And sometimes—not often, but sometimes—I'm positively brilliant. This was one of those positively brilliant moments.

"I have an idea," I said.

"I do, too," Jim said. "You first. I bet we both have the same idea."

I doubt it. After all these years, we never have. I didn't really say that, of course.

I motioned to Jim with my mittened hand. "No, you go ahead. Tell me your idea."

"Claire and Larry are in Florida for most of the winter. We'll ask them if we can stay at their place."

No way! If one of Claire's precious things was in a different place when they got home or, heaven forbid, if we broke something, I'd never hear the end of it. I didn't say that out loud, of course. Jim would never understand.

I shook my head. "You had a good idea but it's not going to work. They come back and forth all the time whenever the spirit moves them. Plus, we have to bring Lucy and Ethel with us. They'd never go along with having the dogs there."

Jim's face fell. "You're right. I didn't think about the dogs. So, what's your idea?"

"We move to the Fairport Inn and Suites. The place even allows dogs. It's perfect."

"It's expensive," Jim countered. "Who the heck's going to pay for that?"

"We have homeowner's insurance," I reminded him. "And part of our coverage is for temporary housing if there's an emergency. It's called 'loss of use.' "

Jim raised his eyebrows. "Are you sure about this? I never heard of it."

"I'm positive. Get our policy from the filing cabinet and check it for yourself. Then call the insurance company and find out what we need to provide to start coverage. I'll call the inn and make reservations, then start organizing what to bring with us. The rooms at the inn have kitchenettes, so that makes it cheaper. We won't have to eat in the restaurant." I swatted my husband and ordered, "Get going. The sooner we leave, the sooner we can move back home."

In less than an hour, the insurance coverage was all set and I'd made a hotel reservation online. We packed up what we thought we'd need, loaded everything into the car, and were on our way to our temporary, and palatial, new home.

Chapter 13

I had my patience tested. I'm negative.

Jim dropped me off at the main entrance to the inn, instructing me to handle the check-in process while he negotiated (argued) about self-parking, rather than handing over his precious car keys to the valet. I was delighted not to be a witness to what was guaranteed to be an unpleasant and embarrassing conversation.

My new pal, April, was nowhere to be seen at the registration desk. I hoped she'd taken the day off to recover from the previous night's ordeal.

The woman currently behind the desk was close to my age (which, again, is none of your business), and had a mass of curly hair that made me green with envy. Intent on her computer screen, she didn't acknowledge my approach.

"I love your hair," I blurted out.

The woman looked up, seeming startled at the interruption. "Can I help you?"

I hastened to cover my gaffe. "I'm sorry if I startled you but I've always been envious of anyone with curly hair. My own is straight as a stick. At least, that's what my mother always called it. She also said to be happy with what the Good Lord gave me and quit complaining."

Sheesh, Carol. Enough about the hair. You're obviously annoying her.

To my surprise, the woman started to laugh. "When I was a child, I wanted straight hair, like yours. In fact, I used to try ironing it to get rid of the curls until my mother caught me doing it and read me the riot act."

Now we were both laughing.

"I apologize for not welcoming you properly to the Fairport Inn and Suites," the woman said. She touched her name badge. "My name is Barbara, but everyone calls me Bobbie. Are you checking in today?"

"Yes," I said. "Carol and Jim Andrews."

Bobbie's fingers zipped across the computer screen, then she looked up, frowning. "I'm sorry, Mrs. Andrews, but I don't seem to have a reservation for you. When did you make it?"

I gripped the registration desk like it was the last life preserver on the *Titanic*. "Our name must be there," I said. "Please, look again."

"When did you make your reservation?" Bobbie asked again.

"This morning," I said, my voice shaking. I was on the verge of a full-blown meltdown, and believe me, it wasn't going to be pretty.

"Did you receive a confirmation email?" Bobbie asked, frowning. "I don't think the reservation went through. And we're now fully booked until the week after Christmas. I'm so sorry."

Now I understood how Mary and Joseph must have felt on the way to Bethlehem. The Christmas story had suddenly taken on a whole new meaning for me.

"Isn't there anything you can do to help us? We have an emergency in our house, and we've had to move out for several days. We have nowhere to go."

Luckily for me, Jim was nowhere to be seen while all this drama was going on. Bobbie's expression softened. "Let me talk to my boss and see what I can do. Wait here." She disappeared into a nearby office.

I couldn't control myself any longer. The waterworks started, despite my best efforts. And I couldn't think of a single saint I could call on for help. In the midst of my misery, I felt a tap on the shoulder and froze. OMG. Jim was back. What was I going to tell him?

"Carol, is that you? Why are you crying? What's wrong?"

Strong arms turned me around, and I stared into Jeremy's kind eyes. "We have nowhere to go," I stammered. "Our furnace died this morning, and we had to move out of the house right away so it could be replaced. I thought we had a reservation here, but the desk clerk says we don't. Jim's going to kill me when he finds out about this."

"I can't believe there's nothing available," Jeremy said. "Let me see what I can do to help." He walked around the check-in desk and disappeared into the same office Bobbie had moments before.

They both emerged an eternity later—which was probably less than ten minutes. "Mrs. Andrews, if you're willing to share, we've found a place for you and your party," Bobbie reported.

"Share? I don't understand." *I'm not so desperate that I'm going to bunk in with strangers. At least, not yet.*

"The only thing we have available now is our corporate suite. No company has reserved the suite this close to Christmas, so it will be completely empty over the holidays. Mr. Dixon is giving up his room, and he and his party will move into the corporate suite and share it with you. It's a huge suite, with three full bedrooms, each with its own bath, a full kitchen, a formal dining room and living room, and personal concierge service. We'll be able to rent the room Mr. Dixon is currently occupying without a problem, and he's already paid for that in full. There's no extra charge for the upgrade because you're all really doing the inn a favor. It's a win-win for everyone."

"Just to be sure, the entire hotel allows dogs, correct? Even the corporate suite? We have our two English cockers, Lucy and Ethel, with us."

"Not a problem," Bobbie assured me. "We're completely pet friendly here."

"Are you sure Margo's okay with this plan to share the suite with us?" I asked Jeremy. "I know Margo's allergic to dogs."

To my complete surprise, Jeremy laughed out loud. "She's not allergic to dogs. I convinced Margo to see a doctor about her allergy problem, because she hadn't been checked out properly. It turned out she's allergic to some of the ingredients in that horrible green concoction she drinks. I texted her already about the room change and she's fine with the idea. She's already packing so we can switch rooms right away. There's a bellman on the way to help her move and give her the new keycard. I love dogs and I can't wait to meet yours."

"What a relief."

"Margo thinks it's a great idea for all of us to share this suite. She said it's the perfect way to pay you back for your hospitality a few months ago."

I took that with the proverbial grain of salt. I figured Margo's sudden burst of good will wouldn't last long, but hopefully Jeremy could keep her in line.

"Let's get you and your husband officially checked in and then I'll give you key cards to the suite," Bobbie said, handing me a registration form to fill in. "This is just for security purposes, so the hotel staff knows you're 'official.' And be sure to put down the names of your two dogs. We like to greet all our guests by name and make them feel welcome."

"On behalf of Lucy and Ethel, thank you," I said, scribbling down all the requested information in the illegible cursive I laughingly refer to as my handwriting.

"I'll just need to run your credit card through, Mrs. Andrews," Bobbie said with a smile.

At my alarmed expression, she clarified, "Don't worry. You won't be charged anything for the suite. It's our policy to always have a credit card on file for each guest, in case there are discrepancies in the billing. It's really a safety measure for the guests."

"If that's your policy," I said, rummaging in my purse and extracting my wallet, "I'm glad to cooperate." I handed over my credit card; Bobbie zipped it through her computer and handed it back to me. "Thank you. You're all set."

Turning her attention to Jeremy, she said, "Here are your new key cards, Mr. Dixon. I'll deactivate the old ones as soon as you move and you can return them at your convenience." She pointed toward an elevator with a bronze door, which set it apart from the others. "Your key card gives you access to this express elevator, which goes directly to the sixth floor. It's our V.I.P. elevator, only for the corporate suite guests."

Wow. At my age, I finally became a V.I.P. Then my completely irrational fear of being stuck in an elevator kicked into high gear.

"What if that elevator stops working with one of us inside? Or what if it stops working and we can't get off the sixth floor? Will we be trapped?" My palms started to sweat as I pictured a possible life and death scenario.

"Relax, Mrs. Andrews. All the other elevators can reach the sixth floor, too. This one is just the fastest and we have exit stairways on every floor. You'll be perfectly safe."

"Oh, I wasn't asking for myself," I lied. "My husband is claustrophobic. I was asking for him."

"It might be time for us to check out our new digs," Jeremy said, holding up his new card. "Margo's probably waiting for us there. Text Jim and give him the suite number. We can meet him up there. Thank you so much for all your help, Bobbie. I'll be sure to put in a good word for you with your boss." And he gave her a killer smile.

Bobbie blushed. "Much appreciated."

"Yes, I'm very grateful to you for all your help, Bobbie," I added. "You've been terrific. Before we go check out the corporate suite, though, I wondered if you knew how April is. Will she be in later today?" To Jeremy, I clarified, "April works at the front desk, and she had an accident last night. Jim and I found her when we were on our way back to our car."

"I'm not sure. She took today off to recover from last night's ordeal. I didn't realize you and your husband were the ones who saved her. She could have frozen to death out there. Thank you so much for what you did."

"She's certainly lucky that you and Jim came along when you did," Jeremy said, looking at me with admiration.

"I'm glad she's staying home today," I said. "If you should

hear from her, please tell her I was asking about her."

Jeremy offered me his arm. "Shall we take a ride on our private elevator?"

"Why not?" I answered, pressing "send" on my phone to text Jim. And away we went to the sixth floor. And Margo.

Chapter 14

There's nothing like a little tomato soup to soothe the soul. Even if it's cold. Over ice. With a celery stalk. And vodka.

The V.I.P. elevator whisked us to the sixth floor so fast I thought my ears would pop. When it stopped suddenly, Jeremy said, "Wow. That was some ride."

"You're not kidding," I said, praying that Jeremy hadn't caught on to how terrified I was.

"I wonder what the ride down will be like."

I looked at him with alarm. "I hope you're not suggesting we try that right now."

"No way," Jeremy said as the doors slid open. "I have to recover from the ride up, first." He bowed and gestured to me. "After you, Carol."

"Your mother sure raised you right," I said, stepping onto terra firma and staring at the spectacular view out the floor-to-ceiling windows that greeted us. "My gosh. I swear I can see Manhattan from here."

"I don't think that's possible," Jeremy said. "It must be Stamford."

"Well, whatever it is, it's gorgeous."

The door opposite the elevator opened, revealing Margo

dressed in a Christmas sweater and black slacks. "Welcome to our home away from home," she said, pulling both of us inside. She gestured around the beautifully furnished living room with sliding glass doors leading to a private terrace. "Isn't this something? Our old room was nice, but this is spectacular." She looked behind us. "Where's Jim? Isn't he with you?"

"He's coming after he walks Lucy and Ethel. Our dogs," I clarified, in case she'd forgotten. "We had to bring them with us."

I suddenly realized that I could have called Mary Alice, and she would have been thrilled to have canine houseguests for as long as necessary. She loves the dogs as much as we do, and the feeling is reciprocated. I tucked that idea away in case things (and dogs) got out of hand here and I needed an emergency backup plan.

"Jeremy told me," Margo said, looking at him fondly. "I found out that I'm not really allergic to dogs. I haven't ever been around many, so I'm nervous around them. Jeremy loves dogs and he's convinced me I will, too, if I just give myself the chance. I'm looking forward to seeing Lucy and Ethel again."

I hope they both return that sentiment, especially Lucy. She can tell when someone doesn't like her, and she's been known to hold a grudge. Like I do.

"Why don't you look around and we'll try to figure out who'll take which bedroom?" Margo suggested. "We have three to choose from. Lucy and Ethel could have their own." Her remark made me laugh, which surprised me. In our previous encounter a few months ago, when CJ was born, there was nothing to laugh about in our relationship.

I heard knocking, then Jim's voice. "Carol, we're here. Let us in. The dogs need water."

I started toward the door, but Margo stopped me. She had a mischievous look on her face. "Let's have a little fun. You two get out of sight and let me open the door and surprise him. Go on, shoo."

Jeremy and I exchanged looks, then I said, "What the heck. Let's do it." We raced into what turned out to be a small half bathroom and closed the door.

"Jim," I heard Margo exclaim, "come in. I'm so glad we'll finally have some time together alone."

I heard the dogs yip, and Jim say, "Margo? What the heck are you doing here? Where's my wife?"

"She's having some alone time with Jeremy. It's a special Christmas celebration just for the four of us."

I could just picture Jim's face. Or maybe I couldn't.

Jeremy was doubled over, laughing, and I swatted him. "Knock it off." I opened the door and said, "Surprise! We have roommates. But don't worry, I'm bunking with you."

The expression on my husband's face was priceless, and I wished I'd had my phone ready so I could capture it for posterity. Meanwhile, Lucy and Ethel were straining at their leashes, eager to check out their new surroundings. I crossed my fingers that they'd behave themselves and Margo wouldn't lose it, the way she did at our house when she first saw them.

I needn't have worried. Jeremy snapped his fingers and beckoned them close. Both dogs obediently trotted over, sat in front of him, and licked his hands. It was amazing, like watching the *Dog Whisperer* in person, instead of on television. He squatted down so he was at their eye level and crooned, "Well, aren't you the two most beautiful dogs I've ever seen?" Lucy immediately rolled over on her back, begging for a tummy rub. She obviously agreed with him. Both dogs were entranced with their new friend and totally ignored me.

"We're all going to be great friends while we're together, aren't we?" he continued. "So come say hello to your other friend. You remember Margo, don't you?"

I held my breath. This was make it or break it time. But once again, Jeremy performed his magic. He snapped his fingers and both dogs immediately trotted over to Margo, who was sitting on the sofa with a nervous look on her face. He snapped his fingers and said, "Be polite, now. Sit and say hello."

To my utter amazement, both dogs immediately obeyed. They even gave Margo a friendly nudge, and she gave them a tentative head scratch.

"See, Margo," Jeremy said, "dogs are wonderful companions, if you just give them a chance. You'll be a dog lover in no time."

Jim finally recovered his voice. "I'm sure one of you will eventually explain to me what the heck is going on. And how we can afford this suite. I know our insurance covers a temporary move, Carol," he said, making it crystal clear which of his roommates he was addressing, "but the daily rate for this must be a fortune."

"I don't blame you for being concerned, dear. But this suite isn't costing us or the insurance company a single penny," I said.

Jeremy interrupted. "Let me explain. I happened to be in the lobby when Carol was checking in, Jim, and we said hello. The room clerk told us that the hotel has limited availability now because of Christmas, and offered us a deal on this suite if we were willing to share it. The hotel can fill our old room right away with guests from their standby list. In fact, we're doing the hotel management a favor. It's a win for all of us."

"It was my idea to play that trick on you, Jim," Margo confessed. "I guess it wasn't as funny as I thought. I'm sorry." She put out her hand. "Shake? If we're going to be roommates for a while, we'd better be friends, too."

"You really threw me for a loop," Jim said, taking her hand. "I didn't know what to think."

"Now that we're all friends," Jeremy said, "why don't we figure out who gets which room, maybe take a quick snooze or unpack, and then get together again in the living room in a little while for a glass of wine? I understand there's a well-stocked bar in the suite. We shouldn't let it go to waste."

"I'll get the luggage cart. I left it out in the hall," Jim said. I was relieved to see that he finally had a smile on his face. "And a glass of wine sounds great. It's been a helluva day."

I had to admit it. I could definitely see why Margo fell head over heels for Jeremy. Don't tell Jim, but I was falling a little bit for him, myself.

A tiny voice popped up in my head, suggesting that Jeremy

might be too good to be true. But I ignored it.

Chapter 15

Sometimes my husband thinks I'm crazy. But I'm not the one who married me.

"You're not still upset, are you?" I gestured around the luxurious bedroom that would be our home sweet home for the next few days. "All things considered, I think we've made out pretty well. Lucy and Ethel obviously think the same thing." Both pooches were deep in slumber on the huge bed. "I've always wanted a king-size bed, but it won't fit in our bedroom."

"Nah, I'm fine now. Sorry I overreacted before, but when I saw Margo in seduction mode at the door, my first instinct was to run away as fast as I could."

"You mean you were shocked to think that Margo was harboring lustful intentions toward you?" I teased.

"We should consider this an unexpected Christmas gift instead of an unexpected home emergency," Jim went on. "Maybe even another honeymoon for the two of us." Jim waggled his eyebrows, just to be sure I got his drift.

"We have roommates, remember?"

"Believe me, I do. But I'm sure they won't mind."

"Well, I'm not going to try and find out right now, so let's get organized," I said. "Where's my cell phone? We should check in with Jenny and Mark and tell them where we are."

"And who we're with," Jim said, pointing to my open purse, where the phone was taking a nice little nap.

"Oh no," I said, scrolling through several texts from our daughter, each one more frantic than the one before. "Jenny's been trying to reach me. I have to call her right now."

"You can handle explaining what's going on without me, right?"

"Sure," I said, already pressing "CALL" on my phone. "Go have a glass of wine. I'll join you as soon as I can."

Jim nodded and headed for the living room as Jenny answered my call.

"Mom! Where are you? Is Dad with you? Are you both okay? We're supposed to pick out Christmas trees tonight, and when I got to the house, it was dark. I used my key and let myself inside. It's freezing in there, and Phyllis Stevens said she saw strange men going in and out of the house all afternoon."

"Phyllis Stevens? How did she get involved?"

"I'll tell you about her after you explain what the heck is going on, and where you both are."

"Fair enough," I said. "I'm sorry we worried you. The furnace officially died this morning and we had to move to a hotel for a few days. We were in such a hurry to leave that I totally forgot about our date tonight. I should have texted you, so you wouldn't worry. Believe it or not, Dad, the dogs and I, are living in the fancy corporate suite at the Fairport Inn and Suites until the furnace is replaced. The men Phyllis saw were the workers from Reliable Fuel." A horrible thought occurred to me. "She didn't call the police, did she?"

"No, not yet. But she said if I didn't hear from you soon, I should call Mark and let him handle it. She scared me to death."

Good old Phyllis.

"She saw me drive up," Jenny continued, "and ran across the street to talk to me right away. You know how she is."

"She's probably been glued to her front window all afternoon. Be sure to tell her we're fine before she assumes the worst."

"Will do. So how did you get to stay in such fancy digs?" Jenny asked. "I can't imagine Dad springing the big bucks it must be costing."

"It's a long story about how we got the suite," I said slowly. "The hotel couldn't find our reservation when we got here. It was a nightmare. But it worked out. Sort of." I paused, then said, "Brace yourself, Jenny. We're sharing the suite with Margo and her new boyfriend, Jeremy Dixon."

Jenny let out a shriek that I was sure our roommates must have heard through the closed bedroom door. Lucy and Ethel both raised their heads and gave me dirty looks for disturbing their slumber.

"Jenny, keep your voice down," I said. "Margo and Jeremy are both in the next room with your father. I don't want them to know we're talking about them." Not taking any chances, I retreated to our bathroom and closed the door.

"I'll do my best to restrain myself," Jenny said. "But you can't blame me for my reaction after you dropped a bombshell like that. I'm in my car in the driveway with the heat on and the windows cracked open. It was too cold to stay in the house."

I did my best to fill Jenny in as quickly as I could. Of course, being my daughter, she kept interrupting me with questions. I left out the part about Margo pretending to seduce Jim, though. I wasn't sure how Jenny would react to that!

"So far, everything's working out very well. Margo's even making an effort to be nice to the dogs. Jeremy is a real miracle worker."

"If you say so," Jenny said. "Mark isn't keen to meet him yet. Or ever. His talk with Margo did not go well. I hope he changes his mind before Christmas. I'm trying to stay out of it, but it breaks my heart to see him so upset. I love him so much, but he's so stubborn sometimes."

"Oh, sweetie," I said, "wish there was something I could do to help."

"Well, since you and Dad are roommates with the happy couple for the next few days, maybe the four of you can come up with a brilliant plan. I sure hope so. I'm checking in with Phyllis now, and then I'm going home. I'll text you first thing tomorrow morning. Please stay out of trouble until then, okay? Mark and Paul were called in to work tonight, and your son-in-law may be willing to look the other way if you act up, but you know his partner isn't your biggest fan."

"And vice-versa," I said, earning a "Mom, be nice!" response from Jenny.

"I promise to be a good girl. Love you."

"Love you, too."

I felt guilty, making Jenny worry so much. Then I scrolled through texts on my phone and found two anxious messages from Nancy and one from Mary Alice, both wondering where I was. Good heavens. I never realized if I went AWOL for even a short time, the effect it would have on people close to me. I fired off answers to both pals, reassuring them, without giving any details, that all was well and I'd be in touch tomorrow. They responded immediately with a thumbs-up emoji. The situation in my family was more serious. Jenny had asked for my help, but what the heck could I do?

The more I thought about it, the more I realized that, so far, Jeremy had proved to be a miracle man at fixing problems. And since he *was* this problem, I was counting on him to come up with its solution

Chapter 16

The older I get, the earlier it gets late.

After drinks and a delicious dinner, courtesy of our own personal chef, both Jim and Margo excused themselves and retired to their respective rooms. "I hope tomorrow is a better day for all of us," Margo said. "Maybe I'll dream about the perfect way to win over my son. Good night."

"I'm going to hook up my computer and check my email," Jim said. He wasn't kidding me. As soon as he walked into our bedroom and saw that inviting king-size bed, he'd stretch out on it and be on his way to dreamland.

That left Jeremy, me, Lucy and Ethel. And since I figured neither of the dogs were willing to put their new pal on the spot by suggesting he figure out a way to fix the current family crisis, it was up to me to play the bad guy.

"Jeremy, I've been giving this problem between Margo and Mark a lot of thought," I began. "I'm sure you know that Mark is very close to Jim and me. We've known him ever since he was in grammar school, and he considers us more surrogate parents than in-laws."

"Your close relationship makes you the perfect person to convince Mark to give Margo's relationship with me a chance," Jeremy said. "He resents me and he hasn't even met me yet. I was hesitant to ask you, but while you were talking just now, I realized that, since you two are so close, you're the perfect person to talk to him for us."

Whoa! This certainly wasn't the direction I'd intended this conversation to go.

How stupid you are, Carol. Jeremy's only been nice to us because he's had an ulterior motive all along. What a rat. I bet Margo put him up to it. I'm not going to let them get away with it.

"Jim and I have discussed this situation, and we refuse to be placed in the middle of the current mother/son drama. This is your problem, yours and Margo's. We didn't create it, both of you did. If you're angry that we're not willing to be the go-betweens for you and want us to leave, we can pack our bags and be out of here right away. We have lots of friends in Fairport who'll be glad to let us stay with them temporarily, no strings attached."

Jeremy looked shocked. "Is that what you think? That I've been generous to you and Jim only because I planned on using you to intercede with Mark? You're totally wrong. I never even thought of doing that. I swear, I'm telling the truth." He seemed so sincere that I almost believed him. Almost.

I decided to sit there, mute, to see what else Jeremy had to say. If he was still the good guy we all thought he was, maybe he'd figure out that it was up to him to talk to Mark, man to man.

The silence was just about killing me. Finally, I said, "There's only one person who should try to explain this situation to Mark, and I'm sure you know who it is." I gave him my Mommy stare, the one that I'd used to strike fear in Jenny and Mike when they were kids.

Jeremy sighed. "I get it. You're right. I have to bite the bullet and talk to Mark myself. This relationship with Margo is very important to me. I have no idea where it's going, or how long it will last, but we have something very precious together right now and I don't want to lose her. I also don't want to come between her and her son. I know they already have a rocky relationship. And it would kill Margo if she couldn't see her grandson."

"I can't imagine anything worse than that," I agreed. I was

beginning to feel very sorry for both Margo and Jeremy. Talk about being between a rock and a hard place.

"If Margo's forced to choose between seeing CJ and a relationship with me, I want you to know that I'll step aside. That's a promise. And if I start to waver, I'm counting on you to remind me of what I said, Carol."

"I will. But I hope it doesn't come to that."

The silence continued, with each of us lost in our own thoughts. The chair I was in was so comfortable that I found myself getting very drowsy. It had been a long day. But before I could enjoy that king-size bed, I had doggie needs to see to. I yawned, stretched, and stood up. "Come on, girls, we have to go out." I looked around the room and frowned. "Providing I can find your leashes."

Jeremy reached under the coffee table. "Here they are. I stashed them here so nobody would trip on them." Both dogs immediately trotted over to him, and he snapped on their leashes. "I'll take one of the dogs and go with you. It's late, and you shouldn't be out alone."

"Thank you," I said. "We appreciate the company."

I suppressed a feeling of panic as I envisioned another express elevator ride, and grabbed Lucy's leash. *At least if we get stuck, you won't be alone. Don't be a baby. You'll be fine.*

In what seemed like a millisecond, we were in the lobby. I glanced toward the reception desk, and was surprised to see that April was on duty.

"I have to see how April's feeling after last night's accident," I said to the dogs. "It's very important, so you both better take care of business right away."

Jeremy raised his eyebrows, but didn't comment. "I talk to them all the time," I said. "We're on the same wavelength as long as I explain why I'm asking them to do something." Or have a few dog biscuits in my pocket.

Both dogs cooperated in record time, which impressed Jeremy. "You'll have to teach me how to do that, in case I can talk Margo into getting a dog."

"Deal," I said, handing him both dogs' leashes. "You can go

97

upstairs with the dogs if you're in a hurry. This conversation may take a little while."

"No problem," Jeremy said. "The dogs and I are fine waiting for you."

I shrugged. "Suit yourself." I headed toward the desk and waited until April was finished checking in a late arrival. When she saw me coming, she said, "It's you! Bobbie told me you and your husband were staying here for a few days. How can I ever thank you for rescuing me?"

I took a good look at her. "You certainly are in better shape than you were last night. How's your eye?"

April pushed back a curtain of dark hair that she'd positioned carefully on the left side of her face, revealing a bruise that was smaller than I expected. "As long as I comb my hair forward a little, it's not visible. So far, none of the guests have commented on it. I'm very lucky." She winced. "Until I put weight on my left ankle. It's in a walking cast because I have a really bad sprain. My boss gave me permission to wear slacks instead of a skirt until I'm all healed."

She looked at Jeremy. "Is this your husband? He looks different from what I remember from last night."

I laughed. "No, Jim's already asleep. This is—"

"I'm Jeremy Dixon," Jeremy said. "I believe we've spoken on the phone, April, but we've never met."

April looked flustered. "Oh, yes, Mr. Dixon."

"You weren't here when I checked in," Jeremy continued. "But I wanted to thank you for taking such excellent care of my reservation."

"I'm very glad to meet you, Mr. Dixon. I'll do my best to ensure that everything works out to your satisfaction."

Lucy yipped, startling me. I was so engrossed in checking on April that I'd forgotten both dogs were there.

"And who are these two beauties?" April asked, walking carefully around the desk to pat the dogs.

"Their names are Lucy and Ethel," I said. "We're so glad the hotel allows dogs."

"We love them," April said. "That's one of the questions management asks at every initial employee interview. If an applicant doesn't like dogs, the interview is over." She reached behind the desk and offered each dog a biscuit, which they scarfed up immediately. "There are plenty more where those came from," she told the dogs. "See me and I'll give you extra ones."

"You've made two friends for life," I said, as both dogs sat and gave April hopeful looks. "But one biscuit per dog at bedtime is enough."

"They don't appear to agree with you," Jeremy said, laughing. "I could swear Lucy just gave you a dirty look."

"She does that a lot," I admitted, yawning. "I'm up way past my usual bedtime, and I'm exhausted."

"Anything you and your party need during your stay with us, just let me know. And thank you again for helping me last night. Sweet dreams."

"What a lovely young woman," I said, making idle conversation during our speedy elevator ride to the sixth floor. "I'm glad she's doing so well."

Jeremy looked troubled; I figured he was thinking about his upcoming conversation with Mark. If I had known what was really on his mind, things might have ended up very differently.

Chapter 17

It's the start of a brand new day, and I'm off like a herd of turtles.

I awoke the next morning, sat up in bed and, for a split second, I didn't know where I was. Then I remembered the furnace's untimely end and groaned. Whatever adventures were in store for us today, I hoped they were more pleasant than yesterday's.

I looked around our palatial bedroom, which was twice the size of the one we had at home. *You have nothing to complain about, Carol Andrews. You may not be in your own house for a while, but you've ended up in a hotel suite that would make all your friends green with envy.*

Except for the roommate situation.

I've rarely shared my personal space with anyone except my immediate family and the dogs. Oh, well. Even the most beautiful roses have thorns. I tossed off the bedsheets and put on my ratty old robe. I hoped our roommates weren't dressing formally for breakfast. With my luck, Margo was in a designer caftan that cost big bucks, already perfectly coiffed and made up. I just hoped Jim had made the coffee.

"There you are, sleepy-head," Jim said when I opened the bedroom door. "The dogs and I were wondering when we'd see you."

"We?" I looked around the living room. "Where are Margo

and Jeremy?"

"Margo is starting her day by exercising at the hotel gym." Jim laughed when he saw me roll my eyes.

"To each her own, I guess. And Jeremy?"

"He and I had a brief chat before he headed out for the day. He told me about your conversation last night."

"I hope you agree with what I told him," I said, fearful that Jim had forgotten our joint decision to stay out of the Margo/Jeremy/Mark family drama as much as we could.

"Don't worry, I backed you up one hundred percent. I urged Jeremy to talk to Mark as soon as possible, and he promised he would."

"I'm glad it's just us for a change," I said. "Is there coffee and breakfast, or do we have to go to the hotel dining room for that?"

"I made the coffee. It's in the kitchen. And a waiter delivered a tray of fresh pastries, fruit, and yogurt. If we want a hot breakfast, we have to order in advance."

"Works for me," I said.

"And before you ask me, I've fed and walked the dogs. I'm rewarding myself with a hot shower now. After that, I want to drive home and see what's going on."

"I'm coming with you," I said. "I'll eat fast and shower even faster. At least I don't have to worry about what to wear today. I only packed one other outfit."

Chapter 18

A wife sat down next to her husband as he was flipping channels. "What's on TV?" she asked. "Dust," he replied. And that's when the fight started.

"Oh, my God," I said, walking into what used to be my beautiful kitchen. "The house is a wreck. I never thought it would be this bad."

Jim's mouth was set in a grim line. He stepped over some pipes that were in the middle of the floor. "I'm going to find who's in charge right now. It's bound to take twice as long and cost twice as much as I was told it would at this rate." He turned to me and barked, "If you want more clothes from the closet, get them now. I'll be back." And he marched away in search of someone to yell at.

"I don't see how this can ever be done by Christmas," I said aloud. "It would take a miracle." I realized that, in my large arsenal of go-to saints, I'd never looked for one who was in charge of plumbing or construction. I made a mental note to find one as soon as I had the chance. Meanwhile, I had to pack.

Luckily, our bedroom remained pretty much intact, so I was able to pull several suitable, interchangeable outfits to wear for the next few days. I grabbed a dozen pairs of socks and some sturdy white cotton underwear (the ones without the holes), thanking my lucky stars that I'd done laundry two days ago when life was "normal." Next came shoes to match the outfits. Then purses to match the shoes. By the time I was finished, I had half my wardrobe in a heap on the bed. I rummaged around in the closet, looking for the oversized suitcase I always use for long trips, and came up empty.

It's in the attic, stupid. You'll have to pack your clothes in a garbage bag, just like what you used to move Mike in and out of his college dorm room years ago.

It was impossible to make my way through the mess all over my kitchen floor to the storage cabinet where I kept the bags, so I grabbed my keys, ran out the side door and cut around to the front of the house.

Bad mistake. As soon as I had my hand on the front door latch, I heard the unmistakable voice of Phyllis Stevens calling my name from across the street. I froze. Literally. The outside temperature was about 35 degrees and I wasn't wearing a coat.

Don't turn around, Carol. Pretend you didn't hear her and get inside the house pronto.

It was just my (bad) luck that my persnickety front door took that exact moment to jam, despite my frantic attempts to make it open. I was busted.

"I called to you from across the street, Carol," Phyllis said, now standing right next to me on my icy front stoop.

"I was concentrating on getting this door open," I said, jiggling the house key and pushing while avoiding eye contact. Some people have said they can tell by looking at my face when I'm telling one of my too-frequent fibs, and I didn't want to take any chances with Phyllis. "I guess I didn't hear you."

"Here, let me help you," said a masculine voice that startled me so much I dropped the keys on the icy steps.

I flushed crimson, which was actually a good thing, because for a quick moment, I warmed up. I bent down to pick up the keys at the same time the man did, and we butted heads.

"I'm so sorry," we both said at the same time.

"I'll get them," Phyllis said. "Don't either of you move."

She bent down, retrieved the keys, and pressed them into my hand. I stood there like an idiot, realizing that I had just made an indelible, painful impression on our new neighbor, Frank Adams. And there was a good chance that Phyllis would have my embarrassing encounter spread all over the neighborhood before lunchtime.

"I hope your head's okay," I said. "My husband always says mine is the hardest one he's ever met."

Brilliant, Carol. Now Frank's going to think you're incredibly ditsy as well as clumsy.

"Funny, my wife says the same thing about me," Frank said with a grin.

"This is Carol Andrews," Phyllis interjected. "She and her family have lived in our neighborhood for years."

"It's nice to see you again, Carol," Frank said. "When Sister Rose introduced us a few nights ago, I didn't realize that we were going to be neighbors."

"How nice that you've already met," Phyllis said, clearly annoyed by having the opportunity to introduce our new neighbor usurped by another person.

I finally remembered my manners. "Welcome to Old Fairport Turnpike, Doctor Adams. I'm very glad you and your wife are here, and I promise not to call you in the middle of the night with a medical emergency."

"Just to clarify," he said, "as I've explained to Sister Rose and Phyllis, 'Doctor' is merely a courtesy title. Neither of us are medical doctors. Please, just call me Frank."

I smiled, all the while trying to think of some way to bring this conversation to a quick close. I didn't know about Phyllis and Frank, but I was freezing. "I'd invite you both inside but there are workmen replacing our furnace and the house is a mess. We've had to move to the Fairport Inn and Suites until the work is done. I just hope we can get home before Christmas. I need to get back inside and pack some clothes."

"You and Jim don't have to stay in a hotel while your furnace is being replaced," Phyllis said. "Bill and I would be happy to have you stay with us. That way, you can keep a close eye on the workmen, to be sure the job is finished on schedule." She turned to Frank and said, "Our neighborhood is just like one big family, as you'll soon discover. When one of us has a problem, everyone else pitches in to help."

I'd rather camp outside in a tent without running water or heat for the rest of my life than live with you for even five seconds. I didn't really say that, of course.

I mustered up the sincerest smile I could. And it was a real effort, let me tell you. "Phyllis, you are such a sweetheart. Jim and I could never impose on you so much." I held up my hand to stop the protest I knew would be coming. "Besides, Lucy and Ethel are with us, and I know Bill is allergic to dogs. Our staying with you would compromise his health, and you know we'd never, ever do that. But thank you so much for offering."

Part of me wondered if Phyllis's surprising burst of hospitality had anything to do with showing how wonderful and generous she was in front of our new neighbor. I quickly banished that thought. It was the holiday season, with joy to the world, peace on earth, and all that good stuff. She was just being nice.

"I'd forgotten about the dogs," Phyllis said. "You're right, of course. Bill does have allergies. But I'm concerned about you staying in a hotel rather than with people who love you, especially at this time of year."

Now, that was really a stretch. I guess I wasn't the only one standing on my front stoop, freezing, who was capable of telling a whopper of a lie.

"We really are a warm and caring neighborhood," I said to Frank. "You'll meet many of them at the party Phyllis and Bill are hosting to welcome you and your wife here. But under the circumstances, Phyllis, I won't be able to provide an appetizer."

"That's not a problem at all," Phyllis assured me. "We're postponing the get-together until after the holidays are over. Everyone is so busy this time of year, and we want to do it properly. That's why Frank and I are walking around the neighborhood this morning. I wanted to introduce him to as many of the neighbors as possible."

Rats. Just when I thought I was off the hook.

"I really should get back inside," I said. "Jim will wonder what's happened to me." *So go away.* I didn't really say that, of course.

"We've kept you too long," Frank said. "And you must be freezing."

"Yes," Phyllis agreed. "You really shouldn't be outside without a coat in this weather, Carol. What were you thinking?"

Trust me, you don't want to know.

Our icy interlude was brought to a close by the unmistakable sound of my dear husband, bellowing my name at the top of his lungs. Before Phyllis had the bright idea of adding Jim to our outdoor get-acquainted party, I mumbled something about an emergency and vanished to the safety of my cold house.

As I was shutting the door on a surprised Phyllis and an amused Frank, I thought I heard Phyllis say, "I'll be in touch with you later, dear, to see if you need anything." I hope I was mistaken.

"Where the heck have you been, Carol? I read those workers the riot act and told them they better get busy fixing this house pronto. I warned them we'd be back later today to check on what they've done." Without giving me a chance to explain, he continued on his rampage. "And what the heck were you doing outside chatting with the neighbors when you should have been in here backing me up?"

Give me a break. Literally.

I knew he wasn't really mad at me. He was merely using me as the object of his frustration with our current situation, so rather than burst into tears—my usual reaction—I gritted my teeth and fought back. "You owe me big-time, buster. I just saved you from an interminable conversation with Phyllis and our new neighbor, Frank Adams. You better not tell me we're leaving in five minutes, because I still have to find large garbage bags and pack up some clothes." I punctuated my rebuttal with the Mommy stare. I rarely use it on my husband, but sometimes, it's appropriate.

Jim threw up his hands. "I'm not even going to ask you why you're using garbage bags for your clothes," he said. "But I'm cold. And hungry. How long will you be? The dogs have been in the car too long. They're probably cold, too."

That did it. If there's one thing I'll never do, it's make our sweet dogs suffer. "I promise I'll be quick. Why don't you walk them in the yard and then wait in the car for me with the heat on? Just be sure you crack a window to let a little fresh air in."

"What about our lunch?"

Honestly, that Jim. "We can eat when we get back to the hotel and charge it to the room. We're Jeremy's guests, remember? I'll only be ten minutes."

Without giving him a split second to protest, I ran into the kitchen (being extra careful not to trip over all the rubble), found the garbage bags, ran to the bedroom and stuffed as many mix and match outfits as I could into my snazzy, soft-sided luggage. And before any of you start to criticize me for being vain, please remember that for the next few days I was rooming with Margo, who usually looked like she'd just stepped out of a fashion magazine. No way was I taking the chance of being criticized with a subtle raised eyebrow or skeptical look.

I hate to brag—you know I never do—but the bags and I were in the car, ready to go, with the heater blasting, in eight minutes. And Jim was still exercising Lucy and Ethel in the backyard.

Am I good or what?

Chapter 19

Does running from my responsibilities count as cardio?

When we arrived back at the hotel, Jim waved at the parking attendant on duty who, to my amazement, sketched a salute and waved us through. Jim checked my shocked reaction, grinned, then headed to a space at the farthest corner of the garage. He hopped out and removed an orange cone, eased the car into the spot, and put the cone off to the side, where it wasn't immediately visible.

I was speechless. I know, it doesn't happen that often. But in all the years Jim and I have been married, we'd never parked in an honest-to-goodness valet-assisted garage before.

"I hope you don't mind that we have a bit of a hike," Jim said. "I can ask the parking attendant to bring us a luggage cart if you want."

"Jim Andrews, how in the world did you manage to pull off a reserved space in the hotel garage?"

Jim dangled the car keys in front of me. "Not only that, I don't have to surrender these, either. We can come and go as we please, whenever we please. I hope you're impressed."

"Impressed? I'm stunned," I admitted. "What's the catch?"

"There's no catch," Jim said, looking very pleased with himself.

"I contacted Mitch Robinson, the insurance agent I'd talked to yesterday, and asked if there was any way we could have a reserved parking spot in the garage. He said no customer had ever asked him about special parking before, but since it wouldn't cost the company any money, he agreed to contact the hotel and see what he could do for us. I gave him the make, color, and license plate of our car; Mitch called the hotel manager and was able to work it out. We're all set."

"You never cease to surprise me," I said with a smile. "I never would have thought of doing that."

"Ditto," he replied. I hoped that was a compliment. "Let's get the two dogs inside now. I'll come back for your bags while you take care of ordering lunch."

"It's a deal," I said. "Let's go."

I'd no sooner grabbed the dogs' leashes and turned around when the parking attendant and a luggage cart magically materialized beside us. "Hi, I'm Ryan Peterson, the head of parking," he said. "I thought you might need some help unloading your car."

I let Jim handle the initial conversation, since it was his contact who was responsible for all this extra service. I just smiled, holding the dogs' leashes, and didn't interrupt as the two guys chatted.

"And this is Carol, Lucy, and Ethel," Jim said, finally noticing I was standing there. "Carol's my wife and Lucy and Ethel are the dogs, in case you were confused."

That Jim. Such a kidder.

"I may be driving our car while we're staying here, too, Ryan," I said. "Please spread the word among the other parking attendants. I don't want to be arrested for carjacking."

Ryan laughed, then bent down and gave Lucy a gentle stroking on the top of her head, which she loved. "What beautiful dogs." Sweet Ethel immediately gave Ryan's hand a sniff, then decided he must be okay and sat down obediently at my side.

"I can tell your dogs and I are going to be great pals," Ryan said, patting both of them. "And you'll both get parking passes at the reception desk that show you're registered guests. There's a matching one to put on your car dashboard. Be sure it's visible to the staff when you drive in, and there'll be no problem. April's at the desk right now, and she'll take good care of you. I'll help load up the cart and take you inside. She should have stayed home to rest, but she insisted. I made her promise that if she was in any pain, she'd leave."

Not that it was any of my business, but it seemed obvious that Ryan and April were a couple. I resisted any follow-up nosy questions, and I hope I get points for that.

The two dogs were now straining at their leashes, demanding attention. "Since you have Ryan to help you, how about if I give Lucy and Ethel one more quick walk and then meet you upstairs?" Jim asked. "Will that work for you?"

I nodded, and as Jim walked away with the dogs, he turned around and yelled, "Don't forget to order lunch."

Good grief.

My laptop was wobbling precariously at the top of the cart, so I grabbed it and followed Ryan. A small wave of panic hit me as I realized we had to take another elevator to get to the main lobby of the hotel. Wasn't anything on the same floor in this place?

Ryan pressed the call button; as we waited, my palms started to sweat. I wished with all my heart that Jim and the dogs were with me.

"Thank you for taking such good care of Jim and me," I said to Ryan. "Our stay here was completely unexpected, as you may have already heard. So far, everybody has been so nice."

"I understand you and your husband found April," Ryan said. "If you hadn't come along when you did, who knows what would have happened? She could have frozen to death out there. I'm glad I had this chance to thank you for being so kind to her."

"We were glad to help," I said. "You obviously care a lot about her."

Ryan nodded. "We're planning on getting married as soon as we can save up enough money. That's why she insists on working so many extra hours here."

"Congratulations," I said. "April seems like a lovely girl."

"She's the best," Ryan said. The elevator arrived at that exact moment, and in no time, we were at the lobby level, only one floor up.

The door opened and the registration desk was in plain view. I stepped out first while Ryan dealt with some of my soft-sided luggage, which was slipping off the luggage cart. April was deep in conversation with a male guest and clearly upset. I wasn't close enough to hear any of the conversation, but I recognized the man as he turned and walked away. It was Jeremy.

For some reason I'll never be able to explain, I didn't call out to him. Instead, I took a quick glance over my shoulder to be sure Ryan hadn't noticed the exchange, then walked to the reception desk and waited for April to pull herself together.

"Just give me a minute," she said. "Some guests are more difficult to deal with than others. But handling difficult guests is part of my job."

Since I'd had only positive interactions with Jeremy, I found it hard to believe that he'd been difficult, but then again, I really didn't know the guy that well, even if we were temporary suitemates.

"You have a tough job," I agreed. "Not everybody's as nice as I am."

That made April smile. "You got that right." She peered over the desk. "Are you alone? Where are your trusty canine sidekicks?"

"My husband's giving them one more walk around the block before he brings them upstairs."

"They're so pretty. I just love them." She gave me a small plastic bag filled with dog treats. "Here's a little gift for your dogs from me."

"On behalf of Lucy and Ethel, thank you." At that moment, my stomach growled, reminding me that I could use some food, too. "I'm here to pick up parking passes for our car. Ryan said you have them." I turned around and saw him waiting on the other side of the lobby. He gave April a quick wave, then, glancing around to see that nobody was watching, blew her a quick kiss, which made her blush.

"He shouldn't have done that publicly," April said. "Please don't mention what you saw to anyone. Dating another staff person is against company policy."

"I promise I won't say a word. I'm good at keeping secrets." I'm even better now that I'm older because I forget so many of them.

"We had a fight a few days ago," April confided. "He was very angry with me. I couldn't understand it. But I guess we're okay now."

The exchange I just had witnessed between April and Jeremy concerned me more than a young lovers quarrel. Although I didn't know the girl very well, I felt strangely protective of her. As she handed me the parking passes, I added, "If there's anything else you need to talk about, please know that I'm a pretty good listener."

"Is everything okay out there?" Bobbie called from the manager's office.

April looked alarmed. Neither of us realized anyone could be in eavesdropping distance. How much had she heard?

"Everything's perfect," I called out in a loud voice. "April's taking good care of us."

"She always takes excellent care of our guests," Bobbie said, joining April behind the registration desk. "That's why she's one of our very favorite employees."

I waved the parking passes, then said, "I'm on my way. Thank you, April, for all your help." And me and my big mouth left before I could cause any more trouble.

Chapter 20

I am who I am. Your approval isn't needed.

Believe it or not, this time the elevator ride to the suite was too fast. When the doors opened on the sixth floor, I still hadn't figured out a devious plan to get Jeremy to tell me what he and April had been talking about. There was no way he could have been complaining about the hotel. The place was paradise as far as I was concerned. Oh, well. I'd just have to improvise.

I'd barely gotten inside our suite when I heard Margo's voice. "We need to talk. I'm so sorry." A bedroom door opened, revealing the usually perfect Margo, hair disheveled and eye makeup streaked, dabbing her eyes with a tissue. My goodness. What in the world was the matter with everybody today?

Her face fell as soon as she caught sight of me. "Oh. It's only you. I thought you were Jeremy."

I tamped down the snarky remark that sprang to my mouth. Definite points for me. I hoped Santa was watching.

"Nope, sorry. Jim and the dogs will be here in a few minutes." I tried to look sympathetic instead of nosy. "Is everything okay?"

Margo pasted a fake smile on her face. "Of course, it is. Jeremy and I had a little...misunderstanding about...." She paused for a second. "About whether or not we were going to exchange Christmas presents. I didn't think that giving me anything was necessary because he's been so generous already."

"And he didn't agree with you," I said, throwing Margo a lifeline to grab onto.

Her face immediately brightened. "Yes. That's it, exactly, Carol. I knew you'd understand."

"I certainly do," I said. *If that's what the argument was really about.* I didn't say the last part out loud, of course.

"Anyway, right in the middle of our...discussion...he got one of his business calls, said he had to go, and left. Just like that." Her eyes filled up. "We've never had an argument before, not in the entire time we've known each other. It's very upsetting."

"Listen, Margo, take some advice from a veteran of these... discussions. Jeremy will be back soon, you'll make up, and all will be well. Don't worry. He's clearly bonkers about you."

"Do you really think so?"

"No doubt about it."

It didn't take a genius to figure out that Jeremy's sudden exit after receiving a mysterious phone call and his chat with April might be connected.

"How long ago did he leave?" I asked.

Margo gave me a disgusted look. "What difference does that make, Carol? He's gone. Period."

Oh, for heaven's sake. It wasn't like Jeremy was a child who'd run away from home. Margo was once again the same annoying person I'd come to know and dislike intensely during her previous visit to Fairport.

I was saved from making a snide comment by the welcome arrival of Jim and the two dogs. Since I'd already used up my daily patience quota dealing with Phyllis Stevens, his timing was perfect.

Margo greeted Jim's arrival with a frosty smile, then retreated to her bedroom and closed the door.

Jim raised his eyebrows. "Did I do something wrong? Is she angry about the dogs?"

"No," I said. Lowering my voice to a whisper, I added, "There's been a little bump in the romance department."

I picked up the house phone. "What do you want for lunch?"

Margo stayed cloistered in the bedroom for the rest of the afternoon. Jim took advantage of the quiet by curling up on our bed for an afternoon snooze. Lucy and Ethel quickly joined him.

I tried to be as quiet as possible, and grabbed a new mystery I'd been looking forward to reading to pass the time. But I was too antsy, and I couldn't concentrate. Dealing with a critical, annoying Margo was bad enough. Dealing with a lovestruck, annoying Margo was even worse. But as long as Jim and I were forced to share this suite, we (I) had to make the best of it.

To distract myself, I finally set up my laptop on the dining room table and answered a few emails. Nothing urgent. Most people I know prefer texting, so a lot of my email is spam, anyway.

Jenny sent a quick text with a picture of CJ wearing a Santa hat. He looked adorable, of course.

I responded with a smile emoji, then took a chance and texted a longer reply.

Me: *Did Mark and Jeremy connect yet?*

Jenny: *No progress. How r things there?*

Me: *House progress slow. Hotel fine.*

Jenny: *Miss you. See you tomorrow?*

Me: *Great. Love you.*

Jenny: *Love you, too.*

I clicked off. Maybe I couldn't fix the darn furnace, or the current Margo-Jeremy situation, but there must be something I could do to end the Mark-Margo stalemate. Mark was being so stubborn. Even donuts wouldn't solve this one.

Then, in a sudden flash of brilliance, I figured out where Jeremy had gone in such a hurry. He'd reached out to Mark (at my suggestion, not that I'm taking any credit) and my stubborn son-in-law had responded. Jeremy didn't want to take a chance on Mark changing his mind, so he'd raced out without giving

Margo the reason why. She was going to be thrilled when she found out that her son and her new love were finally talking. What a wonderful Christmas present for her.

I brushed aside Jeremy's encounter with April as totally irrelevant. Jeremy was in a hurry, and she probably asked him some silly question, which delayed him, and he overreacted. I'd jumped to a completely wrong conclusion—something I do too often.

By 6:00, Jeremy still hadn't come back. I hoped that meant he and Mark were really bonding. Maybe they were even having a beer together, or doing some Christmas shopping to buy presents for Margo.

I was just wondering what we should do about dinner when there was a knock at the door. Margo raced to open it like she was running in the Olympics. Instead of Jeremy, the person was a member of the hotel catering staff with another sumptuous meal. Margo burst into tears when she saw it wasn't Jeremy, and I was bursting to tell her what the love of her life was really up to. But I didn't. Points for me, right?

Jim tucked into the gourmet meal like he hadn't eaten in days (it had been less than three hours since lunch, but who's counting?), and I made a valiant attempt to eat a few bites myself. Okay, more than a few bites. Margo announced she wasn't hungry and was going to bed.

After giving Lucy and Ethel an early evening walk and praying they'd both behave until daylight, Jim and I called it a night, too. Jeremy came back at 11:00 (yes, I checked my cell phone for the time), and I strained to hear his conversation with Margo without waking Jim or the dogs. I'm usually pretty good at eavesdropping, but not this time. Then...I guess I fell asleep.

Chapter 21

Old age is when you still have something on the ball but you're too tired to bounce it.

Something was nudging me awake. Correction: not something; someone. Even in my groggy state, I knew it was Jim. After almost forty years of marriage, I recognized the message. I was taking up too much room in the bed, and he was urging me to give him more space.

Ignoring him the way I always do under these circumstances, I turned on my other side and willed myself to fall back to sleep. Which was not going to happen, because Lucy was the culprit disturbing my sleep, not Jim, and she was letting me know in no uncertain terms that she had to go outside right now or I'd regret it.

I poked Jim, hoping I could persuade him to take over, but it was no use. He grunted, then rolled over. Ethel nestled at his feet, and began to snore. Loudly.

I poked Jim again, a little harder. He finally sat up and, even in the dark, I could feel him glaring at me. "What's wrong, Carol? And it better be a crisis of major proportions."

"It is," I said. "Lucy has to go out. I'll take her, but I don't want to go all by myself. I would if we were home, but we're in a hotel. I'm nervous about being outside alone. I could get mugged."

Jim groaned. "I was sound asleep."

"So was I. Come on. We better bring Ethel, too. The quicker we take them out, the sooner we can all get back to bed."

I heard a heavy sigh. "Oh, all right. I give up. Let's go."

I quickly pulled on a pair of sweatpants and a heavy jacket, then double-checked to be sure I had our room key card. The way our luck was running these days, we'd probably lock ourselves out if we weren't careful. Jim had already clipped leashes onto the two dogs and was creeping across the living room toward the door.

I looked down at Lucy and whispered, "This is all your fault. Don't expect any extra dog biscuits in your Christmas stocking this year."

I could see from my cell phone that it was almost midnight. What a magical time to be walking dogs in an unfamiliar place that required our taking an elevator just to get outside. At least I had my big, tall, strong, brave husband to protect me.

We reached the lower level quickly. Lucy and Ethel tugged at their leashes, anxious to get to the grassy area near the parking garage which served as the hotel dog park. Mercifully, they were both quick to take care of their personal needs. I couldn't wait to get back to the warmth and safety of our room.

Jim and Ethel headed toward the elevator, but Lucy had different ideas. She was now wide awake and ready to have a little fun. I tried to urge her in the direction of the hotel, but instead, she pulled me in the opposite direction, toward the picnic table where the hotel staff ate their break-time snacks. "I know where you're heading," I said. "No dice. You just want to see if anyone dropped some food."

Making it clear that she was in charge, not me, Lucy continued to resist, and I realized that this tug of war would keep going until she got her own way. So, sue me. I was cold, tired, and I gave in to a dog.

"Hang on a second, Jim," I called out. "Lucy and I will be right there. She just wants to check something else out first."

Jim turned around. "Well, hurry up. It's cold out here. You let Lucy boss you around too much. I'll see you at the elevator."

"There's someone sitting at the picnic table over there, and I'm sure Lucy wants to see if they have any food for her. You know how stubborn she can be when she wants to do something. Give her a minute, and then we can go back upstairs."

As Lucy and I got closer, I realized whoever was at the picnic table was taking a power nap. One hand was on the table, the other was hanging free. Lucy was wriggling with excitement, figuring the person was holding a treat for her. She broke away from my grasp and raced to the table before I could stop her.

"Lucy, no!" I yelled. "Come back."

Lucy, of course, ignored me and nuzzled the person's hand, looking for her prize. The movement was just enough to disturb the position of the person at the table, who fell sideways onto the concrete parking garage floor. I recognized her immediately. It was April, and she wasn't taking a power nap. She was dead.

Chapter 22

We come from dust and we'll return to dust. That's why I don't dust. It could be someone I know.

The next thing I knew, I heard loud screams. It took me a few seconds to realize they were coming from me. I took a deep breath and willed myself to be calm. Since Jim's retirement, I seem to be a magnet for dead bodies. Not my fault, I assure you. I just seem to be at the wrong place at the wrong time. But at least this time, Jim was with me.

I pulled the dog leash extra tight, backed away from poor April, and ordered Lucy to sit. Sensing the gravity of the situation, she actually obeyed me.

"Jim, I need you. Right now!"

Fortunately, this wasn't one of those frequent situations where my husband's selective hearing kicks in. "What the heck are you yelling about? We're waiting for you at the elevator. You're loud enough to wake the dead, and some people are trying to sleep!"

Poor choice of words under the circumstances, wouldn't you agree?

I saw Jim coming toward me, accompanied by an excited Ethel, who was having a grand time on her midnight adventure. I knew my husband wasn't sharing Ethel's good mood. Neither was I. But I hoped Jim would assess the situation and immediately take over, like he always did, no matter what. Like the way I did the laundry, for example. Or loaded the dishwasher. This time, I actually welcomed his interference. I hope the irony of that isn't lost on any of you.

"Now, what the...? Oh, my God. Who is that? And why is she lying on the floor?"

I started to cry. "It's April, Jim. I think she's dead. It doesn't look like she's breathing."

Jim went to April's side and knelt beside her. He started to feel for a pulse, and I yelled, "No! Don't touch her or move her. You may make things worse."

Jim gave me a withering look over his shoulder. "I don't see how I can make things any worse, Carol. April fell and hit her head again. And because she was already hurt, this time, the fall killed her." He stood up. "Obviously this was a terrible accident." He handed me Ethel's leash. "Hold this while I call 911."

I nodded, grateful to have a task that distracted me from looking at poor April. Jim was right. Jim was always right. Wasn't he? April had probably come out here for a quick break and put her head down on the table because she felt dizzy. When Lucy nuzzled her hand, she fell sideways onto the concrete floor and hit her head again. OMG! Did that mean we were responsible for her death?

I forced myself to look at April again, and I realized her head had bled from two separate places. One was where her head had hit the concrete garage floor. The other was on the left side of her forehead, in the same place where she'd been hurt from her previous fall. She'd shown me that wound the day after her fall, and it was already scabbing over and partially healed. I'm no expert, but it looked to me like that wound was now fresh. Weird.

Fortunately, by this time Lucy and Ethel had found a suitable snoozing spot, so I was able to loop both leashes around my wrist and concentrate on the ghoulish scene without them interrupting me. I took a deep breath and forced myself to look at both the picnic table and the garage floor more closely. That's when I realized there was also blood in both places, suggesting that April had collapsed and fallen onto the table first, slamming her head hard enough to open the older wound and kill her. It was just bad luck that she happened to land on the same spot. Not that I planned to share my conclusion with the police. No, siree. Not this time. (Unless, of course, they were stumped and asked for my help. In that case, all bets were off.) I prayed April had already passed before Lucy and I arrived, and that she didn't suffer.

I heard the wail of a police siren and stuffed my phone in my pocket, then joined Jim at the entrance to the garage. He was waving his arms like crazy as the cruiser careened around the corner and skidded to a stop. Two patrolmen stepped out and looked at us suspiciously. "It's a little late for folks your age to be out and about. Do you need help finding your car?" one of them asked.

I was about to say something I'd probably regret, but Jim stopped me. "My name is Jim Andrews and this is my wife, Carol. I called 911 to report that we discovered a dead person in the parking garage. I should have called our son-in-law directly instead."

"Our son-in-law is Detective Mark Anderson, and I know he's working tonight," I added. "I'm sure he and Paul Wheeler will be here any minute to take over the investigation." There was enough light in the garage for me to see that I had scored a direct hit with the self-important patrolmen.

"Yes, well, we'll secure the area until they get here," one of them said, looking around. "Where's the body?"

I cringed to hear April referred to as simply "the body." She was a lovely young woman with her whole life ahead of her. It was beyond tragic that she had died alone in a cold parking garage.

I thought I heard Jim mumble something about some town employees being a waste of taxpayers' money, but I could have been mistaken. He pointed to the picnic table on the other side of the garage. "April's on the floor over there."

I knew right away from all those mystery books I read that my husband had made a huge mistake. The first person the authorities always zero in on during a suspicious death investigation is the person who found the body. And the fact that Jim named the victim could make it even worse for us.

Lucy began to tug at her leash, momentarily distracting me. "I know you're cold," I said, "and I'm sorry. So am I. But if it hadn't been for you, we wouldn't be standing here in this garage in the first place."

I heard a car door slam, more footsteps heading our way, and then a man laughing. "I told you she'd be here, Mark. You owe me ten bucks. Your mother-in-law is drawn to dead bodies like a magnet."

"I'm here, too, Mark," Jim said, stepping forward and glaring at Paul Wheeler. "And so are Lucy and Ethel. Lucy had to go out and I didn't want Carol to be outside alone, so I came with her." He put his arm around me protectively. My hero.

I saw Mark shoot Paul a quick look. "Paul didn't mean what he said. We both know you don't get into these situations voluntarily. We'll take a quick look at the victim, and then we need to ask you both a few questions. Okay?"

I nodded as Jim tried and failed to stifle a quick yawn. We were both exhausted, but the only place to sit and rest was the picnic bench, which was currently the scene of April's fatal fall. I wondered if it was possible to sleep standing up. I leaned against a pillar for support, closed my eyes for a second, and felt myself start to pitch forward. Nope. Bad idea.

In about twelve hours—which was probably less than five minutes—Mark was back. "I understand from Officer Taylor that you knew the deceased woman."

"She worked at the hotel reception desk," Jim clarified.

"Her name is April," I said. "I don't know her last name." My eyes filled up. "She was very sweet. I liked her a lot, even though we'd only just met."

"I'm sorry you two had to be the ones who found her," Mark said. "Look, we're going to be here quite a while. Why don't you both go back to your room and try and get some sleep? I'll catch up with you and take your statements another time."

"Thanks, Mark," Jim said, grabbing the leashes and making a speedy exit. "Come on, Carol. Let's go."

"There's one more thing," I said. "We're sharing hotel accommodations with your mother and her...gentleman friend. When you come to interview us, they may be there, too."

Mark was silent for a minute. I could tell by the way he clenched his jaw that he wasn't happy. "I'll have to see them both eventually." He leaned forward and gave me a quick kiss on the cheek. "Thanks for the head's up. I'll see you later."

"Do me a favor and text before you come, okay? I want to be sure we're decent."

"Our shift ends at nine this morning. We'll be there by seven-thirty. Sorry, Carol."

Not as sorry as I am. I didn't really say that, of course.

Chapter 23

My body is a temple. Ancient and crumbling.

Jim, Lucy and Ethel fell asleep right away. I guess discovering a dead body didn't upset them as much as it upset me. Poor April. She was one of the nicest girls I'd ever met.

You really didn't know her that well, Carol. Maybe she just seemed nice. Looks can be deceiving. You're not always the greatest judge of character. Close your eyes and go to sleep.

I was sure she had people who loved her, like her family and co-workers.

My baby blues snapped open. Ryan! He was going to be devastated when he heard what had happened. I wondered if he was working today. And how he'd react to the tragic news.

Maybe you should be the one to tell him about April, Carol.

I immediately realized what a terrible idea that was. I had enough to deal with already, especially if an encounter with Mark, Margo and Jeremy was also on the horizon.

I checked the time on my phone. It was already way after one, and sleep was still eluding me. If I was going to get any rest at all, I needed a little extra help. No, not a quick prayer to whoever the patron saint of sleep was. (It's St. Dymphna, in case you were all wondering. And St. Raphael is the patron saint of sweet dreams.) I made a snap decision and, quiet as a little mouse, I crawled out of bed and rummaged in my travel bag for the over-the-counter sleep aid I only use in cases of extreme stress. If finding a dead body in the middle of the night doesn't qualify as stressful, I don't know what does. I wanted to be sure I slept, so I took two tablets followed by a quick swig of water, then crept back into bed. Neither canines nor husband moved a muscle.

I guess I fell into a deep sleep, and had a terrible dream. People were arguing loudly and then I heard the sound of a woman crying. I tried to wake myself up, but I couldn't seem to do it. I heard Jim's voice calling my name, and I knew I was safe. Whatever was happening in my dream, Jim would protect me, the way he always did.

I felt someone shaking me. "Carol, Carol, wake up. Mark is here to take our statements."

I sat up in bed, fuzzy from sleep, and tried to rid myself of the nightmare. "I just had the worst dream," I told Jim. "People were yelling and saying awful things. It was horrible. I'm so glad you woke me up."

Jim handed me a mug of coffee. "Here, drink a little of this. It'll make you feel better."

I suddenly remembered finding poor April, and pushed the mug away. "No coffee now. I want to give my statement and get it over with." My eyes filled with tears. "Poor girl. Maybe that's why I had such a terrible dream."

"You weren't dreaming. What you heard was Mark and Margo arguing." Jim looked like he'd aged twenty years in the last twelve hours. "And I walked right into the middle of it."

I grabbed the coffee back. It looked like I was going to need it. "Tell me everything," I said, taking a huge gulp of the heavenly brew.

"There's not too much to tell," Jim said. "I got up before you, because I wanted to warn Jeremy and Margo that Mark and Paul would be coming to the suite very soon. I figured I'd take the dogs out and give the lovebirds a chance to decide if they wanted to stay or leave before the boys got here. Unfortunately, the dogs had many outdoor needs, and by the time I got back to the suite,

Mark and Margo were in the middle of a terrible row."

"Where were Jeremy and Paul?"

"Both gone. Margo asked Jeremy to leave so she could talk to Mark alone. Mark told Paul he'd take care of getting our statements by himself."

"The mother-son conversation didn't go well?"

"That's an understatement. Margo's in her bedroom sobbing, and Mark's sitting in the living room wearing a face that looks like it was carved from stone."

I took another sip of coffee and tried to focus. "Jeremy told me yesterday that he was going to have a private conversation with Mark at the station to clear the air," I said. "He obviously didn't do it." *What a coward.* My positive impression of him evaporated instantly, no matter how charming he was.

Don't be so quick to condemn Jeremy, Carol. Maybe he went to the police station to talk to Mark and Mark wasn't there because he'd been reassigned to the night shift. Jeremy would have no way of knowing that in advance.

That made me feel a little better. But not much. I hate it when I argue with myself. I never know which side I'm on.

"I'll take the dogs and go home to check on the work while you deal with Mark," Jim said. "You're better at defusing emotional situations than I am." Before I could protest, he vamoosed.

After taking a little time to make myself presentable, I grabbed my mug of now-lukewarm coffee and ventured out of our bedroom. My son-in-law was now sitting at the dining room table, still stone-faced. Oh, boy. I sat opposite him and prayed that, somehow, the right words would come to me and I wouldn't say something to make things even worse.

Before I could open my mouth, Mark said, "I want you to tell me everything that you remember when you and Jim found the deceased. Don't add anything, and try not to leave anything out, even if you think it isn't important." He held up his cell phone. "I'm going to record your statement as well as write it. That's our new policy, so there are no mistakes. I did the same during Jim's statement."

I know a diversion when I see one. I use the same technique

on Jim when faced with a subject that I want to avoid. If Mark didn't want to talk about his argument with Margo, I'd go along with him. I spent the next several minutes going over every detail I could remember about my late-night activities while Mark took notes. I stuck to the facts, and didn't offer any personal theories or opinions. I couldn't resist throwing in a little dig about how patronizing the two patrolmen who answered the initial 911 call were, though. Then I was ashamed for being so petty when a young woman was lying dead close by.

Mark made a note on his phone. "They're both new hires," he said. "I'll have a word with them."

"Oh, no, please don't do that," I said, worrying that there could be another instance when I'd have an emergency and they were the responding officers. Paul Wheeler already thought I was an interfering, old busybody. I didn't want to add two more to my Fairport Police "un-fan" club. "Some people just rub each other the wrong way, I guess."

Mark's mouth trembled. "You sure got that right, Carol. Like me and Margo."

I grabbed his hand. "Oh, sweetie, I love you, and I'm so sorry to see what you're going through."

"That's just it, Carol. I know you and Jim love me. And Jenny...." He shook his head. "Jenny. I don't know what I'd do without her. She and CJ. When I was there while Jenny was in labor, I suddenly realized the enormity of what a woman has to go through to bring a new life into the world. My mother went through that agony to bring me into the world. I thought we were finally making some headway in our relationship when she came for CJ's birth, even though her arrival was completely unexpected."

I refrained from commenting that "unexpected" hardly covered the trouble Margo's arrival had caused. Points for me, right?

"I was thrilled when Margo said she wanted to come for Christmas, especially since it's CJ's first one. And then she shows up with a guy—who's closer to my age than hers—and she's clearly crazy about him. Why not me? When is she going to love me?"

Mark sat there, silent, and so did I. My heart ached for him. Finally, he said, "I need you to sign this official statement and then I'm leaving." He handed me a pen.

As I wrote my name in what I hoped was legible cursive, I whispered, "Honey, the love Margo has for you has nothing to do with any feelings she may have for Jeremy, no matter what you think. It's like comparing the love I have for Jenny and Mike with the love I have for Jim. There totally different. You need to tell Margo what you've told me, even though it's hard. And all parents make mistakes. Even me, believe it or not." That last part got a brief smile out of him.

"I shouldn't have to tell her how I feel. She's my mother. She should already know." Mark gave me a fierce hug, then he was gone, leaving me with a lot to ponder.

Chapter 24

Patience is a virtue. It's just not one of my virtues.

To interfere, or to not interfere. That was the question.

I shook my head. No. I shouldn't get involved. Margo and Mark were both adults. They needed to work out their relationship on their own.

I'd already given Mark some words of wisdom to ponder. I'd already suggested to Jeremy that he and Mark needed to sit down together and talk. The idea of Margo asking for my help was laughable. So I was done.

My mind wandered from Mark, Margo and Jeremy to last night's terrible event. *The two different head wounds may not mean anything to the police unless you step in and explain about April's previous fall.*

No, Carol! No! Stop it right now. The police can figure this out without any extra help from you. And it's almost Christmas. You have other things to deal with, like being sure the furnace is repaired so you can go home. And you haven't done much holiday shopping.

I heard a door open and swiveled around to see Margo standing there, matching her son's sad look with one of her own. She was dressed in an old sweatsuit that could have come from my own closet, rather than her usual designer duds.

"I guess you heard us," I said. "I'm sorry."

"You have nothing to be sorry about," Margo said. "But it's obvious that I do." She sat on the sofa and dropped her head into her hands. It didn't take a rocket scientist to figure out she was crying and didn't want me to see her. I decided to head into the kitchen and see if there was anything for breakfast. I was starving.

I came back with a plate of two freshly baked muffins, which smelled heavenly. "Can I tempt you with a muffin?" I asked, sliding the plate toward Margo, now sitting upright, eyes closed, with her head resting against the back of the sofa. "A little food, especially something sweet, always cheers me up."

"You should know I don't ever eat baked goods, especially at breakfast," Margo said. "I believe in starting my day with a healthy smoothie, like the ones I made when I was staying with you."

I wrinkled my nose at the memory. "You mean that horrible greenish junk you kept in my refrigerator? Jeremy told me you're allergic to it."

Margo's eyes snapped open and she scowled at me. "It is *not* greenish junk. It's delicious and very good for me. I was allergic to a few of the ingredients, so I changed the recipe a little. You should try some instead of criticizing it."

"Attagirl. That's the Margo I know." A horrible thought struck me and made my stomach churn. "Please tell me you don't have any with you. I don't think I could stand to be that healthy all at once."

Margo laughed out loud. "Truce, Carol?" she said, holding out her hand. "I know we don't agree on too much except how adorable our grandson is, but I could really use a friend right now. That is, if you're willing."

Oh, Lord, no.

I was torn. On the one hand, I *really* wanted to stick to my own life and my own priorities. On the other hand, despite my best intentions to 'Stay Out of Their Business,' I did feel sorry for all of them, and if there was anything more I could do to help resolve such a heartbreaking situation, I should, right? Of course, right. Especially because helping people in need was in the true spirit of Christmas. So, in reality, I was checking a few gifts off my shopping list by being a friend to Margo now. I'd give her the perfect gift—my friendship—and check her right off my list. I hope you're all impressed with my logic. Sometimes my thought process amazes even me.

"I'll make a deal with you," I said, breaking a cranberry muffin apart. Heck, I was still starving, and if I was going to play Mother Confessor, I needed to keep up my strength. I put half the muffin on a napkin and handed it to her. "Share this with me as a token of our new relationship."

Margo broke off a piece of muffin that was so tiny I could barely see it, even with my glasses on, and popped it in her mouth. "Delicious." She pushed the remainder toward me. "Thank you, but that's enough for me."

It took every bit of self-control I had to refrain from scarfing down the rest of the muffin in a single bite. I hope I get extra points for that, because believe me, it was tough.

My phone pinged with a text. I was sure it was from Jim, wanting to know if the coast was clear and he could come back to the suite with the dogs, so I ignored it. I know. You're shaking your head and pretending you'd never do that. But he'd left me to cope with the latest fallout from this "emotional situation" because, according to him, I was much better at this stuff than he was. Ha! Well, I was dealing with it and refused to be interrupted.

"Margo, if you want to tell me more about what happened, I'm here to listen. But if you don't, I'll respect your privacy and just sit here and keep you company for a while."

My phone started pinging again. "Oh, for Pete's sake." The pinging stopped, then began again. "I'm sure this is Jim. If I don't answer him, he'll just keep on texting until I do."

Margo broke off another, larger piece of muffin and waved it at me. "Go ahead and answer, Carol. It's okay. And this is positively my last piece, so please hide the plate from me!"

I smiled, whipped on my glasses, and squinted at the phone. All the texts were from Nancy, not Jim, and they all were the same.

Nancy: *What size is CJ? I'm going Christmas shopping with Mary*

Alice.

Me: *Not sure. Will check.*

Nancy: *Finally! Let me know.*

Me: *Sorry. Lots going on. Where r u?*

Nancy: *At Mary Alice's.*

Me: *Don't leave. We'll be over right away.*

Nancy: *We? Who else? Jenny?*

Me: *No. Margo.*

Nancy: *Hurry up! We want to beat the crowds!*

I sent back a thumbs-up emoji, turned my phone off and stood up. "You and I have an important situation we have to deal with right away. Two of my best friends are going shopping for CJ's Christmas presents, and we're going with them. Get dressed. We're leaving here in fifteen minutes."

"I can't possibly be seen in public until I shower and do my hair and makeup," Margo protested. "That takes me at least an hour."

I laughed out loud. "You're hilarious. Take a quick shower and run a comb through your hair. Get going or I'll leave without you."

"What about Jeremy and Jim?"

Oh, for heaven's sake. "Jim's going back to the house to check on the progress the workmen are making. The dogs are with him. He knows me well enough to realize I'm not going to hang around here when I have a major retail therapy opportunity. Text Jeremy, tell him we're leaving and we'll be back sometime later today. I'll meet you at the elevator." I grabbed the rest of the muffin and headed toward the shower before Margo could respond.

Chapter 25

Chocolate is God's way of telling us He likes us a little chubby.

The lobby registration desk was busy with a line of impatient guests. Bobbie was doing her best to handle the crowd on her own, but from the harried look on her face, she wasn't succeeding to anyone's satisfaction.

"I'm glad we're not checking in today," Margo said. "Look at this crowd. There should be another person at the desk. Isn't April working today?"

I suddenly realized that Margo had no idea what had happened last night to April. I grabbed her arm and pulled her aside so we wouldn't be overheard. "April won't be in today," I said in a low voice. "In fact...." I searched for the right words to describe how Jim and I had discovered April in the parking garage without freaking Margo out. "I'm trying to figure out how to tell you," I said. "It's not easy."

"Oh, for heaven's sake. First you rush me out the door and now you're stalling. What are you trying to say?" Margo turned and spotted Ryan standing near the main entrance. "Well, if you're not going to tell me, I'll ask Ryan. He should know what's going on around here."

"No!" I grabbed Margo's arm so hard the poor woman

screamed in pain. "Please, don't ask Ryan. I'll tell you." I took a deep breath. "April's dead. Jim and I found her in the parking garage last night when we took the dogs for a walk. The police are investigating."

"Oh, my word. How horrible." Margo rubbed her arm. "But you didn't have to grab me so hard."

"I'm sorry."

"Is that why Mark was here this morning? To talk to you and Jim about April?" Margo asked. "I thought he was here to give me an ultimatum about Jeremy. I made things between us even worse by jumping to a completely wrong conclusion."

"It was a natural reaction," I assured her. "Be patient. I'm sure Mark will listen to reason once he has a chance to get to know Jeremy and see how happy you two are. I've been known to jump to the wrong conclusion myself. Everybody does it. The whole situation will straighten itself out and we'll all have a wonderful holiday."

After all, miracles can happen, especially at Christmas, right? Of course, right.

"Ryan and April were a couple," I continued in a low voice, "and I'm sure he's devastated about her death. I didn't want you to upset him by asking innocent questions about why she isn't at work. In fact, I'm surprised that he's even working today."

"Oh, that's so sad. The poor guy."

"It's against hotel policy for employees to date, so nobody here knew they were in a relationship. I shouldn't have told you. Me and my big mouth."

"I promise not to say anything," Margo said, looking peeved that I was suggesting she couldn't keep a secret.

The cowardly part of me was hoping I could sneak out of the hotel without Ryan spotting me. I'd already spent a lot of emotional support trying to help my son-in-law reconcile with his mother. I needed some happy time to recharge my batteries, even if it had to include Margo.

Naturally, the universe had other plans. We'd almost made it to the side door when Ryan appeared at my elbow. "Are you going out this morning, Mrs. Andrews? I'd be glad to get your car for you. Your husband gave me an extra set of keys in case I had to move it."

"My own car? Is it here?"

"Mr. Andrews arranged to have it driven to the hotel yesterday afternoon as a surprise. I can't guarantee another reserved parking spot, though. We're tight on spaces since we can't use part of the garage right now." Ryan's voice broke. I could tell the poor guy was having trouble keeping his emotions under control.

"I'm surprised to see you here at work today after what's happened," Margo said. "It was very brave of you to come in."

I swear, I could have kicked that woman in the shins and nobody would blame me. Ryan's eyes filled with tears. He knew I had betrayed his confidence when he was the most vulnerable. He'd probably take the air out of my tires as punishment for my big mouth. I pushed him out the door before anyone could see what was going on, not caring if Margo the Motormouth was following us or not. "I'm so sorry, Ryan. I feel terrible about everything. I only told Margo about you and April. Even my husband doesn't know. Margo's a mom, too. I thought maybe two moms were better than one to help you get through this."

You should have figured out by now that Margo is the absolute last human being on the face of the earth any sane person would look to for emotional support, and her track record as a mother was a complete disaster. But it was the first thing that popped into my head, and maybe giving Margo a compliment in the parenting department would make her feel better, too.

Fortunately, the garage was empty except for the three of us, so nobody witnessed Ryan sobbing on my shoulder for what seemed long enough to have me wonder if my down coat was truly waterproof. Margo didn't say another word. She just stood there, watching.

After a few minutes, Ryan pulled himself together enough to speak. "I didn't mean to lose control like that, Mrs. Andrews. It's just...I can't express the grief I'm feeling while I'm working or I'll lose my job. When I got that phone call in the middle of the night, my whole world collapsed. I cried all night. April and I had plans to bake Christmas cookies this afternoon. Can you imagine? I already had some of the ingredients on the kitchen counter, ready to go. It's our first Christmas together, and we were planning on making it very special." He wiped his eyes. "It was *going to be* our first Christmas together. I still can't believe it. How did it happen? The police won't tell me anything. Just that she was found dead there." He pointed in the direction of the employee picnic table, which was now ringed with yellow crime scene tape and still busy with police activity.

I felt helpless in the face of such raw grief. "Jim and I were the ones who found her," I said. "I wish we'd been able to help her, but this time, it was too late."

"You found her?" Ryan repeated. "Did she look like she... suffered? I can't handle it if she suffered."

"She looked like she was taking a nap when we found her," I answered, leaving out the rest of the horrible details. He didn't need to know any more.

"That makes me feel a little better, I guess. After the phone call telling me what had happened, a police detective, Mark somebody, showed up at our apartment and asked me all kinds of questions. How long had we known each other? What was the nature of our relationship? Did she have any enemies?" Ryan's voice was getting louder. "Her death was a horrible accident, wasn't it, Mrs. Andrews? It had to be an accident. Nobody in the world would want to hurt her. She was the best thing that ever happened to me. And now she's gone."

"Losing someone you love is always unbearable," I said in a low voice. "I'm sure the police will figure it out. The best thing for you to do right now is keep busy and try to take your mind off your grief, especially while you're at the hotel."

Stop telling the poor guy how to grieve. You don't really know how he's feeling.

Margo gave me a nudge and gestured toward the valet parking desk. There were a few guests standing there now, trying to appear inconspicuous while they were obviously hanging on every word

Ryan was saying. "You have guests waiting for their cars," she said, taking Ryan's hand and squeezing it. "I'm truly sorry for your loss. She was a lovely girl."

"Thank you. She was." Ryan turned to me. "Do you mind getting your own car, Mrs. Andrews? I parked it at the back corner of the garage near the exit. Just be sure to put the orange cone in place when you leave, to reserve the spot. I have to take care of these other guests now."

"Not a problem," I said. "Hang in. We'll see you later." I turned to Margo. "I know what you said about April meant a lot to Ryan."

"A loss like that makes my problems look pretty small," Margo said as we walked toward my car. "I'm realizing the pressure my son must be under every day in his job. I need to be more patient with him, and not expect miracles to happen in our relationship. It's going to take a lot of time."

"I held my breath when Ryan said a detective named Mark questioned him," I said. "I was afraid you'd say he's your son, and I'm not sure what Ryan would have done then."

"I was worried you'd say Mark was your son-in-law," Margo said. "Good thing we both kept quiet."

"You're right," I said, smiling as I unlocked the car doors. "Although...."

"Although, what?" Margo said, fishing around for the seat belt.

"Oh, nothing important." I buckled my seat belt and thanked my lucky stars that, for once, I'd kept my big mouth shut. Because it had just occurred to me that I was in a unique position to "help" the police solve this case. And since Jim and I had discovered poor April together, he couldn't criticize me for falling over another dead body. Maybe we could even work together (for once) to figure out if April's death was an unfortunate accident or something more sinister.

Jim and I would be just like Lord Peter Wimsey and Harriet Vane in Dorothy Sayers' wonderful mystery series. Or Nick and Nora Charles in *The Thin Man* movies (without all the booze). Yes, that was even better, especially since they had a dog, even if Asta was a wire-haired fox terrier and not an English cocker spaniel. Or...yes! We'd be Sherlock Holmes and Dr. Watson! Perfect. I wondered where I could buy a deerstalker hat, and if it'd look better on me or on Jim. Oh, heck, we could both wear them. We never agreed on who was in charge, anyway. Even though I was the one who had more experience in crime-solving than Jim did. Maybe we'd even get our own reality television show.

I was suddenly conscious of someone shaking my arm. "Carol! Aren't you going to start the car? What's wrong with you?"

Oops.

"I was trying to figure out which was the quickest way to Mary Alice's from here. There are several options." I turned the key and the car roared to life. I could check Amazon for deerstalker hats another time.

Chapter 26

I prefer dogs over people.

"This looks like a lovely place to live," Margo commented as I punched the security code into the keypad of Mary Alice's condo community. "I wonder if there are any available units."

My heart dropped to my boots. OMG. I'd never expected that Margo would see a real estate opportunity when I invited her on this "grandmother bonding" adventure.

It's Christmas, Carol. The spirit of peace on earth and all that jazz. Be nice. After all, you, Jim and the dogs are technically her guests until you can go back home.

I swung into a parking spot right next to a shiny, new, black Range Rover, trying hard not to scratch the fender. It was a tight squeeze, and my parking skills are somewhat lacking as I age. (Please don't tell anyone else that.)

"I've heard there's a waiting list for units here," I said, carefully opening my door and easing my way out of the car. I hope Santa was watching when I added, "Nancy would know. She's our local in-house real estate expert. You can ask her."

Margo nodded. "I just might do that."

The Range Rover's tinted window glided open, and I heard a familiar voice. "Where're you going, Carol? Don't you want to ride in luxury for a change?"

"Nancy! How in the world were you able to afford such an expensive car? I know the real estate market is hot right now, but still."

"Nancy doesn't own the car, silly. Hop in and she'll give you all the detail," Mary Alice said from the front passenger seat. "Margo, it's nice to meet you. I'm Mary Alice, by the way, another of Carol's posse."

Margo looked at me questioningly, and I grinned. "Nancy is always full of surprises. I just hope she hasn't stolen the car."

"I heard that," Nancy said, as Margo and I settled ourselves in the back seat, which was bigger than my entire house. (Only a slight exaggeration.)

"Mary Alice is the sweet one in our group," I explained to Margo. "Her job since grammar school has been to keep the rest of us out of trouble."

"And it's not easy," Mary Alice added. "Especially without Claire here to back me up. She's the only one who can really keep Carol in line, and she had to pick now to go to Florida."

"Yeah, she must really be suffering in all that sunshine and warmth," Nancy said, pulling out of the parking lot and heading toward the new upscale shopping center in Fairport. "Don't you want to know about the car?"

"Of course I do," I said. "But I'm not going to beg you to tell me." I shot a glance at Margo, who looked a little dazed. I couldn't blame her.

"Bob gave me this new Range Rover to drive for the month of December as a Christmas present," Nancy continued. "Isn't that the sweetest thing? He even put a big red bow on the hood."

"Bob is Nancy's sort-of husband," I explained. "He manages a high-end local car dealership, and he's always loaning Nancy expensive cars."

"We're still married, but we don't live together. We just date. Believe me, it works out much better this way," Nancy explained. "I've been telling Carol for a long time that she and Jim ought to try this arrangement."

"So when Jeremy and I had dinner with you the other night,

you and Bob were on a date?" Margo asked, trying to clarify Nancy's unique marital situation.

"Yes. We're married and dating. Each other."

"I understand," Margo said, though she clearly didn't. Truth to tell, neither did I.

"This car's promised to one of Bob's customers, although the deal isn't finalized yet. The buyer is some young yuppie who's a financial wizard and loaded with cash. He doesn't want the car until the end of the year, so technically it still belongs to the dealership."

"The buyer probably doesn't want to close the deal now for tax reasons," Mary Alice said. "I've never had to worry about that problem."

I looked at Margo and rolled my eyes. She was trying hard not to laugh. Nancy is always entertaining. "Doesn't Bob worry that a car he's loaned you might be damaged?" she asked.

"Not at all," Nancy said. "He knows that I'm the world's best driver. He trusts me implicitly." Need I tell you that this conversation was taking place while Nancy was weaving in and out of traffic, without signaling first, causing other drivers to honk at her and give her a one finger salute? No, I didn't think I had to tell you that. Honestly, that Nancy.

Chapter 27

I don't think a therapist is supposed to say, "Oh, wow," that many times in the first session, but here we are.

"I'd forgotten how much fun it is to shop for a baby," Nancy said, carefully putting five shopping bags on the hood of the Range Rover while she fumbled for the magical key fob.

"I can't believe how much we bought for CJ today," I said, balancing a huge shopping bag and a box containing a stroller that would keep Jim busy assembling it from now until New Year's.

"It was such a great idea you had to divide our purchases by assigned size, Margo," Mary Alice said. "Otherwise we probably would've all bought clothes that CJ'd outgrow in less than six months."

"I like to be organized," Margo said. "And I, for one, am exhausted. But I loved every minute of our adventure. I'm so glad I was here so I could be part of it."

"Did you also love the fast food we grabbed in the middle of our shopping frenzy?" I teased. "I was worried you wouldn't find anything to eat."

"I loved every morsel of that cheeseburger," Margo said, grinning. "Probably too much. I have to get back on my strict regimen right away or I'll lose all my resolve."

"Oh, lighten up, Margo," Nancy said. "It's Christmas. Time to overindulge in a few extra calories."

"That's just the point. I want to lighten up, and I'm afraid that if I keep eating the way I've done so far today, I'll fatten up instead."

Good grief. The woman was skinny as the proverbial rail. A few extra pounds would look good on her. Unlike me, not that I intended to let that bother me during the holidays.

"You need to open the tailgate, Nancy," I said. "And hurry up. This stuff is heavy."

"I'm trying to! Bob told me something about the car having a gesture tailgate." She left her purchases on the hood, walked to the rear, and began jumping up and down and waving her arms. I'd never seen anything so funny in my whole life.

"May I be of some assistance?" a passerby inquired. "I don't mean to intrude, but it looks like you're having a difficult time."

"Thank you so much," Nancy said, trying to hide her embarrassment. "That would be great."

I recognized our good Samaritan immediately; it was my new across-the-street neighbor. "We have to stop meeting like this," I said. "People are beginning to talk. Everyone, this is Frank Adams. He and his wife are moving into a house across the street from ours. This is the second time he's come to my rescue in a ridiculously short period of time."

"I'm always happy to help a lovely damsel in distress," Frank said, smiling. "We leased a Range Rover for a while. The gesture tailgate function is one of the reasons why we decided not to buy it when our lease was up. My wife said I was embarrassing her every time I used it in public. Watch and learn. First, you have to find the right spot." He walked to the rear corner of the Range Rover and made a smooth kick and return motion beneath a sensor in the outer part of the bumper, then moved away quickly. The lights flashed and the tailgate opened majestically. Amazing.

"You can close it the same way."

"I'm glad it's your Christmas present and not mine, Nancy," Mary Alice said. "I'd be sure to fall and land on my you-know-what every time I tried to open the tailgate."

"So what brings you to this part of town?" I asked Frank as I fought for space to squeeze all my purchases into the car. "This stroller is really heavy."

"Let me help you again," Frank said. "Ladies, if you don't mind, I'll show you the proper way to load a tailgate and have room to spare." He removed all the bags and boxes we'd piled in helter-skelter and placed them on the sidewalk. He studied them, then began reloading, putting the stroller way in the back. In less than five minutes, all our treasures had been stowed, and, as promised, there was still room for a few more purchases.

"How in the world did you do that so efficiently?" Nancy asked. "I can't believe it."

"Years of practice. We've moved around a lot, sometimes on the spur of the moment. I've become somewhat of an expert on how to pack a vehicle."

"I'm impressed," I said. And I was.

"You asked me what I was doing in this part of town," Frank continued. "I have a meeting to discuss financials for the nonprofit program Sally's Closet shop supports. Ellen and I are thinking of making a sizeable donation, but I want to check over the donor list first."

"The thrift shop is a very worthwhile program that does a lot of good in the area," I said.

"So it seems. I hope you all have a wonderful holiday." And he walked away at a brisk pace.

Margo had already claimed her place inside the Range Rover and didn't witness Frank's re-organizing the tailgate. But she must have extra good hearing. "I love thrift shops. How far is it from here?"

I shot Nancy and Mary Alice a look. I had no desire to visit Sally's Closet and risk having a little chat with Sister Rose. I could tell by their body language that they both agreed with me.

I yawned for effect, then said, "Boy, am I tired. I need a quick nap. I didn't sleep very well last night." *Finding a dead body and then being interrogated by the police is hard on a person's sleep pattern. I* didn't really say that out loud, of course.

"Oh, come on, Carol," Margo said. "Don't be such a killjoy. This will be fun. The perfect way to end a perfect shopping trip is scoring major bargains." Without waiting for a response from me, she scurried away and caught up with Frank.

"There's no way to get out of this unless we want to ditch Margo and make her walk back to Mary Alice's," Nancy said in a low voice. She checked her phone. "I'm showing a house in one hour, so let's get going."

Chapter 28

I started out with nothing. I still have most of it.

After a speedy three-block walk during which we were all blown to bits by the punishing north wind, I was actually glad the thrift shop was in sight, no matter what other adventures besides scoring major bargains might be waiting for us inside.

"It's a good thing we didn't move the car," Mary Alice said. "There isn't an empty parking spot anywhere near here."

"Tell that to my freezing face," I said, my teeth chattering. I pushed open the door and was greeted by a horde of frenzied females shopping like they were about to board the last train out of Fairport for the heavenly gates. Frank was nowhere to be seen (who could blame him?), and a harried Sister Rose was at the checkout desk along with Frank's wife, Ellen, who was doing her best to ring up and bag purchases as quickly as possible.

Sister Rose immediately spotted three of her favorite former students (that would be Nancy, Mary Alice and me) and waved us forward. I nudged Nancy. "I told you this was a bad idea. Sister Rose needs more help and we're it."

"Thank the Good Lord you're here," Sister said, her face flushed. "I can always count on you three girls to come to my rescue. It's Customer Appreciation Day, and everything in the shop is half-price. That's why we're so crowded. Our regular afternoon volunteers are mothers who had to cancel their shift because their children were sent home sick from school. I've had no time to recruit anyone else."

She turned to Ellen. "Thank you so much for pitching in, but the cavalry has arrived. We can join your husband in the office now to go over the program financials." Without another word, she and Ellen vanished, leaving the three of us to deal with what was now a *really* impatient line of shoppers.

Nancy and Mary Alice had panicked looks on their faces. I realized they had been loyal customers of the thrift shop, but had never volunteered. Which left me in charge. Oh, boy.

Channeling my best Sister Rose imitation, I clapped my hands the way she used to do when we were in high school and yelled for quiet. To my amazement, everyone obeyed—even the customers who were still shopping.

"All right, everybody," I said in a loud voice, "I know you just want to pay for your purchases and leave. We're stepping in to help, and we've never done this before, so please be patient with us. We'll do our best."

I must have looked as desperate as I felt, because instantly one of the customers yelled, "I can help you."

The line of customers parted faster than Moses parting the Red Sea, and in a jiffy, I realized the woman coming to help us was Margo. "I worked for a while as a retail clerk," she whispered to me. "With any luck, I can figure out this cash register." She fiddled around with a few keys for a minute or two, and I held my breath, then nodded. "I think I can do this. It would be quicker if the line were divided into those paying cash and those using charge cards," she suggested in a loud voice. "And we'll check out the cash customers first, because they'll be faster."

I had immediate misgivings. Nobody I knew used cash any more. Especially me. I just whipped out a credit card when I wanted to buy something, and prayed Jim wouldn't be home when the bill arrived. I hoped Margo knew what she was doing.

"Trust me," she whispered. "Once people find out that paying in cash will get them out faster, you'll be surprised at how fast the money will appear."

I said a quick prayer, then yelled, "Did everyone hear that? People who are paying cash will be checked out first. Nancy, can you...?"

"I'm on it," she said, and immediately began dividing the line. This was a perfect job for her because some of the customers were threatening to leave their merchandise and scram. Nancy's an expert at dealing with difficult people after years of practice as a real estate agent.

"I'll wrap and bag the merchandise," Mary Alice said.

"And I'll read off the prices so you can input them into the system and total each sale as fast as possible," I said to Margo. "Remember, all the merchandise is half-price today."

Working as a team, we had most of the customers taken care of and out the door in less than twenty minutes. Margo was right. When given the right incentive, most of them paid in cash.

"Phew," I said. "We did it." I pointed around the shop. "There are a few more customers shopping, but I doubt there'll be another backup of customers waiting to check out like there was when we got here."

"Now that the mad rush is over," Margo said, "will one of you please tell me why we did what we did? I thought we were just coming in to do a little bargain shopping; the next thing I knew, I looked up and saw the three of you working behind the counter."

"I don't blame you for being confused," Mary Alice said. "Sally's Closet is a nonprofit that benefits a domestic violence crisis center in Fairport."

"That's certainly a very worthy cause," Margo said. "But I still don't see a connection between that and you." Her eyes widened. "Or, maybe I do."

"No, no," Mary Alice said quickly. "That's not it, at all. Sister Rose is the manager of the thrift shop, and also the director of the crisis center."

"She was our high school English teacher at Mount Saint Francis," Nancy continued. "She can pretty much get us to do anything she wants, even all these years after our graduation. Especially Carol. All Sister has to do is give her one look and Carol starts to tremble."

I bit my lip. I realized how ridiculous it must sound to Margo that a grown woman in her "later adult" years would still be intimidated by a long-ago high school teacher. Even if it was true.

"In the spirit of the Christmas season, I'll let that pass, Nancy. Especially since most of the events that I got in trouble for in high school were your idea. You just didn't get caught."

"True," Nancy said. "I always ran faster than you." She snuck a look at her phone. "Oh, my goodness. Just look at the time. I have to leave now, or I'll keep a client waiting. And this one is really demanding." I rolled my eyes. To hear Nancy tell it, all her clients were "really demanding."

"It looks like you and Margo have everything under control now, Carol." She gave me a quick peck on the cheek. "Mary Alice, do you want a lift home? I'm going right by your condo." And before I could object, they were both gone.

I shook my head. "It's a good thing Nancy and I are best friends, or I'd give her an empty box for Christmas instead of an expensive present."

"It must be nice to be best friends for so long," Margo said, looking sad. "I've never had one."

Well, don't look at me. There's no way we're ever going to be besties. I didn't really say that out loud, of course.

"I think it's great for the family that we're getting to know each other better, don't you?" I said, side-stepping the 'best friend' designation. "Although you know the old saying about family—you can pick your friends, but you can't pick your relatives." I clapped my hands over my mouth. "Oh, gosh. That sounded horrible. I'm sorry."

"That's a perfect description of our relationship," Margo said, grinning.

"But we're working on it," I added. "Even though this day started off terribly for both of us, I think sharing a shopping adventure and buying presents for our wonderful grandson is a memory I'll treasure. There's nobody else who would have made the experience so special. CJ's two grandmothers shopping together for his first Christmas." My eyes misted up, and I realized that I was serious about what I'd said.

"You're absolutely right," Margo agreed. "And since we found out today that we can work together on a common project, we're ready for our next one."

"Next one? Jim would have a conniption if I bought any more presents for CJ, even though he loves the little guy as much as you and I do."

"I'm not suggesting we do any more shopping. Let's work together and figure out what happened to April. Maybe our sleuthing might actually impress my son."

Chapter 29

This "killing them with kindness" thing is taking way longer than I expected.

Immediately my blood pressure shot up at least twenty points. Then, I laughed. "I know you're kidding, Margo. You really had me going, though."

"I've never been more serious about anything in my life. This is perfect for the two of us. We could call ourselves the Glamma Squad."

"Huh?"

Now Margo looked impatient. "Don't you remember, Carol? When CJ starts talking, he'll call me Glamma and you Grandma. We already decided."

This woman was going to drive me over the edge, for sure. I was working on a monster headache. *Please, let a customer interrupt this conversation before I say or do something I'll regret. Or, even worse, that I won't regret.*

I was conscious of other voices, and then I saw Sister Rose, Frank and Ellen walking toward the front of the shop, deep in conversation. Hallelujah!

"I'll do my best to pull together the information you asked for tonight," Sister Rose said, bypassing the cashier desk at a fast pace and shepherding the couple out the door. "I'll text you. Thank you so much for your generous donation, and for your interest in our nonprofit program." She closed the door firmly and fanned herself with a piece of paper that looked to me like a check. "My goodness. That was something."

"Sister Rose, are you all right? Your face is all flushed." *And I know you're way past menopause.* You know I didn't say *that* out loud!

"Carol, dear. I'm so glad you're still here. Thank you for pitching in today." She zeroed in on Margo. "I don't believe I know your friend. I'm Sister Rose."

I hastened to cover my breach of etiquette. "This is Margo Anderson, Sister. She's Mark's mother and CJ's other grandmother. She's visiting for the holidays."

"Of course," Sister Rose said, clasping Margo's hands and giving her a big smile. "I thought you looked familiar."

"Nancy and Mary Alice had to leave right after the rush of customers," I put in. "They were a tremendous help, but Margo's knowledge of the cash register really saved the day. We rang up a slew of sales. I think the shop made a lot of money today."

"How wonderful," Sister responded with less enthusiasm than I expected, which was weird. I knew Sally's Closet's profit margin was razor thin.

"I've gotten some amazing news, and I have to share it with someone or I'll burst," she continued, fingering the paper which I now was certain was a check. "You won't believe what's happened. It's like a miracle." She looked around the thrift shop, which mercifully was quiet. "Look at this donation."

I took the check from Sister Rose's shaking hands and read the amount. "This is a check for ten thousand dollars."

"I'm in shock," Sister Rose admitted. "And not only that, Frank and Ellen plan to do a challenge grant to raise a hundred thousand dollars from other donors for the domestic violence program by the end of the year. Frank wants our private donor list so he can contact each of them personally and get them to commit. Isn't that something?"

I put my arms around Sister Rose and hugged her—a first! "It sure is."

I felt the tiniest prickle of concern, because I couldn't figure out how someone who'd just purchased a house that needed tons of work just to make it livable—could afford to be that generous.

I hope the check clears. I didn't say that out loud, of course.

"I won't keep you both any longer," Sister Rose said. "Thank you again for all your help." She peered out the front window of the thrift shop. "I don't see your car, Carol. I hope you didn't have to park far from here on such a cold day."

Reality dawned, a little late. "We came with Nancy and Mary Alice," I said. "My car's still at Mary Alice's condo." I pulled out my phone. "Maybe I can catch Jim, and he can pick us up here."

"But what about all the presents for CJ?" Margo asked. "I wanted to get them back to the hotel tonight so I could start wrapping them."

Ouch! Bad idea. No way was I giving Jim a chance to see everything I'd bought and yell about how I'd spent too much money. My perfect plan of sneaking them into the hotel would be ruined.

"It's time for me to close the shop for the day," Sister Rose said. "I'll be glad to drive you to pick up your car, Carol. It's the least I can do after all your hard work today."

"Are you sure it's no trouble, Sister?" I asked. "We don't want to inconvenience you."

"It's no trouble at all," Sister Rose said. "You know that I don't get to use my car nearly as much as I want to. I don't want my driving skills to get rusty. I'll be with you in a few minutes."

"I'm sure we can figure something else out," I called after her. But she ignored me and disappeared into the back of the shop.

"What's your problem, Carol?" Margo asked. "This really is the easiest solution."

"I had the dubious pleasure of being Sister Rose's passenger about a year ago," I said. "I haven't recovered from the experience yet. You'll see for yourself in a few minutes. I guarantee it'll be a ride you'll never forget."

The Good Lord smiled down on me before I had a chance to beg for help. My phone pinged with a text from my Nancy.

Nancy: *Dropping gifts off in ur suite.*

Me: *OMG! Is Jim there?*

Nancy: *No, silly. Great digs. I'm waiting 4 Bob 2 come.*

Me: *Bob? Why?*

Nancy: *Driving ur car back from Mary Alice's b4 our date 2nite. U're welcome.*

I smiled. Knowing Nancy as well as I do, I was positive her motivation for being so nice—

in addition to doing me a favor—was to check out the corporate suite. "She makes me laugh," I said aloud.

"Who?"

"Nancy just dropped the gifts and my car off at the hotel. Everything's all worked out." A tiny simplification of the facts in the interest of brevity, for which I hope I can be forgiven.

"So Sister Rose will drop us at the hotel, too?"

In a flash, I had another solution. "No way. Text Jeremy, tell him we need a ride, and beg him to come to our rescue."

Margo's face lit up like the Rockefeller Center Christmas tree. "Perfect."

Chapter 30

*You don't realize how old you are until you sit
on the floor and then try to get up again.*

"I'm glad you two had such a wonderful time today," Jeremy said as he navigated through rush hour traffic in the direction of our hotel without a single curse word escaping his lips. (Unlike you-know-who.) Either he was on his best behavior for my benefit, or an example of one of the few men on earth who have the patience all women are born with. He looked at Margo with such love that I even felt it in the back seat of the rental car. "If you're happy, so am I."

I was glad to see that the morning's tiff between the two lovebirds was over.

"We spent a lot of money," Margo said. I almost kicked the back of her seat, but restrained myself just in time.

"*You* spent a lot of money," I corrected. "I was very frugal in my purchases, and I want you both to remember that fact should Jim ask any questions about our shopping spree. Just don't mention how many times I was frugal and everything will be fine."

"So that's the secret to being married for such a long time," Jeremy said. "I always wondered."

"Word choices are very important," I continued. "So are separate bathrooms."

"I agree with that last rule one hundred percent," Margo said. "It's not necessary for a man to see the process a woman goes through to make herself attractive, as long as he appreciates the finished product. A little mystery is good for our relationship, right?"

"Would you prefer that I be a man of mystery to you, my darling?" Jeremy asked.

"As long as I have the same privilege," Margo clarified. She turned in her seat and winked at me.

"What did you do today, Jeremy?" I know, that was nosy. "I bet you did some Christmas shopping, too."

I suddenly realized Jeremy could have gone to the police station to talk to Mark. I don't need any of you to remind me that I wanted him to do just that—yesterday. If he talked to Mark today, after Margo and Mark's terrible argument, his visit could have made things even worse.

"Just a little," he said. "I spent most of the day driving around Fairport and getting to know the town. It's a beautiful place. I can see why you've lived here for so long, Carol. I ended up accidentally driving by your house on my way to the beach. Jim was outside talking to a workman, so I stopped to say hello. We ended up grabbing lunch at the local diner."

"I hope Lucy and Ethel didn't get too cold waiting for you in the car." Okay, sue me. I worry about my dogs, especially when the weather is as cold as it was today.

"Jim was concerned about that, too. The heat's still off in your house, so we couldn't leave them there. Luckily, he found two dog sweaters in your hall closet to keep them warm. We got takeout at the diner, drove to the beach for a picnic, and then took the dogs for a nice walk. I enjoyed it a lot."

Jeremy drove into the hotel parking garage, and I averted my eyes from the picnic table at the rear, still cordoned off with yellow police crime tape. "Ladies, we have arrived."

I checked; Ryan was nowhere to be seen, thank goodness. I hoped he was home, dealing with his grief over April's death in private. I noticed that Jim's car was already in his spot, and wondered where mine was. I hoped Nancy hadn't left all the shopping bags in the living room, where Jim was sure to see them if he got back to the suite before we did. By the time we'd unloaded a few packages from the car and used the stop-and-go local elevator with other guests (the express one was temporarily out of service for maintenance), I could feel my good mood slipping away.

It's Christmas, Carol. Peace on earth and good will toward men. And women. Get in the spirit and stop anticipating the worst possible scenario. Don't let anything, or anyone, spoil your good mood. I squared my shoulders and followed Jeremy and Margo to the door of our suite.

Despite my internal pep talk, I wasn't prepared for the sight that greeted us. Mark was sitting on the sofa, wearing what Jenny calls "his cop face." There was no sign of Jim and the dogs. They were probably hiding in the bedroom, and I wished that I was with them.

Margo stepped forward. "I didn't expect to see you so soon, Mark," she said. "I'm very glad you came back. I'm sure you and Jeremy will become friends once you get to know each other."

I grabbed Margo's hand and squeezed it tight. I knew, even if she didn't, that this was no social call.

"I'm sorry to intrude on your evening," Mark said. "I'm here on official police business." He addressed Jeremy. "Mr. Dixon, we've received some information about an altercation you recently had with the deceased hotel employee, April Swanson. I'm here to take you in for questioning."

Chapter 31

I asked my husband to take me to a restaurant where they make the food in front of you. He took me to Subway.

Margo gave a little cry.

"He's not being arrested," I assured her as the two men walked out the door. "The police just want to ask him a few questions. It's standard procedure. Jim and I had to give a statement this morning." But I knew in my heart that I was lying to make her feel better. Maybe to make myself feel better, too.

"I know you're right," Margo said, trying to smile and failing. "Jeremy wouldn't harm anyone. He's the kindest, most loving man I've ever known."

"He seems like a real sweetheart," I agreed, knowing from personal experience that appearances can be deceptive. "I'm sure he'll be back in no time, so try not to worry."

"I'll try my best," Margo said. "I'm going to lie down for a while."

On impulse, I gave her a quick hug, and she started to cry, which made me feel terrible.

"Excuse me."

Jim's coat was flung carelessly over the back of a dining room chair, so I knew he was here. I'm not going to kid you. I was plenty miffed that he'd chosen to be absent from another major family crisis involving Margo and Mark. I was getting tired of carrying the full emotional support load for them.

I opened the bedroom door and found my husband and two English cocker spaniels, snoring like chainsaws, sprawled on the bed. The three of them were making such a racket that they probably wouldn't have heard a jet plane if it had landed beside them. They looked so cute that I didn't have the heart to wake them, so I tiptoed out of the room, leaving them to their slumber. I knew that, unlike me, if Jim takes a nap during the day, it doesn't interfere with his nighttime rest.

I also knew that as soon as Jim woke up, he'd want dinner. I wondered if Jeremy had pre-ordered anything earlier in the day, the way he frequently did. I tiptoed out of the bedroom, cell phone in hand, to check with the front desk. As if reading my mind—or possibly in answer to my tummy's growling—there was a discreet knock at the suite door, then a woman's voice: "Hello. Is anyone there? I have your dinner."

I could definitely get used to this pampering, especially since it wasn't costing Jim and me a cent.

To my surprise, it was Bobbie, the desk clerk with the great haircut, who wheeled our dinners into the suite. She looked a little harried so, good sport that I am, I pitched in to help her unload the cart in the suite's kitchen.

"I see you're doing extra duty tonight," I quipped as she handed me one of the plates.

"Not by choice," Bobbie said. "We're stretched thin because of what happened to April. Plus, Ryan's gone home early for reasons that I don't understand at all, so the parking garage is also understaffed. I suppose the manager will have me parking cars next."

I tried to look sympathetic, but honest to goodness, April had died and Ryan...well, I couldn't explain his absence without getting him fired, so I didn't respond.

Bobbie leaned a little closer to me and whispered, "Is Mr. Dixon here?"

"Not right now. He had to leave unexpectedly, but I'm sure he'll be back soon. Does he need to sign for this order?"

Bobbie shook her head. "No, you can do that." She handed me the receipt and I scrawled what I laughingly call my signature across the bottom. "I'm wondering where he went. Do you know?"

Some people accuse *me* of being nosy. Honestly, this woman had me beat by a mile.

"I really couldn't say," I hedged. "Why are you asking?"

Bobbie grinned. "I bet the police came a little while ago and took him away. You just don't want to talk about it. Am I right?"

What was wrong with this woman? How did she know that Jeremy was at police headquarters being questioned? And why did she look so happy? And then, I got it.

"You're the one who called the police about a so-called altercation you just happened to overhear," I said, my voice rising. "Do you have any idea how much trouble you've caused for an innocent person? You ought to be ashamed of yourself, instead of gloating about it. I suppose this is a way to make yourself look important. Well, you've certainly reached a new low as far as I'm concerned. I have a good mind to report you to your boss for spreading false information about a guest." I paused to take a breath. I was so mad, I wanted to dump one of our dinners on her head, but my mother taught me never to waste food.

Bobbie took a step back, clearly surprised at my reaction. "I know what I heard," she insisted. "And I realized it was my duty as a good citizen to report what I heard to the authorities."

"When did this so-called altercation take place?" I asked, channeling every defense attorney I'd ever read in mystery books. "And where were you when you heard it?"

"It happened two days ago. I was in the hotel office catching up on some paperwork," Bobbie answered without skipping a beat. "The office is right behind the registration desk."

I nodded. I knew exactly what conversation Bobbie was talking about because I had witnessed it, too. She obviously had forgotten that. "And then...?"

"April and Mr. Dixon were talking at the desk. I always make it a point to listen when another staff member is dealing with a guest, in case there's a problem he or she can't handle and I need to step in."

Bobbie paused, and I wondered if she was thinking about how to spin what she'd overheard to give it the worst possible meaning. Talk about taking a long time to get to the point. Sheesh.

"I could tell from the sound of April's voice that the conversation wasn't going well. Although I couldn't hear the exact words at that point."

"Aha," I said, triumphantly. "You just admitted you didn't hear the exact words." I didn't either, but I didn't say that. I just let Bobbie continue with her fictionalized version of the event.

"If you'll let me finish, I got up and opened the office door wider. I distinctly heard Mr. Dixon threaten April. He told her that she should be careful or she'd be sorry. And that he wouldn't want anything bad to happen to her. Now, what do you say to that, Mrs. Andrews?"

"It's only your opinion that what you overheard was a threat," I countered. "And opinions aren't facts."

"April certainly felt she was being threatened," Bobbie said.

"Did she tell you she felt threatened by Mr. Dixon?"

"No," Bobbie answered. "When I finally talked to her, she refused to talk about their conversation. She just started to cry. That was enough proof for me."

"She could have been upset about something that had happened earlier, and Jeremy was comforting her. Did you ever think of that?"

"You didn't hear his voice, Mrs. Andrews," Bobbie insisted stubbornly. "He didn't sound like he was trying to comfort her."

"I didn't realize you were such an expert on voices," I said. "You certainly are multi-talented." *If you ask me, I think you're just a nosy busybody with an overactive imagination.*

Oh, wait. If that's what she is, what does that make you, Carol? Fortunately, I reined in my mouth before I gave her my opinion.

"Did you try to intervene when you heard the so-called altercation and help April?" I asked. "If she was as upset as you claim she was, that's what I would have done."

"No. Another hotel guest arrived at the desk before I could, and Mr. Dixon had left. Besides," Bobbie said, "in the hospitality business, the guest is always right, even if he's wrong. It's the first rule that every staff member has to learn and obey if they want to keep their job."

"Do you mean, if a guest is belligerent and rude, you just have to stand there and take it? That seems so wrong."

"Tell me about it," Bobbie said. "Although if my personal safety is at risk, I guess it would be okay to protect myself."

"How comforting to know that you'd be able to defend yourself against an attack by an enraged guest," I said. Then, I realized what I'd just said. "Do you think that's what happened to April? That Jeremy attacked her for some reason and she couldn't defend herself? That's just crazy."

"Now maybe you're beginning to understand why I called the police and told them about the conversation I overheard. You may be right. I might have jumped to the wrong conclusions. But what if I didn't? I already feel guilty that I didn't insist April tell me why she was so upset after her conversation with Mr. Dixon. I don't want to feel guilty that I didn't pass on information about a guest who might be responsible for her death."

Bobbie wheeled the food service cart toward the door of the suite, and I stopped her. "The other guest who came to the registration desk that day was me," I said, enjoying the look of shock on her face. "I guess you conveniently forgot that part. It's fascinating that your memory of what happened is so different from mine. I did talk to April, and she in no way indicated that she'd felt threatened by Jeremy. I plan to share that information with the police at the earliest opportunity."

Bobbie wouldn't let it go. "Did you hear any part of their

actual conversation?"

I had to come clean. "No, I didn't."

"I did. And I'm telling you that I heard Mr. Dixon threaten April. I know you and your husband are his guests. Perhaps you should be careful, just in case you're sharing this suite with a murderer."

Chapter 32

A wife was hinting about what she wanted for an upcoming wedding anniversary gift. She asked for something that went from 0 to 150 in about 3 seconds. Her husband got her a bathroom scale. And that's when the fight started.

Jim and I ended up as a party of two for dinner that night. Margo announced that she was too upset to eat a single bite, adding that, after such a high calorie lunch, she might skip meals tomorrow, too. Jeremy was a no-show, and I prayed that Mark wouldn't allow personal issues to interfere with his duty as an officer of the law.

Under normal circumstances (whatever that means), I love eating food that someone else has cooked. But Bobbie's parting remark about our sharing a suite with a possible murderer ruined my appetite. Jim never lets anything interfere with enjoying a good meal, especially one he's not paying for, so even though our de facto host was missing and our hostess was on a self-imposed fast, he ate dinner with his usual gusto. When he finally realized that I was moving my food around the plate instead of eating it, he pointed to the untouched meal and asked, "Are you going to eat that? Otherwise, I will." Honestly, men! So sensitive to their partner's every emotion.

I did cheer myself up by eating two desserts. I'm a sucker for peppermint stick ice cream, and it's only available around the holidays. I figured I deserved a special treat after the day I'd been through. Merry Christmas to me.

After wrapping up the remaining food and storing it in the refrigerator, Jim and I spent the next couple of hours watching a movie on television. Don't ask me what the title was because I wasn't paying much attention. Jim wasn't, either, if his gentle snores were any indication of his interest level. To be honest, I was straining to hear if there was any activity in Margo and Jeremy's room—like a phone conversation that might give me a hint of what was going on.

Despite my best intentions to wait up until Jeremy arrived back so I could casually interrogate him on what was new in his life, I found myself dozing off on the comfy sofa, the two dogs asleep beside me. "I give up," I announced in a loud voice.

Jim stirred, then opened one eye and stared at me. "So do I. Just tell me what we're giving up."

"Staying awake so we can talk to Jeremy, of course."

Jim yawned. "I didn't know that's what we were doing." He pointed at the huge television screen. "I thought you wanted to watch this movie. I was just keeping you company."

"And you were such great company, dear," I said, giving him a kiss on his head. "Let's walk the dogs and go to bed. I'm exhausted."

"I thought you wanted to wait up for Jeremy," Jim said. "I wish you wouldn't change your mind all the time. You confuse the heck out of me."

I could tell we were on the verge of a silly domestic skirmish when Jim added, "What happened at the police station tonight is none of our business," and gave me a stern look.

Rather than quarrel, although I didn't agree with him, I gave in gracefully. "You're absolutely right; it's none of our business." I waved the two leashes and Lucy gave me a dirty look. "I know you're warm and cozy, but you and Ethel both have to go out now. Then, it's off to bed for all of us." *And with any luck, we'll stay inside the suite all night and not find any more dead bodies.* I didn't say that last part out loud, of course. I didn't want to give Lucy any ideas.

After an uneventful walk around the block, where both girls took care of enough doggie needs that they probably wouldn't need to be walked for days (only kidding!), we headed back into the hotel, intent on getting upstairs and into our warm bed as soon as possible.

"Hold the elevator, please, Jim," a male voice called out. "Phew. It's cold out there."

I couldn't believe my luck. Jeremy joined us and leaned down to pet both dogs, who were wriggling with joy at the sight of one of their favorite humans. For once in my life, I willed the elevator to go slowly, so I had a chance to have an innocent chat with Jeremy. The patron saint of elevators, St. Eligius (he's the patron saint of electrical and mechanical engineers, which I figure was close enough) laughed at me, and delivered us to our floor before I could figure out how to frame a single question without appearing too nosy.

Once inside the suite, before we could even take off our coats, Margo flew out of the bedroom and into Jeremy's arms, almost knocking the poor man down, and peppered him with questions. "Are you all right? Was it a terrible experience for you? I've been so worried. I hope Mark wasn't too tough on you because of me. I'm so glad you're back."

"I'm fine," Jeremy assured her. "We cleared up a few questions he had and I signed a statement."

What questions? Inquiring minds want to know. Details! We want details!

Margo, seeing that I was hanging around the living room after Jim and the dogs had disappeared, gave me a disapproving look and gestured in the direction of our bedroom. I hadn't been sent to my room for decades, but I understood her desire for privacy. I just hoped they talked loud enough so that I could eavesdrop from the next room, although it was doubtful since I'd have to close the bedroom door. I yawned and said, "Jim and I are glad you're back too, Jeremy. We saved you dinner. It's in the refrigerator."

"I'll warm it up for you," Margo said before I could volunteer my culinary services.

Jeremy enveloped her in a huge hug. "The only thing I want you to warm up right now is me. Let's turn in. It's been quite a day."

Even I couldn't come up with an appropriate comment for that.

Chapter 33

When we were young, we snuck out of our house to go to parties. When we're old, we sneak out of parties to go home.

Have you ever heard of restless leg syndrome? That night, I had restless body syndrome. It was so bad that I kept Jim awake, and believe me, that man can sleep through anything. He finally sat up in bed, turned on the bedside lamp and glared at me. "For Pete's sake, Carol, will you stop tossing and turning and kicking me? You're driving me crazy. You should be exhausted after getting so little sleep last night. I know I am. What's the matter with you?"

I punched a bed pillow instead of the target I really wanted to aim for. (I'll leave my preferred target choice to your imagination.) "I'm sorry that I'm keeping you awake. I just can't seem to turn off my mind. Every time I close my eyes, I see April lying dead on the parking garage floor. I can't get rid of that horrible image, no matter how hard I try. I wish there was something we could do." I punched the pillow again, a little harder, to emphasize my point.

"Now, Carol," Jim said in that placating tone of voice that always makes me nuts, "calm down. I agree that it's very sad about April. But we have to let the police do their job. It's not our place to get involved."

"We're already involved! We found her! If you could have seen Ryan today, you'd know that his heart is broken over this. We have to find out what happened to that poor girl." Oops. I didn't mean to spill the beans about Ryan and April to Jim. But fortunately, my gaffe passed right over his head. Or else, he didn't hear me—the more likely scenario.

"I haven't forgotten that we're the unfortunate people who found April. I remember the scene vividly, and it's affected me just as much as it has you. Maybe even more, since you seem to go through this kind of thing on a regular basis." I let that comment go. Major points for me, right?

By this time, every light in the bedroom was blazing, and Lucy and Ethel were starting to stir. I had no desire for another late-night walk, so I grabbed Jim's arm and pointed toward the living room. He nodded and tiptoed out of the bedroom, with me and the dogs right behind him. When I started to sit on the sofa, Jim pointed toward the kitchen, then licked his lips. I tried hard not to laugh. No matter what the circumstances are, he can always eat. I knew that a quick snack was a sure guarantee to put him in a good mood, so he'd go along with the brilliant plan I'd suddenly come up with.

The refrigerator had enough leftovers to feed a family of four, so I had no trouble putting together a plate to satisfy Jim's appetite. To keep him company while he was enjoying his midnight "snack," I rewarded myself with another helping of peppermint stick ice cream. I'd worry about the extra calories another time. Or, never. I tossed Lucy and Ethel a few dog biscuits each. After all, they'd been traumatized by finding April, too.

When Jim pushed his plate away, with a contented look on his face, I knew I had to talk fast before he yawned and announced he was ready to hit the hay again. "It's not healthy to go right to sleep after eating a big meal. Doctors say it can cause indigestion or heartburn. Let's talk a little before we turn in."

Jim was struggling to keep his eyes open. I had to come up with a surefire topic to get his attention.

"How did things go at the house today? Are they making any

progress on replacing the furnace?"

That did it. Jim's eyes snapped open and he scowled at me. Oops. It looked like I'd picked the wrong subject for a chat.

"Those bozos. I'm sure they're taking extra time to do the job just so they can pad the bill. The latest update is that two parts of the new furnace are missing and have to be ordered. I ask you, have you ever heard of such a thing? A brand new furnace, straight from the factory, is missing two parts? I didn't want to tell you, but we may not make it home for Christmas."

"You mean we won't be able to celebrate any part of CJ's first Christmas in our own house?" I was willing myself not to cry.

"I knew you'd be upset. But you asked."

Stupid, Carol. You're allowing yourself to get off track. Focus on Jeremy. There's nothing you can do about the furnace.

"With any luck, we'll be home by then," Jim said. "I plan to be there every day until the job is finished. Otherwise, nothing will happen. Look on the bright side, Carol. Thanks to someone we didn't even know a week ago, at least we have a place to stay."

Jim had given me a perfect opening, so without giving myself another minute to wallow in a potential holiday disaster, I plunged ahead. "We're very lucky," I agreed. "But you've brought up an interesting point, dear. We still don't know anything about Jeremy, aside from what Margo's shared with us. And she's clearly bonkers over the guy, so who knows how objective she's being? Maybe Mark's right to be suspicious."

"What exactly are you implying? We're living in a luxurious suite through the entire holiday season if necessary, and it isn't costing us a single dime. As far as I'm concerned, Jeremy's a great guy and we should be grateful."

"I am grateful," I countered. "Believe me, I'm very grateful." *Except for the fact that we also have to share the suite with Margo, but in the spirit of the holidays, I'm not going to bring that up.*

"I'm merely saying that, in the interests of family harmony, it'd be a good idea to learn more about the guy. You two seem to be getting along particularly well. Why don't you see what you can find out about him? I'm not asking you to interfere in Mark's official investigation. This is for our family." I took Jim's hand and gave him my most pleading look. "After all, if he and Margo get married, he'll be CJ's other grandfather."

"Step-grandfather," Jim corrected.

"Yes. So, what do you say? Will you do it? Please?"

Jim yawned. "If I say yes, can we go to bed? And do you promise not to spend the rest of the night kicking me and keeping me awake?"

"I promise," I said, giving him a smooch on the cheek. "Thank you, honey. I'm tired, too. Let's get some sleep." I knew I'd have sweet dreams tonight.

Chapter 34

If you lose a sock in the dryer, it comes back as a Tupperware lid that doesn't fit any of your containers.

I pretended to still be asleep when I heard Jim stirring beside me the next morning. Unfortunately for me, he knows most of my tricks (not all, thank goodness). "I know you're awake, Carol, but I've decided to let you get away with sleeping in this one time. I'll shower and take care of the dogs, then be on my way to the house. Should I take them with me?"

This required an answer on my part, so I mumbled, "K."

"I guess that's a yes. I'll also ask Jeremy to come with me, per your request. But you now owe me big-time for being such a good guy, and I intend to collect later tonight." He bent down and gave me a smooch.

I rolled over and ordered myself back to sleep. It was no use. Big surprise. I never take orders from anyone, even me. After waiting half an hour to be sure the coast was clear, I sat up, stretched, and considered my options for the day. Without any coffee to start my grey cells percolating, I knew exactly what I was going to do. In every mystery novel I've ever read—and I've read hundreds—the detective searches for clues to find out more about the victim and who wanted that person dead. All my interactions with April had been superficial ones at the hotel reception desk—except for finding her hurt after her fall, and then dead in the parking garage the night after. Which was an odd coincidence, the more I thought about it. Perhaps her "fall" hadn't really been an accident, but the first time her nameless attacker tried to kill her. That's assuming her death was a deliberate attack and not an accident. Mark hadn't come right out and said so, but he did take Jeremy in for questioning. Was I just jumping to conclusions again, without any proof to back me up?

I made a snap decision. I would spend the day finding out all I could about April.

I heard a discreet tap on the bedroom door, then Margo's voice, "Carol, are you up? Jim and Jeremy are gone. What do you want to do today?"

Oh, boy. I'd never anticipated that I'd still have to deal with Margo. A day of just us two grannies bonding held no appeal whatsoever. At least yesterday, I had two of my besties to make our shopping trip more fun. I had to ditch her. If she even caught a hint of what I was up to, she'd suggest that she play Watson to my Holmes.

"I'm getting myself together," I called back, stalling for time. "I'll be out in a little while."

Think, Carol! You have to come up with a perfect place for her to spend today.

The Good Lord gave me the answer in the form of a text from my daughter, reminding me that I was scheduled to take care of CJ at 11:00 today. I knew the Good Lord was testing me, because suggesting that Margo spend her day babysitting CJ instead of my doing it would require an act of supreme selflessness and charity. Oh, well. She deserved some quality time with our grandson, and besides, she and Jeremy would (hopefully) be gone after the holidays.

Me: *Change of plans. I think Margo should babysit instead.*
Jenny: *R u kidding?*
Me: No. *Time 4 her to know CJ.*
Jenny: *Will u come 2?*

Me: *Sure. But won't stay. OK?*
Jenny: *OK.*

I patted myself on the back (metaphorically, so as not to cause a pain spasm), made myself as presentable as I could in five minutes, and greeted the Other Grandmother with a huge smile.

Margo handed me a mug of steaming coffee, and I ignored the look of surprise on her face. Or maybe it was suspicion. Anyway, I knew she'd be thrilled when I told her today's plan.

I sipped the coffee, then said, "Good morning. I hope things went well between you and Jeremy last night."

Margo blushed crimson, and I realized what I had implied. Oh, well, we're all adults here. Moving on.

"I'm glad Jeremy and Mark talked, and that Mark got the answers he needed. Maybe they'll finally become friends. I'm sorry if I'm being too nosy. My family says it's one of my worst faults."

"I don't know if the word 'friends' will ever be applied to their relationship," Margo said. "Jeremy told me that he clarified several issues that were bothering Mark. And he didn't spend the night in jail, so I guess that's a good thing."

"Definitely," I agreed. "Now I'm going to make you an offer about how to spend your day that you can't refuse. The best way ever." I grinned. "Believe me, I know what I'm talking about. Even though it may involve changing a diaper or two."

Margo's eyes widened. For a brief moment, I wondered if she'd had cosmetic surgery, then dismissed the idea and mentally slapped myself. "Do you mean what I think you mean?"

"If you think I'm talking about a solo date with the most adorable grandchild ever born, you'd be right. So, what do you say, Margo? It better be yes!"

To my surprise, Margo looked hesitant. "I'm not sure I can take responsibility for CJ all by myself. What if I do something wrong? That'll give Mark one more thing to hold against me."

"You're not going to do anything wrong. I'll hang around for a little while, if you want me to, until you're comfortable. It'll be fun. Jenny can't wait to see you."

Okay, so that last part was a total fib. I could picture my darling daughter at this very moment: vacuuming, dusting, straightening, and generally racing around the condo like a madwoman before the arrival of her mother-in-law. And probably cursing her own mother for inviting her. Oh, well. I'd make it up to Jenny as soon as I could.

"Come on, Margo. You'd be crazy to skip this golden opportunity for one-on-one time with CJ." Honestly, what was wrong with the woman?

"I do want to spend some time with CJ," Margo insisted. "But I'd hoped you and I could investigate April's death today. Jeremy tried very hard last night to convince me he was in the clear. I could tell he was only trying to make me feel better. I want so much to help him, and you're the one with all the sleuthing experience."

"I've heard that setting a problem aside for a while, and coming back to it later, can give a whole new perspective," I said. *Not that I've ever tried it. I'm more the type who stews over a problem until I've driven myself and my loved ones, even the dogs, to the brink of insanity.*

"How about if we both try that today? If either of us has an idea, we could make a note on our cell phones to share later. What do you say?"

"All right. Give me a few minutes to get dressed."

"Don't wear one of your designer outfits," I called after her. "You're taking care of an infant, and sometimes even perfect ones like CJ can be a little messy."

Congratulating myself on pulling off a major coup, I scarfed down two raisin muffins (healthy, yes?) and finished my coffee just as Margo emerged, clad in a gray sweatsuit that was a mirror image of my own.

"We look like twins," I said, laughing. "In my case, this is the only thing I have left to wear that's still clean. What's your excuse?"

"Every now and then, comfort rules over fashion sense. This is one of those times."

"I'll take that as a compliment," I said, grabbing my purse and hustling Margo on our way before she found an excuse to change her mind.

Chapter 35

You are about to exceed the limits of my medication.

I made a quick scan of the lobby when the elevator doors opened. Bobbie wasn't visible at the reception desk, thank goodness. Margo didn't need to have Bobbie repeat her suspicions that Jeremy could be a murderer. That'd send her over the edge, for sure.

We were speed-walking to the parking garage when Margo suddenly pulled on my arm, bringing me to a screeching halt. "Carol, look," she said, pointing toward the newspaper kiosk near the exit. The front-page headline on the latest edition of the *Fairport News* read: "College Student Found Dead at Local Hotel."

"This must be about April's death. I'll buy a copy and read it out loud on our way to Mark and Jenny's," Margo said, walking to the kiosk and taking a copy before I could stop her. "I hope Jeremy's name isn't mentioned."

"So do I," I said, grabbing the paper and forcing myself to stay calm until we got to my car.

"Mrs. Andrews, wait. I have to talk to you!"

"It's Ryan," Margo said.

Rats. I was hoping to make a speedy exit without any more drama. I slowed down and waited for Ryan to catch up to us.

Margo threw her arms around him and gave him a hug. "Oh, you poor boy. How are you today?"

Ryan flinched a little and pulled away, not that I could blame him. He probably didn't even remember Margo's name, since she didn't have a car parked in the garage.

"I decided to come in today, instead of staying home," he said, addressing me. "All I can think about is what happened to April. Not that being here is any better, even though I have work to distract me. All I have to do is look toward the picnic table and I start replaying her death over and over in my mind. It must have been terrible for you, finding her. Can you tell me anything more?" His eyes filled with tears, and he brushed them away angrily.

Now it was my turn to give Ryan a hug. I forced myself to remember that awful scene. "I think her death was very quick."

"Thank God for that," Ryan said. "I guess that makes me feel a little better. The police came to our apartment again last night and asked me even more questions. They wanted to know how long April and I had known each other, how we'd met, stuff like that. Also how she got along with the hotel guests. Was she well thought of at work? Did she have any enemies? That shocked me. I thought her death was an accident. But maybe it wasn't. I don't know what to believe now."

"I'm sure it was an accident," I said, shooting Margo a warning look to keep her mouth shut.

"But what if it wasn't? The police who've questioned me didn't even know her. They have no idea what a wonderful person she was. What if they don't work hard enough to find out what really happened? I can't stand by and take that chance. I want to hire you to find out the truth. You're the only one I can depend on."

It's a good thing I was leaning against my car at this point, or I probably would have landed on the cement floor of the garage. "Hire me?" I repeated. "What do you mean?"

"I don't make a lot of money, but I'll pay you what I can if you promise to help me get justice for April." He pulled an envelope out of his windbreaker pocket and thrust it into my hand. "Here, take this as your retainer."

"Ryan, this is ridiculous. I can't take money from you. I'm not a detective."

"That's not what I've heard. I understand you've been helpful to the local police several times in the past. Will you help me?"

As I tried to figure out a way out of this uncomfortable situation, Margo inserted herself, unasked and unwanted, into the conversation. "Perhaps Carol and I could both keep our ears open, and if we hear anything that we think is important, we could pass it on to you."

Honestly, I wanted to kick her. But in the interests of family harmony, I didn't. This time.

"I haven't had as much experience solving crimes as Carol has," Margo continued. "But I'm very intuitive about people, and I frequently pick up nuances in conversations that others might miss. What do you say? Do we have a deal?"

OMG. I had to do something, and quick!

"Just to set the record straight," I said, stepping in front of Margo so Ryan and I were eyeball to eyeball, "there have been a few instances in the past when I've been able to provide some amateur help to the authorities in similar situations, but only because I've been in the right place at the right time." I shot Margo a warning look. "As I've already said, I'm not a detective. Neither of us are. But I certainly want to see justice done for April. If I should happen to hear something that I can share with you, I will. But not for money," I said, giving him back the envelope.

"Why don't you give us a dollar to make it official?" Margo suggested. "How's that for a compromise?"

Honestly, that woman! But Ryan looked so relieved. I couldn't say no.

"I guess that'll work," I said, taking the dollar bill and tucking it in my pocket. "And now, we both have to leave." I yanked open the passenger door and gestured to Margo. "Coming?"

Believe it or not, Margo finally got the hint. "Bye, Ryan. We'll be in touch," she said, settling herself beside me. Without bothering to see if her seat belt was securely fastened, I revved the engine and drove out of the parking garage.

After about five minutes of stony silence on my part, punctuated by a few attempts by the Other Grandmother to make amends (which I ignored), I finally pulled onto a side street and parked the car.

"This isn't Jenny and Mark's," Margo said. "Why are we stopping here?"

I turned and faced her. "Look, Margo, I know you're worried sick about Jeremy and his possible connection to what happened to April. So am I. I also feel terrible about April's death, and poor Ryan, who's lost the love of his life. But let's get one thing straight right now. We're not going to play detective and snoop around to find out what happened to April. If either of us should *accidentally* find out something that could help the police investigation, we're telling Mark right away. No matter what it is. Got it? Otherwise, you're on your own, and good luck to you."

Please don't bother to remind me that I was forbidding Margo to do exactly what I intended to do. Or that my ultimatum might land Jim, the dogs, and me out on the street in the bitter December cold if Margo told Jeremy what I'd said. I knew I was taking a chance. On the other hand, I was the Grandmother-in-Situ, so to speak, and I was giving Margo a chance to get to know our grandson all by herself, for the first time. I think that gave me the upper hand in this "discussion."

"I'm sorry. You're right. I should have kept quiet. But Ryan wants the same thing we do, to find out what happened to April. I could tell you were getting angry with me, but I couldn't stop myself. Haven't you ever said something out loud and then regretted it?"

Let me count the times.

Ignoring that question, I held out my hand. "I want to take a peek at the newspaper article about April. I'll be distracted if you read it to me while we're driving, and I don't want us to have an accident." I scanned the story quickly, happy that my husband hadn't written it and forgotten to tell me. The article was pretty bland, considering its prominent position on the front page. Jim says there's an old saying in the news business, "If it bleeds, it leads," which certainly was the case here. I found out that April was a part-time student at Fairport College. Hmm. Interesting. If I was really lucky, Jenny might know her; or, even better, April might have been a student in one of her classes. I just had to figure out a way to ask Jenny without Margo catching on. I didn't want to risk setting Margo off again.

"There's nothing much new in the story," I said, sliding the paper back to Margo. "Jeremy's name isn't mentioned, and neither is the name of the hotel where April was found." I found the latter omission very interesting, and filed that fact away in my mental filing cabinet, hoping I'd remember which drawer it was in. "I'm glad we've cleared the air. Now let's spend some time with the most wonderful baby in the world."

Chapter 36

Lord, keep Your arm on my shoulder and Your hand on my mouth.

"This is a beautiful place," Margo said as we pulled into a guest parking space at Jenny and Mark's condo development. "I wonder if there are any available units here. It would be fun to live so close to the kids."

Yikes! Margo had made a similar comment yesterday. What if she was really serious about moving back to Fairport? In the spirit of the season, I quelled the feeling of jealousy rearing its head at the idea of Margo living so close to my (our) precious grandson.

Think, Carol! You can come up with a way to quash this idea if you just concentrate for a second.

Suddenly, I had the perfect solution. "You liked Mary Alice's condo complex, too," I reminded Margo. "Maybe you should talk to Jeremy first, if you're thinking about moving back here. He might have something to say about where you should live."

"I'll have to think about that," Margo said.

"Moving?" I asked, hoping that Santa had just given me an early Christmas present.

"Yes, but also talking to Jeremy. We haven't known each other that long, and I don't want to push him into a commitment he may not be comfortable making."

He may be forced to make a change in his own living arrangements if he's arrested for murder. I didn't really say that to her, of course.

"That's very wise of you," I said, as Jenny opened the condo door, a crying CJ in her arms. "I fed him a little while ago and kept him up so you could both see him instead of putting him down for a nap."

"I guess he didn't like your plan," I said, holding out my arms to take the cranky baby, then stopping myself. "Margo? Want to try calming him down?"

"Usually I walk around the condo with him and pat him on the back in case he has a gas bubble, and after a little while, he settles right down," Jenny said. She turned CJ around a little bit. The baby saw me and smiled. Atta boy! His big blue eyes settled on Margo, and he looked at her curiously. (By the way, Margo's eyes are brown. Mine are baby blue. Just thought I'd mention that.)

"He's not crying now," I said. Because he saw me, not that I was going to point that out to Margo.

"I'll try walking him," Margo said, holding out her arms. "Hi, CJ. It's me, your Glamma." She hugged him tight, her eyes brimming with tears. "This means so much to me. You both have no idea how often I've dreamed about holding him in my arms."

How could I begrudge the Other Grandmother a chance to bond with CJ, even if she insisted on being called "Glamma." What a stupid nickname.

"Turn around," I said, fumbling in my purse for my phone. "I'll take some pictures of you two. If I get a good one, I'll forward it to you."

Margo didn't answer. She was already on her way around the condo with CJ.

"You're good to do this for her, Mom."

"She's CJ's grandmother, too, even though I try to deny it."

I realized I had a golden opportunity for a private conversation about April, and I shouldn't waste a minute. "Just between us, did you know April Swanson? She was a student at the college."

"Yes, she was in two of my classes. I saw in this morning's paper that she died. Mark mentioned her name to me, too. He's involved because it was an unattended death, although he says it's a routine investigation. She was found at the hotel where you and Dad are staying by two guests...." Jenny's voice trailed off and the visible lightbulb went off. "Tell me what I'm thinking isn't true."

"If you're thinking that Dad and I found her, unfortunately, you're correct. Thank goodness your father was with me. We'd taken the dogs out for a late night walk, and Lucy discovered April." I shivered at the memory. "It was horrible."

"I have more to tell you about April, but not right now," Jenny said in a low voice.

I nodded as Margo came back into view, cradling CJ and humming softly. I smiled at the sight and realized that, for the first time (and possibly the last), the sight of the two of them together didn't bother me. Much.

"You're a natural at this grandmother gig," I said.

"Coming from you, that's a true compliment. I guess this is like riding a bicycle. Once you've cradled a baby, no matter how long ago that was, the natural instinct comes right back."

"I'm glad you're doing so well, because I have to leave now," Jenny said.

"We'll be fine," Margo said. "Carol, you don't have to stay, either. If there are any problems, I'll text you." She turned and started the walk around the condo again. I could see that CJ's eyelids were drooping, and he'd soon be ready for a nap. But then he opened his eyes, stared right at me, and I could swear, he winked at me. Or maybe it was a trick of the light.

"We'll be on our way then," Jenny said, hoisting her backpack over her shoulder. "I hate leaving him, but I have to go. I don't want to be late for class."

"I'll walk you out," I said.

As soon as we were outside the condo, Jenny picked up her pace. "I really have to hustle, but here's what I wanted to tell you about April. The first class she took with me was Introduction to Creative Writing a year ago. She was a terrific student, eager to learn, always had her work finished on time. She was juggling a full-time job along with school and it became too much for her, so she didn't come back for another class until the summer semester. We caught up a bit and she told me she'd left her old job and was starting work at the new Fairport Inn and Suites. But she seemed different. Very nervous, and not nearly as motivated as she was before. She didn't participate in class much, either."

"I only talked with April a few times, and she seemed very outgoing and upbeat to me," I said. "That's curious. You're always a good judge of character."

"There's one more thing," Jenny said, her hand already on her car door. "Her old full-time job was at the car dealership run by Bob Green, Nancy's husband. I have a sneaking suspicion something happened between them while she was there, but I never asked her about it. Maybe I should have."

Chapter 37

It's probably my age that tricks people into thinking I'm an adult.

There's a familiar saying, "You can choose your friends, but you can't choose your relatives." I'd like to tweak that a bit. You can choose your friends, but you can't choose your friends' husbands. As Exhibit A, I offer Bob Green, my very best friend Nancy's sort-of husband.

Nancy and I have been closer than sisters ever since our early days in grammar school, and there's nothing in the world I wouldn't do to support her. When she introduced me to her new boyfriend, Bob, I kept my big mouth shut. When she announced she and Bob were getting married, and asked me to be her maid of honor, I agreed and pretended I was happy for her. My decision to keep silent and not tell her how I really felt—that Bob was a narcissistic, self-indulgent jerk—was a huge mistake, so it's understandable why I now offer my opinion on a variety of subjects (even if I'm not asked) every chance I get.

Things really came to a head right before Jenny and Mark's wedding on Nantucket. Perhaps a few of you remember that, but in case your memory is unreliable these days, Bob was caught having an affair with the wedding planner, and then suspected of her murder. I didn't want to lift a finger to help him, but when

Nancy begged me, what could I do? Through particularly clever sleuthing, plus a little help from Lucy and Ethel, I saved the jerk from spending the rest of his life in prison. As I recall, Nancy was pathetically grateful, but I don't believe I ever heard a word of thanks from Bob. Not that I bear him a grudge for that. I tried to forgive and forget, but the forgetting part is much harder for me.

Claire and Mary Alice share my negative feelings about Bob, just in case you think I'm being too judgmental. We've all tried our very best to hide our dislike for Nancy's spousal choice to preserve our lifelong friendship. Two of us have been successful. I'll let you guess which one of us has failed.

As I mulled over my next move, it suddenly occurred to me that the reason Bob never thanked me for saving his bacon a few years ago was because he could have been suspicious of my motives. If I had any hope of getting Bob to open up about April Swanson, I had to prove that he could trust me, instead of suspecting that my questions were to get information that would convince Nancy to finally divorce him.

This was going to be tough.

I came up with a few ideas, each one more ridiculous than the last. My most creative one was that I'd pretend I was shopping for a Christmas gift for Jim, except that Bob would immediately know I could never afford to buy an expensive car like a Range Rover. I sighed. It would have been so much fun taking one for a test drive.

I suddenly had another of My Truly Brilliant Ideas. Bob had loaned Nancy an expensive car for a short time because he loved her. (Also because his grand gesture didn't cost him anything since his dealership technically owned the vehicle.) Nancy was having the time of her life tooling around town in her fancy new SUV. Why shouldn't I give my dear husband the same opportunity as a Christmas present? Jim's eyes would pop out of his head if he spotted a shiny, new Range Rover SUV in our driveway Christmas morning with a bright red bow on the hood.

Bad idea, Carol. Jim is guaranteed to have a heart attack and die right on the spot if you do this. Is this the way you want to celebrate CJ's first Christmas, by killing his grandfather?

Hmm. Okay, there were a few flaws in this plan. I'd work them out on my way to the dealership.

I drove onto the parking lot of Luxury Cars of Fairport with no idea of how to approach Bob Green. Me, the master of creative thinking, was stymied. It was a humbling experience. I slammed my car door in frustration. I had to come up with something right now.

You could try telling the truth for a change, Carol. Sometimes that actually works. Explain about April and tell Bob you need his help.

It was a novel idea, but maybe it would work. There was only one way to find out. I opened the dealership door and was greeted by an attractive woman dressed professionally in a navy blue pantsuit. A good first impression for customers, to be sure.

"I'm Carol Andrews," I said, extending my hand before she could start what I presumed would be a tasteful sales pitch. "Is Mr. Green in? I'm a personal friend, and I'd like to speak to him."

Okay, calling myself Bob's "personal friend" stretched the truth a lot, but I was trying to set the tone for our conversation in advance. As in: "I come in peace, so please don't shoot me."

Bob appeared before the woman had even paged him. I was betting he'd seen me in the parking lot. Points for him that he didn't lock the door before I could get inside.

"Carol," he said, taking my cold hands in his nice, warm ones, "what a pleasant surprise. Are you looking for a new vehicle?"

"I'd love to look for a new vehicle," I said, gazing around the showroom at the impressive array of beautiful automobiles. "But first, there's something else I want to talk to you about."

Bob got a panicked look on his face, probably fearing I'd discovered a recent discretion he didn't want Nancy to know about. He recovered himself quickly. "Of course, Carol. Come into my office where we can speak privately."

When I was comfortably seated in what was a pretty fancy office for a car dealership, Bob cleared his throat, then said, "I never thanked you for helping me out on Nantucket a few years ago. If it's not too late, I'd like to thank you now. I know you did it more for Nancy than for me, but I love her, too. And she loves me. I wonder if you'll ever forgive me for that."

I stiffened. This conversation wasn't going the way I'd planned, assuming I'd actually planned one.

"I haven't been the world's best husband," Bob continued. "The possibility of spending the rest of my life in prison for a crime I didn't commit forced me to evaluate myself. I didn't like what I saw, and I can understand why Claire, Mary Alice, and you disliked me so much. You all thought I wasn't good enough for Nancy when I married her, and I've done nothing to change your opinion. If anything, my actions made you three even more positive that you were right."

"Bob, please stop. I didn't come here to tell you what a horrible person I think you are. Anyway, as long as we're clearing the air, I have to admit that some of the responsibility for this situation is mine." I looked down at my hands. They were shaking. "You and Nancy got engaged before the rest of us did. I guess I was jealous. I thought I was losing my best friend because of you. I hated you for that, and I was wrong. I'm sorry. Can you forgive me?"

"It's time we forgive each other," Bob said. "I've been jealous of Claire and Mary Alice, but especially of you, for years because you're so close to Nancy. I know she tells you things she'd never tell me."

"That's what women do," I said. "Believe me, I tell them things I'd never tell Jim."

That got a smile out of Bob, and he rose and extended his hand. "Friends now?"

"Yes." I was surprised to realize I meant it. We had a quick bonding moment, and then it was back to the purpose of my visit.

"Okay," Bob said, "so why did you come here today? The real reason?"

"I want to ask you about April Swanson. I understand she

used to work for you, and now she's dead."

Bob looked alarmed, and I realized the huge gaffe I'd just made. "I shouldn't have put the two events together like that," I said. "I'm not accusing you of murdering her."

"That's good. You had me scared for a second. Nancy's told me how your mind works sometimes."

"I wish someone could explain that to Jim," I said, laughing.

"I read in today's paper that April was found dead by hotel guests in the facility's parking garage. I was absolutely shocked. Just to be clear, I know nothing about that."

"I'm sure you don't," I said. "I'm trying to understand who April really was. What the newspaper article doesn't mention is that the hotel was the Fairport Inn and Suites and the guests who found April are Jim and me. It was horrible. We're trying to figure out what happened. I guess a part of me wonders that if we'd just gotten there a little sooner, we could have saved her." I teared up.

"The last time I saw April was when Nancy and I went to dinner at the Fairport Inn and Suites earlier this week. I didn't know she was working there. We had a quick talk, and she seemed happy. I was glad about that."

"How long did she work here? And what did she do?"

"April was our official greeter," Bob said. "She has...had such a bubbly, outgoing personality, and the job was a natural fit for her. She put customers at ease from the minute they walked into the dealership." He thought for a minute, then added, "I'd have to check her employment record to be sure, but I think she was with us about eight months. She just walked in one day, without an appointment, and asked if we had any job openings. We didn't, but she was persistent, in a sweet sort of way. Not pushy, just persistent. I had a good feeling about her, so I created the 'Hospitality Hostess' position. Everybody here loved her."

"Why did she leave?"

"One day, out of the blue, she announced she'd accepted another position with the potential to make a lot more money than she was making here. I tried to talk her out of it, but it didn't do any good. She got angry, and told me I shouldn't try to run her life. Then she walked out the door. I didn't see her again, until that night at the hotel. She didn't even come back to collect her last check, so I mailed it to her."

"That's very curious," I said. "April seemed like such a responsible young woman, and walking out of a job with no notice is very unprofessional. Did the hotel contact you for a reference?"

Bob shook his head. "Nope. That's why I was so surprised to see her that night. And I still can't figure out how working at a hotel registration desk had the potential for a lot more money than she was making here. It just doesn't add up."

"No, it doesn't." My phone pinged with an incoming text, interrupting my thought process. I was sure it was Margo, needing help with CJ, so I didn't bother reading it then.

"Bob, you've been great, but grandmother duty calls. I have to leave. I'm so glad we talked."

"I am, too. If I think of anything else about April, I'll let you know. And Carol...Merry Christmas."

Chapter 38

If you can't think of a word, just say, "I forgot the English word for it." That way people will think you're bilingual instead of stupid.

I sat in my car for a minute and digested the fact that, for the first time in almost forty years, Bob Green and I were finally friends. "Miracles do happen at the holidays," I told myself.

I couldn't wait to tell Nancy about my conversation with Bob, so I fished my phone out of my purse to text her. First, though, continuing in my ho-ho-holiday mood, I had to answer Margo's text and reassure her that reinforcements were on the way.

I was surprised that the text I'd just gotten was from Sister Rose, not Margo. Just like that, my holiday mood went up the chimney faster than Santa on Christmas Eve.

SR: *I need your help. Please stop by the shop as soon as you can.*

Interesting. The Good Sister actually said "please," so this was a request for help, not one of her usual commands. Maybe she was feeling the holiday spirit, too. I decided I'd better get over to Sally's Closet quickly, so I could benefit from as much of Sister's good cheer as possible before she changed her mind.

There was only one car in the customer lot when I arrived at the thrift shop, so I took a chance and parked there. (One of Sister Rose's many rules is that her "girls"—meaning former students and shop volunteers—not take up room in the regular parking lot. That was reserved for "real" customers.)

Ignoring the sparkly red sweater in the window that would look so great on me, I squared my shoulders and went in the front door. Sister Rose pounced on me so fast that she took my breath away. I had a feeling of foreboding, as I suddenly remembered that the holiday reception for thrift shop volunteers was tomorrow. Cursing my own stupidity, I was positive she was going to strongarm me into helping out at the party. Rats. How stupid I was. I fell right into her trap.

"Hello, Sister," I said, wrenching my hand free from her vise-like grip. "I came as soon as I read your text. What kind of help do you need?" *As if I didn't already know.*

Ignoring my question, Sister Rose called out to the volunteer cashier at the checkout desk, "I'll be in the back with Carol Andrews for a little while, Marcie. If you need me, just buzz and I'll come right out." She speed-walked to the door separating the behind-the-scenes work area from the shop, itself, with me trailing behind her. "We don't have much time to talk, and this is really important."

Parking my posterior on one of the uncomfortable donated chairs, I said, "Sister, before you start, I have to tell you that I'd love to help you with the volunteer reception, but I can't. Jim and I are still staying at the hotel, and my life isn't my own these days. I can't make any extra plans."

"Volunteer reception? Is that why you think I texted you? I only wish it was that simple."

I took a good look at my former high school English teacher and realized she was very nervous. I braced myself for what I figured was bad news.

"What I'm about to tell you is highly confidential, and it's entirely possible that I'm wrong. I hope you'll be able to give me some suggestions on how to deal with the problem. If it's really a problem. I'm not even sure about that."

"I won't know what I'm promising to keep quiet about until you tell me. So...?"

"It's about your new neighbor; Frank Adams."

"Was there a problem with the donation check?" I asked, praying I was wrong.

"No, Carol, the ten-thousand-dollar donation to Sally's Closet has cleared. But some of our board members and donors are complaining about his fundraising calls. And other things." She looked down at her hands. "It could all just be a series of unfortunate coincidences, I suppose."

"What *other* things, Sister?"

"Remember how Frank asked me for personal data on our donors, and how I was uncomfortable doing that? I believe you were here when that discussion took place."

"I wasn't present for the discussion," I clarified. "But you did tell me later."

"Frank made a series of fundraising calls last evening. This morning, a few donors noticed some suspicious activity on their credit cards. They cancelled their cards right away, and called to alert me. I had to tell them that I'd shared information with Frank, and they were not happy. The card misuse could be connected to Frank, or not. But no matter what, I'm responsible. I used bad judgment in sharing personal financial information with someone I barely know. We may lose donors because of this, rather than gain more. I don't know what to do. So I'm turning to you for help."

"I don't know what I can do," I said, remembering how I'd felt uneasy about Frank's request at the time but didn't say anything. Was this partly my fault for keeping my mouth shut?

"I feel better just telling you about my concerns, because I have absolutely no proof Frank's done anything wrong. A man is innocent until proven guilty, isn't that right?"

"Have you talked to Frank? Maybe it's just a simple coincidence and he can clear everything up."

"I'm not comfortable doing that now," Sister Rose said. "I don't want to even suggest that the man could be dishonest and risk him suing me for slander if he's innocent."

"As someone who frequently jumps to conclusions without any

supporting evidence," I said, "it seems to me that the most logical approach is to find out more about Frank and Ellen Adams. I don't know anything about them."

Maybe that's your job, Carol. Don't you owe it to Sister Rose to help her now?

I was about to open my mouth and volunteer to do just that when I remembered I also was trying to figure out what happened to April, and if the love of Margo's life was a murderer. I may be a superwoman, but there are a limited number of hours in every day.

"Sister, I'd really like to help you, but my life is in complete chaos right now. Did you read about the death of a college student at a local hotel in today's paper? It was at the Fairport Inn and Suites."

"Is that where she died?" Sister Rose asked, crossing herself. "The article didn't mention the hotel. God rest that poor girl's soul. So young."

"The article also didn't mention that the hotel guests who found her were Jim and me," I said. "It was very traumatic."

"Oh, Carol, I had no idea. Here I am, adding to your troubles when you have so much else to deal with."

"I hope the police conclude April's death was an accident," I said. "But I keep thinking it's odd that she also fell outside not far from the hotel the night before she died. Jim and I were walking back to our car after having dinner there and found her then, too. That was the same night I saw you with Frank and Ellen Adams, remember?" Then I laughed. "Of course you remember. You never forget anything!"

Sister Rose laughed. "I do forget some things, but I remember that."

I shook my head to clear it. "I'm letting my imagination run wild. I'm telling you that coincidences happen and you shouldn't jump to conclusions without any proof, yet here I am, doing the exact same thing."

"Since I just unburdened myself on you, feel free to do the same," Sister Rose said. "I mean it. Tell me what's bothering you. Aside from finding that poor girl, of course. That's enough to traumatize anyone."

"April had apparently slipped on ice and fallen. We were able to get her back to the hotel and get her some help. But I wonder... what if she didn't fall on her own that night? What if somebody pushed her and left her outside in the cold to freeze to death? It was just luck that Jim and I took a shortcut to get to our car and found her. That same person could have attacked her again in the parking garage, and this time, April died."

"I suppose that is possible," Sister Rose said, her face clearly reflecting that my theory sounded like another example of my imagination working overtime. "Explain to me how you knew April. Was she a friend of Jenny's or Mike's?"

"April worked at the Fairport Inn and Suites reception desk. I met her for the first time when Jim and I were there for dinner the same night I saw you."

"I do remember her." Sister Rose looked troubled. "When I walked into the hotel, she was in the middle of a conversation with Frank and Ellen Adams. Frank was very angry about something, and she was trying to calm him down."

Another odd coincidence. First, April had a confrontation with Frank and Ellen Adams, then another one with Jeremy. I didn't understand that. In our few interactions, I found April to be very professional and accommodating. Lucy and Ethel loved her, and dogs can usually sniff out an unpleasant person, even if humans can't.

"How awkward for you," I said. *Did you overhear anything?* I mentally slapped myself. Sister Rose would never do that.

"Frank and Ellen were potential donors, and I didn't want to appear as though I was listening to their conversation."

"I'm sorry you didn't hear what they were saying."

"That's not exactly what I said, Carol. Remember, I was a high school teacher for years. I became an expert at reading lips and eavesdropping on secret conversations without anyone catching on." She laughed. "Now you know why you were sent to detention so many times. You thought you were being so clever, but I usually knew what you were up to."

"You really are something," I said. "And I mean that as a compliment. Wait 'til I tell Nancy."

"We're getting off track here," Sister Rose said.

Not my fault. I erased that criticism from my brain instantly. With my luck, Sister Rose could read minds, too.

"Ever since I received those upsetting phone calls about Frank from my board members, I've tried to remember exactly what I observed at the hotel that night. I even made a few random notes. Do you want to read them?"

"Why don't you give me your general impression instead," I suggested. "You're not on the witness stand, after all."

"Oh, my goodness, I hope it doesn't come to that."

"I wasn't serious," I said. "I was giving you another compliment. You must also be a pro at observing human behavior and body language after teaching for so many years."

"I remember that Frank was quite agitated," Sister Rose said. "At one point, I saw him give April some money, and assumed he was paying his bill. She refused to take it. I heard Frank say something about paying her to do something for them, as agreed."

"But what did he want her to do?"

"Unfortunately, he was speaking more quietly at that point, so I couldn't hear that part," Sister Rose said. "Then I heard Frank say she'd better stick to her part of their arrangement."

"What happened next?" I asked, my brain whirling with infinite possibilities without any proof whatsoever.

Ellen grabbed Frank's arm and told him to calm down. She said something to April, too, but I couldn't hear that part. Then she turned around and saw me. I pretended I'd just arrived, and we all went into the restaurant and had dinner. When we were leaving I saw you and I introduced everyone. That's all." Her eyes bore into me just like they used to when I was late turning in a homework assignment. "The question is, what do we do now?"

We? There's no "we." Pretend you don't understand what she means, Carol. Then get the heck out of here.

I checked the time on my phone. "Oh, my goodness. Jenny's teaching a class this afternoon and I'm scheduled to take care of

CJ until she gets home. It's a problem for her if I'm late." (For those of you who are sticklers for the truth, allow me to point out that the above statements are absolutely true, as far as they went. I made a snap decision not to confuse Sister Rose, who was already upset enough, by telling her that Mark's mother was taking care of CJ, but Mark and his mother were currently not speaking because of her new boyfriend. If I didn't get there to pick Margo up before Mark got home, there was bound to be another huge argument. In the interest of family harmony, I shaded the truth a little. That's my story, and I'm sticking to it.)

"Let me think a little about what you've told me, Sister. I may be able to come up with a few ideas. I'll get back to you as soon as I can." I was becoming more and more convinced that Frank Adams could be the bad guy here, not Jeremy. For all I knew, maybe he and Ellen teamed up to eliminate April. I needed time to process this new information.

"Carol, dear, please understand how much I'm counting on you to help me."

"I'd really like to…"

"Good," Sister Rose said. "I knew you wouldn't disappoint me. I'm sure Jenny will forgive you for being a little late, so by all means, text her before we sit down and plan a strategy. Take your time. Meanwhile, I'll go relieve the cashier."

"I'm trying to tell you that I'd like to help, but I can't," I yelled to her retreating back. I knew she heard me, because she picked up her pace and left me alone in the back room to bang my head on the sorting table and tell myself how stupid I was. Once again, I'd allowed myself to be manipulated by Sister Rose, when all I wanted was to move back into my own house and enjoy the upcoming holidays with my family.

"Is that asking too much?" I asked myself. "No, it isn't. Darn it."

Chapter 39

The easiest way to find something you've lost is to buy a replacement for it.

I knew an internet sleuthing expert who could find out about Frank and Ellen Adams in a jiffy and get Sister Rose off my back, because he knew exactly what sites to access—my son, Mike. Assuming, of course, I caught him with a few extra minutes on his hands to do a favor for his dear old mom. Plus, I could also ask—subtly, not to put any extra pressure on him—if his holiday plans included a trip to Fairport to see his loving family, especially his nephew CJ on his very first Christmas.

I dashed off a quick text telling him to expect an emergency phone call from me, then pressed his name in my contacts.

"What's wrong?" Mike said, answering on the very first ring. "Your text scared the daylights out of me. Are you okay? Dad? Jenny and Mark? Oh, God, it's not CJ, is it?"

And people think *I* jump to conclusions. Maybe it's hereditary.

"I didn't mean to alarm you," I said, feeling guilty. "Everyone's fine. We're having trouble with the furnace in the house and staying at a hotel temporarily. We expect to be back home by Christmas. I know how busy you are at Cosmo's, so I figured giving you a head's up that I was going to call was a good idea."

There was silence, then Mike spoke, "Okay, I forgive you. But

I also know you. Are you calling to guilt me into coming home for the holidays? I've already booked a flight, and I wanted to surprise you. I'll be home by Christmas Eve for three days. Now, I gotta go."

"Wait! That's wonderful news, but not the real reason why I called. Sister Rose and I need you to do some internet sleuthing. There are some new big bucks' donors to the domestic violence program, and she's worried that they may not be on the up-and-up."

"That's concerning, Mom. The holidays are the peak season for all kinds of cons, identity theft, you name it. I'll poke around for the next few minutes and see what I can find out. As a matter of fact..." Mike's voice trailed off.

"Are you still there, honey? I think you're breaking up a little."

"I'm here. I was just remembering a story I read in the *Miami Sun* about a brother and sister con artist team preying on unsuspecting people and bilking them out of thousands of dollars. None of their victims could give an accurate description of the pair, and as soon as they realized the police were looking for them, they disappeared."

"Frank never mentioned having a sister. His wife's name is Ellen. Last name Adams."

"Unless now, they're pretending to be married," Mike pointed out. "Or when they were in Florida, they pretended to be siblings."

"I'm sure you're wrong. It can't be the same people. Besides, Frank and Ellen are spending a fortune renovating the Old Parsonage across the street from us. They're our new neighbors."

"That's really interesting," Mike said. "When the con artists were in Miami, they rented a large old house in a classy neighborhood that had been vacant for years and pretended they were going to restore it. That was part of their con, to make it look like they had lots of money to throw around. Once they fleeced their victims out of thousands and thousands of dollars, they disappeared. I remember only one of their victims came forward to report them to the police, but there were many others involved. I guess they were too embarrassed to admit they'd been taken in. It was a pretty slick operation, like something you'd see in a movie."

My unease meter was beginning to ratchet up. It all sounded exactly like what Frank and Ellen had been doing, except this time, they were using Sister Rose's nonprofit as a way to find their victims.

Carol, you're being ridiculous. They're a nice couple, and they're going to be terrific neighbors.

"I may ask Nancy to check Frank and Ellen's real estate transaction, too.""

"I think that's a good idea, Mom. I'll see if I can find out anything about Frank and Ellen Adams to ease Sister Rose's mind. I'll text you later."

"Before you go: Is there a photo or description of this couple anywhere? Did the police ask for the public's help in finding them? Maybe release photos? Or did the victim who reported them give any kind of description?"

"I don't remember any photos, but it was a few months ago, so I could be wrong. Hang on a sec." I heard a few clicks of a keyboard and figured Mike was searching for the original newspaper article.

"According to the newspaper story, they called themselves Fred and Emily Englehart. Late middle-aged. Not much of a physical description. Were very well liked in the community. Many locals were shocked when it came out that they were con artists. It sounds like they're pretty smooth operators. That's all I can find on a quick pass."

Hearing Sister Rose's voice in my head, I said to Mike, "Let's not get off track here. Why don't you stick to finding out more about Frank and Ellen Adams?"

"Will do. But didn't you always tell me that if it looks like a duck and quacks like a duck, it must be a duck? Catch you later."

"Quack, quack," I said, laughing as I disconnected the call. Honestly, that Mike. He can always make me laugh, no matter how stressed I am.

I was sure Sister Rose would freak out if I shared what Mike just told me. As would Phyllis Stevens. I had a momentary image of Phyllis hosting a "Welcome to our Neighborhood" party which was interrupted by the Fairport police storming her house and arresting the two guests of honor.

The argument Sister Rose had witnessed between Frank and April was troubling, but didn't necessarily mean anything. For all I knew, Frank wanted tickets to see a Broadway show that week and April forgot to make the arrangements. And where did Jeremy fit into all this? Or didn't he? Was Mark quick to single him out as a prime suspect only because he didn't approve of his relationship with Margo?

A prime suspect? You don't know that the police have even ruled April's death a homicide. Unless the autopsy results are in and....

I should have shared my theory with Mark about April's duplicate head wound.

You know what would have happened then, Carol. Mark would dismiss it, and give you another lecture about interfering in police business. It's a good thing that, for once, you kept quiet. Let the police do their job.

I realized I hadn't heard anything from Margo, so I sent her a check-in text. I had mixed emotions when she responded so quickly that she and CJ were getting along wonderfully, and that she'd let me know when she was ready to leave.

Next on my to-do list was contacting Nancy. I knew her real estate database was another way to check out Frank and Ellen. I also knew that she couldn't be trusted to keep a secret. Once I shared the reason why I was asking, she'd insist on playing my sleuthing assistant. I already had Margo and Sister Rose vying for that role.

In an unusual flash of genius, I found the answer: pair up Sister Rose and Nancy to figure out if the good sister's suspicions were true and leave me out of it. With both of them reporting to me, as the busybody-in-chief, naturally. Perfect.

Chapter 40

When I was a kid, I wanted to be older. This is not what I expected.

"Nancy, I'm not asking you to do anything illegal, for heaven's sake," I hissed into my phone. "Why can't you just tap into your real estate database and find out the sale details for the Old Parsonage? Sister Rose is worried that there's something fishy about Frank and Ellen Adams and asked me to help her. I figured this was an easy way to see if they're legit or not. You've done this for me a few times before. What's the big deal now?"

I shifted the phone to my other ear. My simple text message had prompted an immediate phone call from Nancy, which'd turned into a covert operation worthy of 007. I had no idea why.

"My boss is cracking down on all of us right now. According to him, someone has been leaking secure information, like bank account and credit card numbers, from listing contracts using our internal office code. He's thinks it's identity theft, and until the person is caught, we're only allowed to work on our own internal listings. All the local real estate offices are on high alert until they figure out who's behind it. It's terrible. If I was caught searching for information on a previous sale brokered by another office, I might be fired. Or even arrested. Crazy."

Good grief.

"Carol? Are you still there?"

"Yes. I was thinking."

"That explains the long silence. Where are you now?"

"I'm at Sally's Closet, where I was summoned by you-know-who, and where I'm doomed to spend the rest of my life unless I can figure out a plan."

"Stay right there," Nancy ordered. "I just had a terrific idea that can't fail. I'll see you soon."

Uh, oh. The instant Nancy breezed into Sally's Closet, I knew I was in big trouble. I hadn't seen that look on her face since the night before our high school graduation, when she talked Claire, Mary Alice, and me into sneaking into the cloister—while all the nuns were in the chapel—and short-sheeting Reverend Mother Agnes Miriam's bed. It seemed like a great idea at the time, a fitting goodbye to our happy, carefree high school days at Mount Saint Francis Academy. We would have gotten away with it, too, except that when we were making our getaway, Mary Alice accidentally bumped into the statue of Saint Francis that was outside the chapel and knocked it off its pedestal. I was lucky enough to catch him before he hit the floor and shattered into a million pieces, and the only one *unlucky* enough to get caught. I almost didn't graduate for that infraction!

"I don't like that look," I said. "Whatever idea you've come up with, count me out. I'm a respectable citizen now, and a grandmother to boot. I have a reputation to protect and I'm not going to risk it for one of your hair-brained ideas."

"Oh, pish," Nancy said dismissively. "You haven't even heard it yet. Don't be such a Debbie Downer. Do you want to help Sister Rose or not?"

"I am not a Debbie Downer," I protested. "And I refuse to agree to anything until you give me all the details of your 'can't fail' plan."

"I'm curious to hear what you have in mind, too, Nancy," Sister Rose said from the doorway. "I haven't forgotten all the times in high school that the two of you teamed up with disastrous results." She rolled her eyes heavenward to make her point.

"See? Sister Rose is suspicious of your plan without even hearing it, too."

Nancy looked hurt. "Well, if you're both going to be that negative, I don't know why I bothered rushing over here."

Sister Rose pulled out a chair and offered it to Nancy. "Sit down, dear. I know you want to help." She sat next to me and folded her hands. I was sure she was praying for guidance. As was I.

"I assume Carol has given you the particulars of my problem."

Nancy nodded. "And I've figured out a way to find out if Frank and Ellen Adams are on the level or not. Do you remember *The Sting*? The movie with Paul Newman and Robert Redford?"

"Who could forget any movie with those two in it?" I laughed. "They were both so handsome."

"Never mind that part," Nancy said. "I'm talking about the movie plot. Newman and Redford set up an elaborate sting operation to trap the bad guy."

Sister Rose coughed. "As I recall, the plot involved swindling the villain out of a lot of money by setting up a pretend horse betting operation. I hope you're not proposing that I set up an off-track betting site here."

"Of course not," Nancy said. "I'm suggesting you tell Frank that Carol has just inherited a large amount of money and has agreed to join the board of the domestic violence program. Give Frank her financial information so he can follow up for an additional donation. If her bank account or any of her credit cards are compromised, we'll know he's a crook. Isn't that a brilliant plan?"

"Words fail me," I said, reeling from the implications and possible fallout from one of the stupidest ideas I'd ever heard.

"I know, right?" Nancy said, looking very pleased with herself. "And if this works, we may also be able to prove that Frank and

Ellen are the ones who are hacking into the real estate databases, too. Which will make me a hero to my boss, and he'll probably give me a gigantic raise. It's a win for everybody."

"Nancy, dear," Sister Rose said, using the stern tone of voice usually reserved for me, "although I appreciate your enthusiasm and your...creativity, what you're asking of Carol is something I'm not comfortable with at all. I suggest you rethink your plan."

I flashed Sister Rose a grateful smile. How interesting to have her on my side for once.

Nancy looked like a little girl who just found out there was no Santa Claus. (I hope you already knew that. If you didn't, please accept my apologies for outing him.) "I think this is a terrific idea," she insisted. "It isn't like I'm suggesting Carol give Frank her credit card and bank account information as a Christmas gift. Banks and credit card companies are always on alert for scams. You'll be notified about any suspicious activity right away."

"Just because there's suspicious activity on my bank account or credit card doesn't prove Frank and Ellen are behind it. And if Jim finds out, he'll have a conniption." I sat back and folded my arms. "I'm not doing it."

"Okay, then I'll do it," Nancy said.

"Nancy, do you understand what you're saying?"

"Of course I do. I should have thought of this before. I'll be Nancy Kendrick instead of Nancy Green."

"You're going to use a phony name? Isn't that against the law, too?" I turned to Sister Rose who, to my surprise, was smiling. "I haven't heard that name in years. Think about it, Carol, and you'll get it."

"Here's a hint," Nancy said, grinning. "Why were we always seated next to each other in school?"

It took me a minute, but I figured it out. "Because my last name then was Kerr." I started to laugh. "I haven't thought of you as Nancy Kendrick since you got married."

"This may be TMI for you, Sister," Nancy explained, "but my husband Bob and I don't have what could be called a conventional marriage. We've been on the brink of divorce several times over the past few years. To protect myself financially, I set up bank and credit card accounts in my maiden name. All the money I've made in real estate goes directly into those bank accounts. I also have a sizable investment portfolio in my name that Bob doesn't know anything about. I don't want to brag, but I've done very well."

I looked at Nancy in admiration. "I have to admit, that's a smart idea. Especially knowing Bob's track record."

Nancy flushed. "Carol, please don't start trashing Bob again, especially in front of Sister Rose. I know you don't like him. You never have."

"You may be in for a pleasant Christmas surprise," I said, smiling. "But I'll tell you about that another time. Meanwhile, let's set this trap and see what happens."

"How will it work?" Sister Rose asked. "And what exactly will I have to do?"

"Relax, Sister," Nancy said. "This will be fun. Just pretend that we're starring in a movie."

I was getting into the spirit of the "movie." I always wanted to be in show business. "What's my role?" I asked.

"You could have been one of the stars," my ex-best friend pointed out. "But now, you're just a member of the audience."

Humph.

Sister Rose still looked hesitant. I couldn't blame her, although she was the one who reached out for help in the first place. She already knew I had an impressive, creative thinking process, and when Nancy was added to the team, anything was possible.

"All you have to do is send Frank this," Nancy said. Sister Rose's phone immediately pinged with a text. "Just change the name from Carol Andrews to Nancy Kendrick."

Sister Rose looked at it briefly, then handed her phone to me. "What do you think?"

Nancy flashed me an impatient look, which I ignored. I scanned the text briefly, then said, "I'd add that Frank helped Nancy with her SUV yesterday on Fairport Turnpike when she was having trouble closing the tailgate. I'm sure he'll remember. The SUV is an expensive Range Rover, which adds credence to her recent inheritance."

"I like that," Sister Rose said, pressing *send* on her phone. "I hope this works."

"I've also asked Mike to do an Internet search on Frank and Ellen. If anyone can find out about them, it's him." I patted Sister Rose's hand. "Don't worry, Sister. We'll figure this out for you."

"I'll wait to hear from both of you," Sister Rose said. "And pray that I don't get any more complaints from board members in the meantime." After a flurry of assurances that all would be well (fingers crossed!), Nancy and I finally made our escape.

"I hope you know what you're doing," I said, as we walked toward our cars. I couldn't help but notice that Nancy was now driving a sporty Mercedes sedan rather than the luxurious SUV. "Where's the Range Rover? You didn't have an accident with it, did you?"

"No, Carol. I don't know why you always criticize my driving. Fortunately, nobody else ever does. Bob needed it back for his customer. I was sad to let it go so soon, but business is business."

"And speaking of business," Nancy said, "I did a quick search on my phone and found out that the buyer for the Old Parsonage is listed as the Robin Hood Trust LLC. I have no way of getting any more information without risking my job, so that's not happening."

"What about Frank and Ellen Adams?"

"They're probably the trustees, but I can't confirm that. I do know that the transaction was all cash, which is unusual but not unheard of."

"All cash? You're kidding. How does that work?"

"It's pretty simple. Just a wire transfer of funds from one bank account to another." Nancy waved her car keys. "I have to go. Bob and I have a date." She gave me a suspicious look. "And what did you mean about Bob and a special Christmas surprise?"

"I think Bob should be the one to tell you. Ask him."

Chapter 41

My ability to remember song lyrics from the 60s far exceeds my ability to remember why I walked into the kitchen.

The shadows were lengthening, and soon it would be dark. The older I get, the less I like driving at night. After the day I'd had, all I wanted to do now was head back to the hotel, take a nice hot bath, and crawl under the covers for a quick nap before enjoying a dinner which I would not have to cook. Ah, luxury. Except I couldn't because Margo was still depending on me to pick her up. Rats. I just hoped that all that time with CJ had completely erased her cockamamie scheme to help me play detective. I already had my trusted posse in place whenever I needed them, and she had definitely not passed the audition.

With any luck, Jim might still be home "supervising" the workmen, and he could pick up Margo and take her back to the hotel instead of me. I was sure he wouldn't miss the opportunity for a visit with CJ, and if Mark happened to arrive home and find his mother there, it was Jim's turn to defuse the tension between them. Man to man, so to speak.

As I eased my car onto Fairport Turnpike, I heard Christmas carolers and saw a crowd gathering on the town green in front of the gazebo. I realized the annual Fairport Christmas tree lighting would be happening in less than half an hour, and traffic in the center of town would be gridlocked.

On impulse, I slowed down, awestruck at the huge Christmas tree in the middle of the green. Maybe I could find a parking spot on a side street and join the fun. When Mike and Jenny were little, taking them to the tree lighting was always the official beginning of the holiday season in the Andrews house. My dawdling earned several blasts of the horn from the car behind me, so I sped up and turned onto Old Fairport Turnpike instead. I figured I could park in my own driveway and walk back to the ceremony. As I rounded the corner, I caught sight of my dear husband walking toward the green, deep in conversation with Frank and Ellen Adams. I had to catch up with them before Jim gave them all our financial information and the deed to our house. (I know, I have an active imagination and always think the worst.) Fate (a.k.a., the nosiest busybody in the neighborhood), had other plans for me just as I stepped out of my car.

"Carol, dear," Phyllis Stevens trilled from her front door, "I'm so glad to see you."

I waved, then started walking. "I don't have time to chat now, Phyllis. I'm on my way to catch up with Jim. He's walking to the tree lighting with Frank and Ellen Adams."

Phyllis beckoned me to cross the street. Rats. I had no time for this. She was probably going to complain about the unsightly trucks that were parked in our driveway.

It's Christmas. Be a good sport for once.

"Carol," Phyllis said in a low voice when I reached her front steps, "I need to bring you up to date on what's been going on at the Old Parsonage." She opened her door wider. "Inside. Please."

I know a golden opportunity when I see one. If anyone had her finger on the pulse of what was going on with our new neighbors, it was dear old Phyllis. I smiled as brightly as the holiday lights on the town Christmas tree and, in a jiffy, found myself sitting across from Phyllis in her immaculate (and probably never used) living room.

"Let me hang up your coat," my hostess said, obviously

anticipating a longer stay than I had in mind.

"I'm fine, thank you," I said, perching on the edge of a chair. "You had something you wanted to talk about?"

"Yes," Phyllis said, "those people next door. Bill noticed odd things going on over there and was concerned."

Since Phyllis's long-suffering husband rarely had anything to say that hadn't been pre-approved by his wife, I took that with several grains of salt. I was sure that Phyllis was the one who thought something odd was happening, and Bill didn't dare disagree with her. Not that I'd point that out.

I settled back in my chair and removed my coat. This was going to take a while, and I wasn't about to rush her. Instead of peppering Phyllis with questions, like I wanted to, I forced myself to sit quietly until she continued. I've read in some of my favorite mystery novels that this technique is most effective in getting information.

"You haven't been home for a while," Phyllis said, making it sound like I'd abandoned my house and family and run away to Tahiti years ago.

"The furnace repair is taking longer than we expected." Mea culpa.

Phyllis sniffed in disapproval. Whether the disapproval was directed at me or the workmen was unclear.

"Bill has pointed out several times that there are people coming and going next door at all hours of the day and night. He's observed people in cars and pickup trucks arriving at midnight and then leaving at seven a.m. Others come at seven and leave at four in the afternoon. And others arrive at four and leave at midnight. What do you have to say about that?"

Poor Bill. He must be very tired. I didn't really say that out loud, of course.

I knew Phyllis had a telescope hidden behind the full-length drapes adorning the picture window at the front of her house, which she used on a regular basis to keep tabs on what was going on in the neighborhood. Now I realized she must have another one in the upstairs master bedroom, too.

"I haven't any idea," I said. And I didn't. "What does Bill think? Is he home now? Shouldn't we ask him?"

"Bill's gone to the post office to mail some holiday cards," Phyllis said. "He asked me to talk to you instead."

I'll bet.

"I agree the activity is unusual," I said. "But Frank and Ellen seem to be lovely people. I remember how excited you were to introduce them around the neighborhood."

"I always thought there was something suspicious about them," Phyllis said, startling me so much that I almost fell off the chair.

"I'm shocked to hear you say that," I said. "I don't want to contradict you, but if you thought they were suspicious, why did you want to give them a welcome to the neighborhood party?"

Phyllis dismissed that with a wave of her hand. "Oh, that. I would think that you of all people would know the answer."

"Nope. Not a clue."

"I wanted to give them a party so they'd let their guard down and you and I could check them out," she said. "I was suspicious of them from the moment they bought the Old Parsonage. I'm surprised that you weren't, too, Carol." Phyllis sniffed again to punctuate her disapproval. Or maybe she was catching a cold.

Calling my across-the-street neighbor an out-and-out liar was not a good idea, so I clamped my lips together and willed them to stay that way. On the one hand, I had to admire Phyllis's creative thinking process, which was even more impressive than mine. On the other hand, her version of the party-that-never-was certainly differed from mine. But if I could learn some things about Frank and Ellen that could help Sister Rose, I was willing to play along.

Falling back on the old adage, 'Flattery will get you everywhere,' I smiled and made an effort to look contrite. "I guess I'm not as intuitive as you are, Phyllis. I completely misread the situation."

"That's understandable, dear. You always have so much on your mind."

I was sure that wasn't a compliment, but I let it pass.

"I believe in giving credit where credit is due," Phyllis went on. "As I said before, it was Bill who called my attention to the unusual goings on at the Old Parsonage. After he mentioned his concern, I decided to go next door with one of my apple crumb cakes as a neighborly gesture. You'll never guess what happened!" She paused and waited for me to respond.

"What?" I know a cue when I hear one.

"I knocked on the door, nice as you please, with a big smile on my face, and nobody answered. I could see through the window that there were people inside. So I knocked again. Finally, Frank Adams came to the door." She paused again.

Good grief. By this time, I was ready to shake the rest of the story out of Phyllis. When was she ever going to get to the point?

"He stepped outside and shut the door behind him so I couldn't see inside. Didn't even invite me into the house." Another sniff. At least, this time, it wasn't directed at me.

"They'd just moved in," I pointed out. "I doubt they were ready for company."

Hold it, Carol. Whose side are you on here? Keep quiet and let Phyllis talk.

"We had a very brief chat on the front porch, I gave him the apple crumb cake, and that's it."

"That's it?" I repeated. "What do you mean?"

"I mean that Frank barely thanked me. He couldn't wait for me to leave. That's when I knew something fishy could be going on, and I started to watch the house." She leaned toward me. "You know, I really never do that sort of thing. But in the interest of neighborhood security, I felt it was my duty to keep an eye on things."

I covered my mouth, pretending to cough, so she couldn't see me laughing. While I got myself under control, I gestured for her to continue.

"I think they're running a boiler house in there," Phyllis said. "I want you to call your son-in-law and report them."

"A boiler house? What the heck is that? I never heard of it."

"Don't you ever watch television, Carol? I saw a special report all about boiler houses on *Sixty Minutes*. Or maybe it was *America's*

Most Wanted. Anyway, one of those news magazine tv shows did a big story about call centers that sell phony investments by telephone. I can't believe you've never heard about them."

The lightbulb went off in my head. "Do you mean a boiler room?"

"Maybe that's what the show called them. I can't remember the specifics. But it makes sense. People are there all hours of the day and night. What else could they be doing?"

What, indeed? All sorts of things, none of which I planned to mention to Phyllis.

"And another thing, Carol. You really need to warn Jim about Frank and Ellen Adams right away. Jim and Frank have become very chummy. I happened to notice them chatting together several times over the past few days. Sometimes Jim even invites Frank into your house. Do you know about that?" She folded her arms and glared at me. "I'd put a stop to that right away, if I were you. Who knows what they could be talking about? Jim could even become an accessory after the fact and end up in jail. That would be terrible."

I'd had enough of Phyllis's theories. I had to get out of there before I lost my mind. At least Sister Rose's concerns were grounded in reality. Phyllis's were inspired by reality television.

I stood up and pulled my coat around me. "Thank you so much for sharing all this information. You've given me a lot to think about. I'll be sure to talk to Jim about his new friendship with Frank and Ellen, so please don't worry."

"You must talk to Mark as soon as possible," Phyllis insisted. "Please tell him I'd be glad to have him stop by so I could share my information with him in person. In fact, if he wants to do a stakeout, he's welcome to use our home. I'm sure Bill would approve."

Oh, good lord. Somehow, I doubted Mark would jump at that invitation. He had enough to deal with already.

Be patient, Carol. Phyllis is just a lonely old woman who has nothing else in her life. Maybe you'll be like that someday, if you're not careful. Or maybe you already are!

I banished that thought from my mind ASAP. My phone pinged, then pinged again. I was sure it was Jim. I wish he wouldn't text me repeatedly until I answer him. It annoys the heck out of me. I waved my phone at Phyllis. "Jim's asking me when I'll be back at the hotel. I wanted to check on the house and pick up a few more things before I left, but I'll have to do it tomorrow instead."

"I'd be glad to check for you if you're in a hurry," Phyllis said. "If you give me a list of what you want, I can pack a bag for you, too. That would save you time tomorrow. I know how busy you always are. Think of it as my way of thanking you for reporting the suspicious activity next door to your son-in-law."

That's all I need. Phyllis going through my closet and my underwear drawer. No thank you.

I shoved my phone in my coat pocket and pulled on my gloves. "I'll think about everything you told me," I said. "If I come up with any brilliant ideas, I'll let you know." And I got the heck out of there as fast as I could.

Once inside the safety of my car, I let the heater do its thing while I checked my messages. To add to my annoyance, the darn thing refused to recognize my fingerprint, forcing me to actually use my password for the first time in almost a year. Thank goodness I remembered what it was.

The first text was from my sleuthing son.

Mike: *Thousands of people have that name, so it's impossible to track your neighbor down. But no crooks popped up, so that's good. Sorry I couldn't help this time.*

And this update from my darling daughter:

Jenny: *Margo's staying for dinner. I'll drive her back to the hotel. Love you.*

And finally, as expected:

Jim: *Traffic bad. Staying in town. Dogs back at hotel with Jeremy. Meet me at Maria's for dinner. I'm hungry.*

I smiled as I texted back a smile emoji. Nothing comes between Jim and his appetite.

Chapter 42

I don't mean to interrupt people. I just randomly remember things and get really excited.

If you've been to Fairport before, you've already visited Maria's Trattoria, which serves the best Italian food in the Nutmeg State as far as I'm concerned. Maria Lesco was a much loved (and feared) teacher in our town for years. Her parent-teacher conferences were the stuff of legend and the source of many agonizing sleepless nights for Fairport parents, including me. An excellent cook, when she finally retired several years ago, she pursued her dream of opening a restaurant on Fairport Turnpike, our town's main commercial artery, and the rest is history. The Trattoria quickly became the go-to place for locals and out-of-towners alike, and reservations are often difficult to get, especially at this time of year. Maria has also become a dear friend, much to our mutual surprise.

Scoring a parking spot in the small lot behind the restaurant, I hurried inside, expecting to see Jim impatiently standing in a long line, waiting for a table. To my surprise, he was already seated at a prime table in an otherwise empty restaurant, sipping a glass of red wine.

"What's going on?" I asked as I parked my keister in a chair opposite him and grabbed his glass. Taking a quick sip, I sighed.

"I needed that. I'm cold." I looked around. "Where is everybody?"

"I guess you didn't see the sign I put on the door," Maria said, miraculously materializing beside me. "We have a big off-premise catering job tonight, and handling both the regular restaurant guests and the party was too much stress. I closed the Trattoria for tonight. That's one of the advantages of being your own boss. But when Jim tapped on the door, looking so forlorn, of course I opened the door for him."

I laughed. "I guess I'm not the only one who's seen that look before."

Maria placed a glass of chardonnay in front of me, then began her version of the Inquisition. "Where've you been? I haven't seen you in weeks."

As I started to explain, Jim interrupted. Big surprise. "Before Carol updates you on our life, which may take a while," he shot me a loving glance, "could we order something to eat? The aromas coming from your kitchen are making me salivate. Everything here is always so delicious."

Maria laughed. "How about samples of what the staff will be serving at the party later? You can be my official tasters."

I kicked Jim under the table. I could tell from the expression on his face that, in his mind, "samples" translated to small portions. But let me ask you, have you ever had an Italian meal and left the table hungry? No, I didn't think so.

Maria caught his expression and laughed. "You won't starve, Jim. I promise. In fact, I may take a quick break and join you. I'll be right back." As she pushed open the kitchen door, I thought I heard the unmistakable sound of one of my favorite television shows. I love watching anything on HGTV, but my favorites are the ones that show magical transformations from downright ugly to fantastically gorgeous. Jim hates it when I watch anything on HGTV, claiming the shows give me ridiculous (expensive) remodeling ideas about our own house.

I was surprised that Maria allowed her staff to spend time watching television while they were technically "on the clock." I knew what a hard taskmaster she could be. I strained my ears and realized the show was, *My Lottery Dream Home*, about the lucky winners of a million dollars (or more) who are then searching for the home of their dreams. My eyes glazed over as I wondered what I'd do, should that ever happen to me.

Before I had a chance to decide what style house I'd look for if money was no object, Maria was back, bearing a delicious antipasto to start off what turned out to be one of the most memorable meals Jim and I ever had. (I'm not going to share the complete menu, because I don't want to make all of you jealous.)

"This looks yummy," I said, as Maria served me from the heaping platter. "The party guests are in for a tasty treat."

"We aim to please," she said, sliding the antipasto platter in Jim's direction. "I'm sure you don't mind helping yourself. I wanted to be sure Carol got her share."

"You don't have to tell me twice," Jim said, smiling as he filled his plate. I glared at him, and then he added, "Thank you. This is so generous of you."

"As I said, we aim to please." Maria turned her attention to me. "So, why haven't I seen you lately? I thought you were mad at me."

I spent the next few minutes (between bites of antipasto) bringing Maria up to date on our house's furnace disaster. "I hope we'll be able to get home before Christmas," I said. All of a sudden, I remembered that, at the snail's pace the workmen were going, Jim thought there was a good possibility we wouldn't. What a horrible thought.

Nobody can whip up a disaster scenario as quickly as I can. My eyes filled up and spilled over. "We should have just sold our old house when we had the chance and found something new instead. Then we wouldn't be homeless for CJ's first Christmas."

"Trust me, Carol doesn't really mean that," Jim said to a shocked Maria. "She's just having a case of the 'I May Not Be Home For Christmas' blues, probably made worse by hearing part of one of those ridiculous HGTV shows just now. Pay no attention to her. She'll get over it soon."

As much as I wanted to contradict Jim, I knew he was right. Not that I'd ever admit it. Instead, I dried my eyes, took another dainty sip of wine and changed the subject.

"I had a quick visit with our neighbor, Phyllis Stevens, a little while ago," I said to Maria. "She loves watching reality television shows like *America's Most Wanted.* I see your taste runs more toward the Home and Garden network, like mine."

"I should have turned it off," Maria said. "But everyone needed a break from the prep, and a quick television fix seemed like a good idea. That's one of my favorite shows."

"What would you do if you won the lottery, Carol?" Jim asked, surprising me that he'd been paying attention to something other than what was on his plate.

"That's easy," I said. "After I paid all the taxes on my winnings, I'd put most of it away for CJ's college education."

Jim nodded. "Depending on how much we won, there might be a lot left over for us to do some big-time traveling, too." (Notice, please, how the pronoun in that sentence changed from the singular, in mine, to a plural.)

"What about you, Maria? What would you do if you won big bucks in the lottery?"

"I'd pay off the mortgage on the Trattoria and give my staff a well-deserved raise." She looked thoughtful. "And help any of my former students who might be in financial trouble. But I wouldn't want them to know it was me. I'd want to do it anonymously. I'd have to talk to a lawyer about setting up a foundation, or a trust, to distribute the money."

"What a wonderful idea," I said. And I meant it.

"It is," Jim agreed. "But if you wanted to remain completely anonymous, it's wise to plan ahead. I've read that smart people who win a huge amount in a lottery set up an LLC first, before they claim the prize. The LLC is named as the official winner, not the person." He patted my hand. "Maybe we should set one up ourselves, Carol. Just in case."

Ho, ho.

"This has been a nice break," Maria said. "But it's time for me to get back to the kitchen. In case I don't see you again before the holidays, Merry Christmas."

"Will the Trattoria be open on Christmas?"

"I always close the restaurant at three o'clock on Christmas Eve, so the staff can spend time with their families. We're closed Christmas Day, too. And then it's nonstop until after New Year's."

"What about you, Maria? What do you do for the holiday?" It suddenly occurred to me that, as far as I knew, Maria had no family in the area. As a matter of fact, I wasn't sure she had any living family at all. As close as we'd become, the subject had never come up.

"It's an unusual chance for me to relax. I'm looking forward to every minute."

"I have a better idea," I said. "We're hoping that the work will be finished in our house before Christmas so we can move back home. How about spending the holiday with us? We'd love to have you, wouldn't we, Jim?" And I gave him 'The Look' to be sure he was on board.

"We sure would," Jim said. "Some of the festivities will be at Jenny and Mark's condo," reminding me of that fact in case I'd forgotten. "Carol and Jenny plan to cook dinner together at our house."

"Fingers crossed that we have a kitchen to cook in," I said.

"Are you serious about the invitation, Carol?"

"Of course I am," I said. "After all the meals we've enjoyed here, it's way past time for us to repay the favor. But keep your standards low, please. I'm certainly no gourmet cook."

"I'd love to come. I'll keep my fingers crossed that the furnace work is finished on time and you can move home. If it isn't, we can cook everything here."

"That's a terrific idea," I said, smiling. "Much better than cooking in Jenny's tiny one. Or at the hotel."

"It's a plan," Maria said. "And this meal is on the house. How about some tiramisu for dessert? I remember that it's one of your favorites."

"Mine, too," Jim said, grinning.

"In that case, I'll be sure the portions are extra generous."

We capped off the evening back at the hotel with one of Jim's favorite activities. I didn't ruin the mood by sharing how horrible my day was, Sister Rose's suspicions, or Phyllis's ridiculous accusations. And that's all I'm going to say about that.

Chapter 43

Four out of three people struggle with math.

I awoke the next morning to the heavenly aroma of fresh brewed coffee. For a split second, I thought I was back home. But alas, when my baby blues focused, I realized I was still at the Fairport Inn and Suites. I suppose I shouldn't complain. Most women my age (or any age) would be thrilled to be the recipient of an all-expense-paid luxurious hotel stay, complete with gourmet meals that required no cooking or clean-up. I'll let you in on a little secret: Luxury that's forced on a person wears off pretty quickly. At least, it does for me. (Feel free to remind me I said that the next time I start complaining about making another home-cooked meal.)

I snuck a peek out the bedroom door to see who was up in addition to my usual roommates—Jim, Lucy and Ethel. Fortunately, Jeremy and Margo were nowhere to be seen, so I took a chance they'd gone out and made a beeline for the coffee while still wearing my nighttime attire—sweatpants and a sweatshirt. I was running low on fashion choices. I either had to go back to my house and get more clothes (risking another wacky conversation with Phyllis), do a load of laundry pronto or go shopping. Believe it or not, the comforting task of doing laundry held the most appeal.

Barely looking up from going through a stack of mail, my

freshly showered and dressed-for-the-day husband pointed me in the direction of the coffee pot. "I ordered half decaf, half caffeinated today, because I know that's the way you prefer it."

I leaned over and gave him a kiss on the top of his head. "You're the best. Thank you."

"It's nice of you to say so," Jim said. He pushed the mail toward me. "Mostly Christmas cards and a few bills. Probably some holiday letters from people we barely know."

"Never mind the mail for now," I said. "Are we alone?"

"I never realized the effect that half caf-half decaf coffee had on you," Jim said, his eyes twinkling. "Yes, we're alone. Jeremy and Margo left early and plan to spend the whole day Christmas shopping. What did you have in mind?"

"Not what you're thinking," I clarified. "At least, not right now. I need to talk to you confidentially, and I want your complete attention. This is important."

Jim sighed. "Okay, but this better be good."

I knew I had to handle this conversation very carefully, especially if Jim really liked Frank Adams. He didn't have a best buddy or two of his very own; most of his friends were the husbands of my friends. I prayed that Jim hadn't chosen Frank to fill the best friend role.

I took another sip of coffee to fortify myself, then plunged right in. "I don't know a lot about Frank and Ellen Adams, and people have been asking me questions that I can't answer."

Jim's expression changed from happy to guarded. "Who's been asking about them?" His voice was getting high, a sure sign that I'd already upset him or made him angry. Either way, this was going to be an even tougher conversation than I'd anticipated.

"Calm down, Jim. People are naturally curious about new neighbors. I saw you chatting with them last night on the way to the town tree-lighting, and I thought they might have talked about where they moved from, for example."

"They never mentioned where they lived before, and I didn't ask. We talked more about Fairport, what a great place it is to live, how nice our neighborhood is—that kind of thing. Oh, you'll laugh at this. Ellen wanted to know how often she could expect a visit from Phyllis Stevens." Jim grinned. "I guess it didn't take them long to figure out that Phyllis is the local busybody."

"Speaking of Phyllis," I said, "I stopped home late yesterday to pick up a few more clothes and she caught me before I could get into the house. She insisted that we talk privately, and there was no way I could get out of it. She had some interesting information to share."

Jim raised his eyebrows. "At least this time she's not spying on us, because we're not home."

"True. She's become fixated on Frank and Ellen. She's decided they're crooks and wants me to report them to Mark."

Jim choked on his coffee. "You didn't, did you?"

"Please, give me a little credit. At first, I thought this was just another Phyllis fantasy, especially when she used things she'd seen on reality television shows to back up her theory."

"What theory?"

"She claimed that Bill's noticed groups of people coming and going at the Old Parsonage on a regular basis, like shifts. She's decided they're running a boiler room in the house, with scammers making telephone calls to swindle people out of money or steal their credit cards."

"We both know that Bill's not even allowed to look out a window without Phyllis's permission." Jim shook his head. "She's really gone off the deep end this time. And what does she know about a boiler room?"

"She called it a boiler house, and it took me a while to catch on to what she was talking about. She said she saw a feature about scam artists on *America's Most Wanted*."

"A credible source of information," Jim said, rolling his eyes. "It's actually kind of funny, in a sad kind of way. Phyllis just doesn't have enough in her life to keep her busy. Poor woman." He yawned, then stood—a signal that meant, for him, this conversation was over.

But it wasn't for me.

"I agree the whole boiler room thing is ridiculous. I wouldn't have even bothered mentioning it to you except for Sister Rose."

"Sister Rose? What's she got to do with this? Next you're going to tell me that Frank and Ellen asked to use the thrift shop as a front to launder money."

Uh, oh. I could tell by Jim's dismissive tone of voice that this discussion was getting us (me) nowhere.

"Please, just listen to what Sister Rose told me." I quickly sketched out the fundraising calls Frank had made to board members, his request for their personal financial information, and the subsequent cyberattacks on their bank and credit card accounts. "The board members called Sister Rose and demanded Frank be investigated immediately. They threatened to quit the board if he was still involved. She's really worried and reached out to me for help."

"I hope this doesn't involve you planning one of your crazy schemes to trap Frank and Ellen Adams," Jim said.

"I can assure you that I'm not planning any schemes, crazy or otherwise, to help Sister Rose. That's why I'm telling you about her concerns. I'm asking you for your opinion." Note that, for once, I was telling Jim the absolute truth. Nancy was the one who'd cooked up a scheme that even *I* thought was crazy.

"Sister Rose may have a legitimate concern. Or the whole thing could just be a series of unfortunate coincidences. Although I can tell you that Frank is pretty convincing when it comes to financial matters. He offered me an investment opportunity yesterday, and I was giving it some thought."

"You're not serious! Especially after what I just told you." I had visions of our entire bank account wiped out in an instant.

"Don't worry. I promise I won't do anything without checking with you first."

"And if I say no?"

"Then, it's no. Don't worry so much. By the way, I'm surprised you're not pestering me about Jeremy. As I recall, you assigned me to pump him for personal information yesterday. Don't you want to know what happened?"

"Of course I do! I want every tiny detail."

Jim grinned. "I was able to convince Mark to join Jeremy and me for lunch yesterday. By the end of lunch, he and Jeremy had made some real progress in their relationship."

"That's wonderful. How did you do it?" I was on the edge of my chair, waiting for details.

"All I can say for now is that you're in for a big surprise about Jeremy. It's his secret to share when the time is right."

"Oh, no. He's married! That's going to break Margo's heart."

She'll end up staying in Fairport forever and drive us all crazy. And I was the one who suggested she babysit for CJ yesterday. She's going to take over completely. How could I be so stupid?

Jim looked at me like I was nuts. "I can assure you, Carol, that you are completely wrong. Jeremy is not married, and he truly cares for Margo. And as far as Frank and Ellen are concerned, let me handle it. I might give Mark a head's up and ask him if he has some time to check them out. Will that satisfy you and Sister Rose? I know nothing can satisfy Phyllis short of a SWAT team storming the Old Parsonage, so I'm going to ignore that part of your story."

"But Jim, what if...?"

"I said I'll handle it. And by the way, you might want to spend the rest of today organizing all the things you brought here from our house. I got a text before you got up that the furnace parts have arrived, so the work is supposed to be finished today. It looks like we'll be able to move home tomorrow morning." I forgot about Frank and Ellen, Jeremy, Margo, Sister Rose, and even Phyllis. Instead, I gave my husband a big smooch, startling Lucy and Ethel, who were sleeping under the table. We were going home for Christmas.

Chapter 44

Never laugh at your wife's choices. You're one of them.

I looked at the heap of clothes piled on the bed. How could I have accumulated all this stuff in such a short period of time? I rummaged around and managed to find a red sweater that looked presentable enough to be seen in public, plus a pair of black stretch pants. I was down to my last two pairs of clean undies, but by tomorrow, I'd be able to do a few loads of laundry in my own house. Yay!

As I was stuffing some of the dirty clothes into a black garbage bag, a horrible thought popped into my mind. What if the repairmen found another furnace problem today and we had to stay here longer?

It won't take you long to pack, Carol. You could be asking for bad luck if you do it too soon.

Choosing not to tempt fate, I decided to take advantage of some unexpected alone time and go through the pile of mail Jim had left behind. Perish the thought that there was an overdue bill Jim hadn't noticed. Our holiday mail delivery was sometimes unreliable. Plus, I get a kick out of reading other people's holiday letters. Fiction writing at its most creative.

I poured another cup of coffee, cleared away a space on the

table, and began to sort the mail into junk (for recycling), bills (only one from the power company that wasn't due until January), and first class. The first class mail was easy to spot because it was in red or green envelopes.

I paused when I found a plain white envelope addressed to me, with no return address. Hmm. A lot of junk mail is cleverly disguised as first class these days. It could be a scam. Or maybe I just had scams on the brain.

Curious, I ripped the envelope open. Not junk mail, but a personal letter to me.

Dear Mrs. Andrews,
I hope this letter reaches you. We barely know each other, but I have no one else I can turn to. I trust you because you remind me of my mom. I've gotten myself involved in something bad. I don't know what to do, or who to trust. I've tried to do the right thing now, but it may be too late. I finally told Ryan, and at first he got really angry. Then he calmed down and said he'll support me no matter what. But the last few days, he doesn't act the same toward me. What should I do? I'm scared. Can you help me?

April

My hands were shaking. I just sat there, holding the letter. *She reached out to you for help, and you let her down. Now she's dead. It's your fault.*

I knew I had to show the letter to Mark right away. This proved, at least to me, that April's death was no accident. Somebody murdered her. And I was going to do whatever I could to be sure that person was punished.

I showered and dressed in record time, fired off a text to Mark to be sure he was working, and told him I'd be there in twenty minutes.

I was lucky there was no sign of Ryan when I reached the ground floor of the hotel. As I scurried across the lobby, I heard Bobbie call my name. Rats. I had no time to chat with her, nor did I want to.

"Mrs. Andrews, I wanted to let you know that there's no parking attendant on duty today. Ryan was fired last night. He's gone."

Well, that stopped me cold.

I turned slowly and approached the registration desk. "Fired? Why?"

Bobbie leaned across the counter for a confidential chat. "Management was informed that he was in a relationship with April Swanson. That's against company policy."

"But April's dead," I stammered. "What possible difference could the fact that they were in a relationship make now?"

"Rules are rules," Bobbie said.

The poor guy. First he loses the love of his life, then he loses his job. "I think this rule stinks," I said. "I can find my car on my own."

Chapter 45

A little gray hair is a small price to pay for all this wisdom.

"Thank you, Carol. This letter reinforces a theory we've been working on." Mark rose to his feet, indicating that our time together was over.

Not so fast.

"I wish I'd read it sooner. I feel very guilty about that. Maybe I could have saved her life."

"Please don't beat yourself up about that, Carol. You brought the letter to me as soon as you found it. You've done all you could."

"It's the part where she said I reminded her of her mom," I said. "That just breaks my heart. Did she have any family?"

Mark sighed and sat down again. He knew I wasn't going to leave until I had more information. "We haven't been able to trace any close relations so far. We know she'd been living with a guy named Ryan Peterson. He may be the closest thing to family she had."

"Yes, word about their relationship seems to be spreading," I said, wondering if the police were the ones who tipped off the hotel management, resulting in Ryan's termination. "It's so sad."

"Yes." Mark stood again.

"I understand you, Jim, and Jeremy had a nice lunch

yesterday," I said, ignoring his hint that our time together was definitely over. "I'm glad it went well. I hope you're feeling better about his relationship with Margo now."

"It was productive. That's all I'm saying."

Goodness. My son-in-law certainly was a man of few words today.

Now that I had my emotions under control, I had one more topic to discuss with Mark and, you know me, I just forged ahead. "Several people, including Sister Rose, have expressed concern about Frank and Ellen Adams. Some of her board members had credit card and bank information stolen soon after talking with Frank. Do you think he and his wife could be con artists?" I resisted sharing Phyllis's offer of using her house as a stakeout location.

"Nobody's filed a formal complaint against them. And now, Carol," Mark said, his hand on my elbow, "I have to get back to work. Thank you again for the letter." The next thing I knew, I was on the other side of his closed office door.

"This is the last time you show up without a dozen donuts," I chastised myself aloud as I sat in my car five minutes later, stewing, in the police department parking lot. "At least when you bring food, Mark isn't quite so anxious to get rid of you."

And that's exactly how my son-in-law behaved. Gave me a cursory "thank you," which he probably didn't mean, and then practically threw me out without giving me a chance to share any of my theories with him.

What theories, Carol? You don't have any.

I checked for the time; it was only 10:00. I had the whole day ahead of me with nothing to do except throw my clothes in a garbage bag and then be sure I didn't throw the bag out by mistake. (That actually happened to a friend of mine. She was cleaning out her late mother's house, got confused, and threw away a garment bag of valuable designer dresses instead of a garbage bag stuffed with old rags.)

I could take some time to do a little food shopping. I hadn't been in my own kitchen for several days, so only heaven knew if there was anything edible left in the house. I put that on my to-do list, but down near the bottom. I was sure I could come up with more fun things to do than pushing a cart around a grocery store.

Maybe some additional Christmas shopping was in the cards. Mike said he would be home for the holiday, and I hadn't bought him a single thing. Perfect.

Because it was still early, I was able to cruise into a spot in the usually jammed parking lot of Handsome Gents, Fairport's trendy men's clothing shop. The merchandise it carried was bound to give me sticker shock, but it was Christmas, the time for splurging. And Mike deserved something special from dear old Mom (and Dad). It didn't take me long to find a V-neck cashmere sweater in a shade of burgundy that I knew would look spectacular on my son. There was only one sweater in that color, and I was thrilled to see it was a medium—Mike's size. Score one for Carol! I decided to buy it, and also pay extra for store gift wrapping. (I have the shopping gene, but the gift wrapping gene has eluded me.)

The yuppie salesperson at the cash register, who had more white teeth than I thought could fit in an average male mouth, ran my credit card through with a big smile. As well he should—the sweater cost over $400, plus an extra $15 for gift wrapping. (Can you understand now why I never shop here?) He frowned, ran the card through again, then handed it back to me. "I'm terribly sorry, Mrs. Andrews, but your card has been declined. Twice. Do you have another one you can use for this purchase?"

"But that's impossible," I sputtered. "There must be a glitch in your computer system."

"I suggest you call your bank and straighten out the problem, then come back. I'm glad to hold the sweater for you until we close at five p.m."

I was mortified, but what could I do? "That's very kind of you. I'll get in touch with my bank and be back to pay and pick up my son's sweater."

"We close at five o'clock sharp," he called after me as I left the store.

Chapter 46

It's hard being the same age as old people.

"Think, don't react," I ordered myself. "Before you go off the deep end and accuse Frank and Ellen of scamming your credit card, ask yourself if there's any logical way Jim's ratcheted up an astronomical charge without your knowledge." Maybe he'd used this card to pay for the furnace repairs and forgotten to tell me. Yes, that made perfect sense. He had to pay the furnace bill and this was the only card he had in his wallet.

The more I thought about this possibility, I realized that Jim would never pay in full for anything as important as a new furnace until he was certain it was going to work perfectly. Plus, he said the servicemen hoped the work would be completed today, not that it had already been completed.

I had to face the unpleasant fact that someone else must have used our credit card. There was no way around it. I had to call our bank and cancel the card right away.

I dialed the 1-800 customer service number, then punched in a variety of passwords and answered ridiculous questions to prove that I was me. Having passed those hurdles, I then suffered through five minutes of horrible music while I screamed: "Representative! Representative!" My call was finally answered by an honest-to-goodness human being, whose name was Christie.

"Oh, Mrs. Andrews, we've been trying to reach you," she said. "We've left several messages on your phone." She rattled off my home number, and I realized she was telling the truth. My bad. I'd never updated my contact information for this account.

"My credit card was just denied," I said. "I was told that the credit limit has been reached. Someone unauthorized must be using my card, and I want it cancelled immediately."

"Of course, Mrs. Andrews," Christie said. "We've been trying to contact you since we noticed suspicious activity on the card last night. I'm so glad you've gotten in touch with us. I'm cancelling this card immediately and the bank will mail out a new one right away. And don't worry, you're not liable for the car purchase."

"*Car?* What car?"

"Your credit card was used for a ten thousand dollar deposit on a Range Rover SUV at Luxury Cars of Fairport."

The scammer certainly had expensive taste in cars. I almost laughed out loud, except this wasn't funny.

"I appreciate your prompt action, Christie. It's good to know the bank is on alert for scammers." I rattled off my cell phone number as my primary contact from now on, then terminated the call.

"You were very lucky, Carol Andrews. Thank goodness the bank realized something was wrong." Although a luxury SUV would look pretty snazzy sitting in our driveway. All the neighbors would be impressed.

The light dawned. I remembered Nancy struggling to open the tailgate of her borrowed Range Rover, and Frank Adams coming to her rescue. He said they'd once had a similar model. Maybe he decided they needed a new one, and our credit card was the perfect way to pay for it. Except I couldn't figure out how he'd done it.

I opened my wallet and saw that my own card was safely tucked away inside. "As soon as I can lay my hands on a pair of scissors, I'm cutting you up and throwing you away." Had Frank gotten his hands on Jim's card? Maybe picked Jim's pocket on the walk to the tree lighting?

I looked at my credit card again, and suddenly remembered the lecture Jim had given me when I wanted to apply for it. He went on and on about how we had far too many credit cards already, we didn't need another one, we'd never use it...blah, blah, blah. I applied for the card on my own; Jim's name wasn't on the account. The only card for the account was the one sitting in my wallet.

I only used this credit card for travel-related purchases, which is hilarious because we never go anywhere. (I remain hopeful, though.) I was only carrying it now so I could use it for our emergency hotel reservations. I didn't charge anything on it, thanks to Jeremy's generosity, although Bobbie insisted on swiping it anyway, saying that hotel policy required credit information for each guest.

If it looks like a duck and quacks like a duck, it's a duck!

That's how Frank got hold of our credit card information—he had an accomplice at the hotel. Who knew how many times he and his wife had pulled this scam before? With someone constantly feeding them credit card information from unsuspecting guests, Frank and Ellen (if those were their real names) always had new sources of income. It was brilliant. And April must have been their accomplice. She finally wanted out, and one of them killed her to keep her quiet.

Don't focus on that now, Carol. First, you need to stop Frank and Ellen from picking up the Range Rover and getting away.

I started to call Bob Green, then decided it would take too long to explain what was going on. I had to drive to the dealership myself. I'd figure out my game plan when I got there.

Breaking who knows how many speeding laws, I got to the Luxury Cars dealership in record time. When I pulled into the parking lot, I saw two of Bob's servicemen shining a black Range Rover, probably getting it ready for Frank to pick up. Ha! Not going to happen.

I took a few deep breaths to calm myself. I needed to be concise when I talked to Bob Green, not emotional and all over the place, the way I usually am. Just the facts, ma'am.

Imagine my surprise when I rushed in the door and saw Nancy sitting at the reception desk. "What the heck are you doing here?" she demanded. "Are you checking up on me? You haven't heard from me today because, so far, I have nothing to report about your brilliant idea to help Sister Rose. I've been busy with other things."

My brilliant idea?

"Forget all about that. I need to talk to Bob right away. Is he in his office?"

"Why? You never have anything positive to talk to him about. You've made your feelings very clear over the years."

"We're friends now. Didn't he tell you?"

"It's true, Nancy," Bob said, coming up behind me. "We both love you and decided it was time we acted like grown-ups."

"At last," Nancy said, crying and hugging us both.

"Yes," I agreed, extricating myself from the joint hug. "But right now, we have more important things to talk about. Bob, that black Range Rover SUV was charged to a credit card stolen from me by Frank Adams. He's not only a con artist, but I think he's also a murderer." I whipped out my cell phone. "I'm calling the police right away."

Bob looked like our budding new friendship had hit a snag, no doubt visualizing his sales commission vanishing before he even got it. "No way, Carol. That's ridiculous."

"I'm not blaming you, Bob. You had no way of knowing the card was stolen. Which raises the question of how the sale happened. Did a customer actually come into the dealership?"

"No," Bob admitted. "The entire transaction was conducted online. Even the signature on the contract was done electronically."

"Isn't that a little unusual?"

"It's become a common way to conduct business, especially for our wealthier customers. All the information provided checked out okay. I didn't think anything about it. Sometimes I don't even meet the actual customer. Someone on the customer's staff picks the vehicle up instead. It's never been a problem."

"Until now," I said. "There's no time to waste." I punched in Mark's number, praying the call wouldn't go to voicemail.

"Put the phone down right now."

Think fast, Carol. Maybe Frank just got here and didn't overhear the conversation. Be casual. Pretend everything's normal. Whatever works.

As it turned out, there was no way I could pretend everything was normal. Surprised, shocked, stupefied—pick any one of these— barely covered my reaction when I realized there was a person holding a gun to Nancy's head. And it wasn't Frank Adams. It was Ryan.

Chapter 47

*Some days my supply of curse words is
insufficient to meet my needs.*

"What the heck is wrong with you?" I screamed. "Nancy didn't
have anything to do with you being fired. I'm the one with the
big mouth, not her. Right, Nancy? Tell him it was me. Then he'll
let you go and we can talk this over reasonably."

Nancy started to nod her head, but that only made Ryan
angry.

Bob was no help at all. He was just standing there. I guess his
customer service training never covered this kind of situation.
But I wasn't going to let my very best friend be hurt over a stupid
misunderstanding. After all, Ryan could always find another job
in another hotel. This seemed to be a bit of an overreaction on
his part.

"People lose their jobs all the time, Ryan," I said, trying to
sound supportive. "I'm sure you can find another one in no time."
Right after you take an anger management course. You know I didn't
say that out loud.

"Why don't you put the gun down and we can talk about this?
Maybe Bob has an opening here at the dealership. You know so
much about cars. That might work out great for both of you. What
do you say, Bob?"

"You really are hilarious, Mrs. Andrews," Ryan said. "I thought you'd caught onto me this morning when I followed you from the hotel to the police station. But instead you're babbling on and on like an idiot about my being fired. Is that what you think this is all about?"

"Okay, then why don't you tell me what's going on."

"There's no time for that. I just want to get out of this hick town as fast as I can. But first, I have to figure out what to do with the three of you. I'd really hate to kill you, like I did April."

"April! You killed her? Why? You said she was the love of your life."

"She was, for a little while. But she got an attack of conscience about the credit card scam and went to the cops. I couldn't risk her figuring out that I was the person behind it and turning me in." He shrugged. "It was a business decision. Nothing personal."

"Nothing personal?" I screeched. "April loved you and you *murdered* her."

"Yeah, I did. Do you want to hear all the gory details? You're lucky I'm not going to kill all of you, too, but I don't have enough time."

"You disgust me," I said. I wanted to smack his face, but I didn't dare try.

"Some innocent customer may walk in at any minute," Bob said, finally finding his voice. "Let me put the closed sign on the door so we're not disturbed." He held his hands up high. "You can follow me to the door if you don't trust me, but you have my word there's no way I'd make a break for it and leave Nancy and Carol alone with you."

"All right. But be quick." Ryan scanned the showroom and spotted a red Range Rover SUV. "Find me something I can use to tie all of you to this car so I can get out of here."

Bob rummaged around in a desk and found a few bungee cords. "Will these do?"

"They'll have to. Tie Mrs. Andrews to one of the door handles. Be sure the knot's secure so she can't wiggle out of it."

"Sorry about all this, Carol," Bob whispered. "Don't worry.

I promise that everything's going to work out okay. You have to trust me."

"I don't have much choice," I muttered.

"No talking," Ryan barked. "I want the key fob to the black Range Rover that's parked outside. Now."

Bob scurried over to the reception desk and held something up for Ryan to see. "Right here."

"Put it on the desk, then back away," Ryan ordered. "Move to the other side of the SUV and don't move. This woman is going to tie you to the tailgate."

As Ryan maneuvered the terrified Nancy toward the back of the car, I remembered how Frank opened the Range Rover tailgate by waving his foot. I kicked my leg up and down a few times like a Radio City Music Hall Rockette, praying Nancy could see me. With a little luck and good timing, the tailgate would fly up and nail Ryan right in the head.

As I explained to Jim later, that's exactly when the front door of the dealership burst open and the two servicemen who'd been detailing the black Range Rover barreled inside, guns drawn. I then heard Jeremy's familiar voice: "FBI. The place is surrounded. It's over, Ryan. Hands on top of your head. Now."

Chapter 48

Marriage Counselor: Your wife says you never buy her flowers.
Husband: To be honest, I never knew she sold flowers.

I'm sure all of you have lots of questions. I know the feeling. I wish with all my heart that I had all the answers. I'll tell you what I can, but I've been sworn to secrecy on a few sensitive issues. Don't try to drag anything more out of me, either. I don't want the Feds coming after me.

In no particular order, here goes: The Fairport police received a tip that a huge identity theft scam was operating in Fairfield County and contacted the FBI for assistance. Agent Jeremy Dixon was sent undercover to investigate. Along the way, in a darkened parking airport lot, he rescued a damsel in distress, proving once again that business and pleasure should never be combined.

Jeremy arrived in Fairport, accompanied by Margo Anderson, the new love of his life and my personal nemesis. Unfortunately for Jeremy, his local contact turned out to be Detective Mark Anderson, Margo's son. Sorting out the emotional baggage between the two took some time (an understatement). Moving on....

The FBI had provided Fairport merchants with an emergency

number to contact if they suspected a scam. When $10k was charged to my credit card for the deposit on a Range Rover, Bob Green knew right away that my card had been stolen. I believe his exact words to the authorities were, "I knew Jim Andrews was much too cheap to buy such an expensive vehicle." He immediately called the emergency number, and was given specific instructions on how to deal with the "customer" when he arrived to pick up the car. I have to admit, Bob really kept his cool through the whole ordeal, even when Nancy and I showed up unexpectedly to add to his stress level. When he posted the "closed" sign on the dealership door, that was the signal to the FBI and police, who were posted outside masquerading as dealership employees, that the "customer" had arrived.

Nancy was praised as a hero for her quick action that knocked Ryan out. Generous friend that I am, I let her take the entire credit.

I understand from Jeremy that he plans to single me out in his final report for having the presence of mind to keep my cell phone on during the confrontation and record Ryan's confession. I know (and those of you who were paying attention do, too) that the fact my cell phone was still on was just dumb luck, but when I tried to tell him so, Jeremy said I was only being modest. Oh, well.

Remember Frank and Ellen Adams? Surprise! Those aren't their real names, nor are they doctors or scam artists. Don't get any crazy ideas—they're not in the Witness Protection Program, either. They're Mega Millions lottery winners who, on the advice of an attorney, set up the Robin Hood Foundation LLC to claim their prize, and are using the money to help the less fortunate. They're restoring the Old Parsonage and then donating it to our hospital to be used as a bed and breakfast for out-of-town families to be close to their sick loved ones during treatment. All the family's expenses will be covered by the Robin Hood Foundation. I'm sorry I suspected them of such nefarious deeds, and was relieved that they left town before they found out what a bad neighbor I was.

Just between us, I was furious with myself for being so off

the mark in my sleuthing this time. Ryan was never on my radar screen for a split second. (BTW, I haven't shared the news about Ryan with Lucy and Ethel. I'm afraid they'll both be so upset when they find out what a rat Ryan was that they'll both need therapy, and I know Jim would never pay for it.)

I've heard from Jeremy that Ryan continues to brag about how clever he and his gang of cyber thieves were, targeting luxury hotel chains and using front desk clerks to steal credit card information from wealthy guests during the check-in process. Ryan recruited his band of merry thieves over the Internet, so his own identity as the Big Boss was shrouded in mystery. When April told Ryan what she was involved in, and wanted to quit, she had no idea about his real identity. Ryan killed her to protect himself, but he had no idea that she'd already contacted the authorities.

Even though there's no doubt Ryan will be spending the rest of his life behind bars for a long list of crimes, I heard—through a source I can't name—that he's hired a talent agent to sell his story to Hollywood and is writing the script between court appearances. Go figure.

The good news is that we were able to move back home right before Christmas, in time to buy a tree (at a bargain price, so Jim was thrilled), decorate the house with mistletoe and holly, wrap some presents, and organize last minute cooking assignments among Jenny, Maria Lesco, and me for The Big Day. Mike was home (yay!) and Jenny and Mark decided to stay overnight at our house for the holidays. CJ's very first Christmas would be here, the way I always wanted. Margo's only job was to stay at the hotel with Jeremy and keep out of our way until Santa came down the chimney. I don't think she minded.

I was in a merry mood on Christmas Eve afternoon as I set the dining room table with my Spode Christmas china and Waterford glasses for the feasts to come. Jim was doing battle with the Christmas tree in the family room—an Andrews sacred holiday tradition—and Mike was doing his best to assist without getting in his father's way. I ignored the colorful choice of words that always accompanies the man versus tree struggle. The tree would be straight, decorated with all the beautiful ornaments we've collected over the years, and the stockings would be hung by the chimney with care. (Actually, they'd be hung on the fireplace mantle in the family room.)

Suddenly, Mike yelled, "Mom, look out the window. It's snowing!"

I ran to the window and pulled up the sash (actually, opened the drapes). And what to my wondering eyes did appear? Old Fairport Turnpike, already covered with a light coating of snow. It was beautiful.

Smiling at what a perfect addition the snow made to what was going to be a perfect holiday for all my loved ones, I began to sing, "White Christmas." I was a little off-key, but so what?

I counted the number of places I'd set at the table and realized I was short three settings. Out of the goodness of my heart, I'd also invited Phyllis and Bill Stevens, plus Sister Rose, to join us. There was no way all those people could squeeze around the table comfortably.

I pulled out a chair and sat down. At least I'd figured out there was a space problem in advance, while I could still fix it. I'm ashamed to admit this, but that dining room chair was so comfortable, and I was so worn out from all the prep work I'd already done, that I closed my eyes for just a few minutes. Or, possibly more than a few.

I awoke to something beating against the windows. The snow had changed to ice and sleet, and the wind was picking up. There was a loud cracking sound, and all the lights in our house went out. I peeked out the window again. There wasn't a light burning on the entire street.

Since I hadn't had the presence of mind to bring a flashlight with me when I began to set the table, I sat down in the dark and cried. We New Englanders are a hearty lot, and we're used to dealing with power outages, but on Christmas Eve? I figured this one would take a longer time than usual to repair, because many of the regular crews could be off for the holiday.

I was interrupted in my misery by the beam of a flashlight

and my husband's voice. "Carol, why are you just sitting there? Come on. We're leaving."

"What? Where are we going? And what about the food?"

"It's all taken care of. When the sleet started, Mark immediately realized we could be headed for a big problem, and took over. He and Mike are packing up all the food and the presents. Jenny and CJ left before the storm got really bad, so they're safe. It's only our part of town that's been affected, and it looks like the storm is moving away from us. It didn't last long." He handed me my coat and boots. "Put these on and let's get out of here."

"But...the dogs?"

"Jenny took them with her. They're fine."

"Where are we going?" I asked again as I fussed with my boots.

"The good news is that we'll all be together," Jim said. "We alerted Maria Lesco, Phyllis and Bill Stevens, and Sister Rose to the change in plans. Maria and Sister Rose have power. Bill and Phyllis have decided to stay home, which I think is foolish, but that's their choice."

"Jim Andrews," I said, standing so I could button my coat, "do I have to ask you this again? Where are we going for Christmas?"

"Why, to our home away from home, of course. We're bunking in with Margo and Jeremy at the Fairport Inn and Suites." Jim held a piece of mistletoe over my head and gave me a smooch. "Merry Christmas, Carol."

Recipes from Carol's Kitchen

Okay, who are we kidding here? Everyone knows that the favorite foods from Carol Andrews' kitchen are the ones prepared by somebody else. However, in the spirit of the holiday season, here are two "recipes" that are so simple, she actually makes them herself without complaining.

The first has become known over the years as...

Carol's Killer Meatballs

This questionable nickname was achieved because of its handy dandy use in Book 2 of this series, *Moving Can Be Murder*. If you don't remember it, or—horrors—you haven't read that title yet (shame on you!), Jim now tells everyone this was Carol's recipe originally, but we all know that's not true.

Ingredients:

One jar of chili sauce

One can of jellied cranberry sauce

One bag, frozen turkey meatballs, appetizer size. (The original recipe called for Italian meatballs, but in the spirit of the season, Carol's changed it to turkey. She's so creative!) Any brand meatballs will do, but in the Andrews house, Jim insists Carol use whatever's on sale, he has a coupon for, or store-brand. Your choice.

Cooking Directions:

Combine first two ingredients in pot and mix thoroughly to break up the cranberry sauce. Add frozen meatballs and cook on stove top or in crock pot until the meatballs are heated all the way through.

Serve in a holiday-themed bowl (Carol likes the Spode Christmas pattern best) or chafing dish. Carol *never* gives out this recipe to her awed guests. She believes it's none of their business how easy this dish is to prepare.

Carol's Easy Peasy Pumpkin Pie

We've all heard the expression, "easy as pie," right? This pie recipe gives that old cliché new meaning.

Ingredients:

One frozen pie shell
Dannon Light and Fit Greek Style Pumpkin Yogurt

Cooking Directions:

Bake pie shell according to package instructions, then cool.

Empty 5-6 containers of pumpkin yogurt into a bowl and mix thoroughly.

Fill pie shell with pumpkin yogurt.

Chill in refrigerator until ready to serve.

Carol's note: Dannon only makes pumpkin yogurt at the holidays. The pie can also be made with any other yogurt flavors. Jim likes the tiramisu, but Carol prefers the chocolate raspberry. Be sure to mix the yogurt up first, before filling the pie shell.

If Carol really wants to splurge, she makes parfaits by alternating a scoop of yogurt with a scoop of Cool Whip, and serves them in a fluted wine glass. (Waterford, of course).

Credit Card Fraud Runs Rampant Around the Holidays

Notes and Suggestions from Jim Andrews:

Globally, losses from payment card fraud have soared to $28.65 billion a year, according to recent data, of which the U.S. accounted for $9 billion in fraud losses.

Especially during the holidays, crooks have more opportunity to commit credit or debit card fraud, as shoppers spend lots of money, often buying online or over the phone, and from unfamiliar websites.

The Federal Trade Commission offers tips to help consumers avoid being ripped off by credit card scammers around the holidays and all year long.

For example, keep a record in a secure place of your account numbers, their expiration dates, and the phone numbers to report fraud for each company. Don't lend your card to anyone—even your kids or roommates—and don't leave your cards, receipts, or statements around your home or office. When you no longer need them, shred them before throwing them away.

Other Fraud Protection Practices:

Don't give your account number to anyone on the phone unless you've made the call to a company you know to be reputable. If you've never done business with them before, do an online search first for reviews or complaints.

Carry your cards separately from your wallet. It can minimize your losses if someone steals your wallet or purse. And carry only the card you need for that outing.

During a transaction, keep your eye on your card. Make sure you get it back before you walk away.

Never sign a blank receipt. Draw a line through any blank spaces above the total.

Save your receipts to compare with your statement.

Open your bills promptly—or check them online often—and reconcile them with the purchases you've made.

Report any questionable charges to the card issuer immediately.

Notify your card issuer if your address changes or if you will be traveling.

Don't write your account number on the outside of an envelope.

Report Losses and Fraud:

Call the card issuer as soon as you realize your card has been lost or stolen. Many companies have toll-free numbers and 24-hour service to deal with this. Once you report the loss or theft, the law says you have no additional responsibility for charges you didn't make; in any case, your liability for each card lost or stolen is $50. If you suspect that the card was used fraudulently, you may have to sign a statement under oath that you didn't make the purchases in question.

Credit card fraud is a form of a broader crime called "Identity Theft," where criminals use your personal information to open accounts, steal your money, and wreck your finances. The FTC states:

Recovering from Identity Theft: Is someone using your personal information to open accounts, file taxes, or make purchases? Visit

IdentityTheft.gov, the federal government's one-stop resource to help you report and recover from identity theft.

About the Author

Susan Santangelo is the author of the best-selling *Baby Boomer Mystery* series. She is a member of Sisters in Crime, International Thriller Writers, and the Cape Cod Writers Center, and also reviews mysteries for *Suspense Magazine*. She divides her time between Clearwater, Florida and Cape Cod, Massachusetts, and shares her life with her husband Joe and two very spoiled English cocker spaniels, Boomer and Lilly, who also serve as models for the books' covers. Susan is also a proud, lucky two-time breast cancer survivor, and credits early detection by regular mammograms with saving her life twice.

CPSIA information can be obtained
at www.ICGtesting.com
Printed in the USA
JSHW012008070922
30078JS00002B/8